SC

THREE TIMES THE TROUBLE

TATE PUBLISHING
AND ENTERPRISES, LLC

Published by Tate Publishing & Enterprises, LLC
127 E. Trade Center Terrace | Mustang, Oklahoma 73064 USA
1.888.361.9473 | www.tatepublishing.com

Tate Publishing is committed to excellence in the publishing industry. The company reflects the philosophy established by the founders, based on Psalm 68:11,
"The Lord gave the word and great was the company of those who published it."

Published in the United States of America

ISBN: 978-1-68237-684-3
1. Fiction / Westerns
2. Fiction / Historical
16.09.14

To:

God, the Author and Finisher of our faith.
He is the One who gave me this storyline and
gave me the motivation to complete it.

Priscilla, my wife. No man could be more blessed than
I to have such a loyal and faithful wife. "Through
many dangers, toils, and snares, I have already come"
and she, like God, has always been by my side.

Acknowledgments

I want to thank three men in particular. Glenn Grinnell, who helped get me hooked on westerns; Paul Reinhart who taught me a great deal about the old west and the western genre; and Jason Hosner, who worked with me and together we helped each other through some difficult times. Jason will always be like a son to me.

I also want to say thanks to Earl Two Bulls who helped me with the Lakota translation. Any errors are strictly my own.

The folks at Tate Publishing have been super. Charles "Kirk" Calloway, Acquisitions Editor, took a chance on an unknown. Beatriz Bustamante, Project Manager, worked hard to get this book put together and ready for sale. And many others there have been great in working with me.

There are many others who deserve recognition for what they have meant to me. I don't have the space to name them all, but I especially want to thank the members of Explore

Church who stuck with me through the most difficult period of my life. The pastor, Clay Burgess, believed in me and has helped others understand that we all make mistakes in life, it's what we do with the aftermath that sets us apart. I particularly want to thank Stephanie Burgess; Wayne and Linda Burgess; Andy Poe; Chip, Karen, and Lydia Cornell; and Mike Ramsey for all their support and love. I also say thanks to Danielle Craver who took time out of a very busy schedule to read my manuscript and provide valuable input.

Contents

Prologue

Salina, Kansas, April 14, 1876

THE BLACK-DRESSED FIGURE stepped back into the shadows of the narrow area between the general store and the town barbershop. In the pre-midnight dark, two other figures darted across the hard-packed dirt street outside the Dog Ear Saloon and stopped at the front corner of the building. One gave a boost to their companion, who held on to the bottom edge of the balcony and quickly pulled up and over the railing. The one still on the ground slipped back along the side of the beer hall and then went around to the backdoor.

Cautiously, the lithe figure on the balcony took a quick peek through one of the upper floor windows. Since the room was empty, a slim knife was used to unlock the simple catch, opening the window, giving access to the room. The figure then looked out the window and lit a match, signaling the person standing across the street.

At the back of the saloon, the third figure, after ascertaining that the backdoor was unlocked, peeked around the corner. Just as the one on the second floor did, the third figure lit a match, a signal to the one across the street that all was ready.

The first figure waited momentarily, making sure that there were no other people out on the town's Main Street before emerging from the shadows. Concealing a Winchester rifle beneath his black duster, he walked across the dirt road to the front entrance of the Dog Ear Saloon. Pushing open the batwing doors, he quietly slipped inside and, with a quick glance, located his two companions—one on the balcony overlooking the main floor and the other just inside the backdoor of the saloon.

Ike Sturgis was in the middle of a not-quite-friendly poker game with two other members of his gang. Surrounding him at other tables were the remaining thirteen members of his group of murderers, cutthroats, bank and train robbers, and just plain old miscreants. All the men were so engrossed in their drinking and gambling that none of them noticed the slim figure in the dark clothing at first. Then Sturgis caught some movement at the corner of his eye, and he turned to look at the figure standing straight and tall in a wide stance.

"Wal lookee har, boys," the grizzled gang leader drawled. "Looks like we's got us a new honey to play wit'."

Speaking to the darkly dressed young woman, he continued, "Whys doncha com har and sits on my lap and—"

The sudden appearance of a Winchester rifle from beneath the woman's black duster stopped Ike in the middle of his sentence.

"Ike Sturgis, I'm US Marshal Matilda Cochran and you and your gang are under arrest for murder and bank robbery," the blue-eyed blonde informed him. "Place your hands on top of the tables. Anyone who comes up with anything other than empty hands is going to die right here. Do I make myself clear?"

"Yeah, but it's one against sixteen, Marshal. Looks like you're outnumbered," Sturgis replied.

With a nod toward the top of the stairs, Mattie said, "Maybe you should count again. Let me introduce you to my sister US Marshal Camille Cochran."

Cami stood on the landing at the top of the stairs, a walnut-handled Colt .45 in each hand. As they turned their eyes toward the matching sister, some of the men spotted Danielle standing by the open backdoor, a double-barreled, twelve-gauge shotgun pointing at them. Seeing the look of sternness on Dani's face, the men instinctively knew this was trouble of the worst kind. Stunned by the fact that they were facing three women rather than men and realizing that the women were identical, the men froze in place. Ike was the first to speak, switching back to his exaggerated accent.

"Listin' har, missy—"

"I am not your 'missy' or your 'honey' or any other term of endearment you might conjure up, and if I don't see some hands grabbing tabletop pretty quick, my fellow deputies and I are gonna get *real itchy*, if you know what I mean," she taunted. To demonstrate the seriousness of her threat, she ratcheted a round into the chamber of the Winchester.

Ike Sturgis swiveled his head back and forth, taking in the situation and assessing the probability of survival should there be a shootout. He wasn't ready to surrender—especially to women—nor be fitted for a hangman's noose just yet. With a slight nod to his men, Sturgis rose from his seat, his right hand moving to the handle of his six-shooter.

The big gang leader blinked uncomprehendingly when he felt someone punch him in the chest. Looking down, he was surprised by the growing red circle that appeared in the middle of his shirt. Then he heard gunfire all around him but didn't understand why his own gun wasn't firing too. Before long, it dawned on him that his gun was still in his holster. As he started to reach for it again, he saw that his right palm was covered in something red.

Slowly, his mind put it together: he had been shot, and it was his blood covering his palm and fingers. Suddenly feeling tired, he sank back down into his chair and laid his head down. His forehead bounced off the table once and then came to rest. Blood dribbled from the corner of his mouth, his breath coming in wheezy gasps as his body convulsed to his death.

Like most gunfights, this one lasted only about fifteen seconds before the room was filled with utter silence. The smell of cordite in the air was strong. Eleven of the gang members lay dead or dying on the floor before the rest raised their hands and dropped their guns in surrender.

"Cami, you okay?" Mattie shouted when she spotted blood on her sister's left arm.

"Yeah! It's just a scratch. I'll be fine," the blonde deputy replied.

"Dani?" Mattie called out.

"I'm okay, Sis," Dani replied.

The three deputies cautiously approached the remaining outlaws and secured their weapons. Dani got a large box from the backroom and began placing the gang's guns in it. Cami kept an eye on their captives, and Mattie carefully checked out her wounded dog. Amid cleanup, the town sheriff arrived with two of his deputies. Camille introduced herself to him and him to her sisters.

"You're triplets?" the sheriff asked.

"That's correct," Danielle responded.

"And you're deputy US marshals?" he asked, incredulity clear in his voice.

"Is there a problem here, Sheriff?" Cami asked, sensing the sheriff's dislike of the fact.

"Who's the idiot who made three women—triplets, no less—*deputies*?"

"That would be Marshal Tobias Winters, and if I were you, I'd be careful about calling him an idiot, especially to his face."

"Honey, anyone who would put a gun in a woman's hand and a badge on her chest is an idiot. And I'd have no problem telling Marshal Winters or *any* other marshal that to their face!"

"Like my sister told Sturgis, I'm not your honey. And considering that the three of us tracked down and arrested Kansas's most wanted outlaw gang, it seems to me that Marshal Winters made a pretty good choice. Now, why don't you and your deputies take our five prisoners over to your jail cell and lock them up until the marshal can make arrangements to have them transported to Topeka for trial?"

"There's no way I'm going to start taking orders from some snotty-nosed little girl, badge or no badge! You want them in my jail? You can take them there yourself."

The sheriff's attitude rankled Cami and her sisters, but they refused to show it.

1

BEGINNINGS

Dewitt, Iowa, October, 1869

FOR THE SEVEN hundred or so residents of Dewitt, Iowa, located approximately 125 miles from Des Moines in the northeast corner of Henry County, corn was the main crop the farmers raised. And the annual Harvest Dance was the biggest entertainment event of the year. Held each October right after the fall harvest, it drew in both the young and the old.

Held in Dewitt's town hall, the dance was not only an opportunity for the community's families to have fun and socialize, but traditionally, it was also a time for young people of acceptable age to begin courting. For that reason, if no other, the Cochran triplets had been looking forward to this particular year's dance and the annual ritual. Prior to 1869, before the girl's sixteenth birthday, their father, Charles, only allowed them to dance with other girls. Tonight, they would get to dance with boys their own age (or maybe even those a couple years older).

Matilda, Camille, and Danielle were the prettiest three girls in all of Dewitt (maybe the entire county even). When they entered the town hall meeting room that late October evening, there wasn't a boy who didn't turn their heads to watch. Many of the young women also watched, but it was really more out of envy than desire. Charles noted the attention his daughters were attracting—both the good and the bad. He knew that these three were soon going to be breaking more hearts than the average girl. For their part, the three teens were only vaguely aware of the jealous stares but superficially aware of the stares coming from the boys.

For the dance, the three were dressed in brand new dresses that were identical in every aspect except for the color: Danielle's dress was her favorite color, yellow; Camille wore green; and Matilda wore her go-to color, purple. Feigning nonchalance, the girls circulated the crowd, sizing up prospects and competition as only teenagers can. Eventually Mattie, who was the natural-born leader, led them over to the food table, where they each got a cup of punch and surveyed the crowd.

It took Nelly Grayson, the girl who would have been this year's Harvest Queen if Danielle hadn't turned sixteen, about thirty seconds to wend her way through the masses and "accidentally" bump into her, spilling punch all over the teen's yellow dress. However, it took Mattie only three seconds to deck Nelly with her vicious right hook.

The blue-eyed blonde Matilda stood over the evil, jealous seventeen-year-old, practically begging her to stand up so that she could slug her again. As Charles gently pulled his daughter away, Nelly's mother knelt down next to the crying brunette. Mister Grayson turned to Charles and accused him of "raising vicious devil girls."

"Seems to me, Grayson," Charles responded with a bemused look on his narrow, sun-browned face, "that your daughter has been begging for trouble for over a year now. She's been taunting and bullying Danielle since school began last year. If one seeks trouble, one should not be surprised to find trouble."

"So you're not going to do anything about Matilda striking my Nelly," Grayson asked belligerently.

"Yes, I am! I'm going to tell Mattie how proud I am of her that she stood up for her sister."

"Well, I never!" Nelly's father sputtered then turned and walked away.

"No, I imagine you never did," Charles mumbled.

Mattie sensed someone standing close behind her. Looking back over her shoulder, she tensed, ready to defend herself if necessary.

"You're not going to punch me too, are you?" a soft, mellow voice spoke.

The blonde was unable to respond as her eyes took in the deep, sapphire blue eyes of a young man. His shoulder-length wavy black hair framed a face containing a pug nose, a sensuous mouth, and those incredible eyes.

Waving a hand in front of her face, he spoke again.

"Hello? Anybody in there?" he asked, smiling.

"Wha—oh, hi!" Mattie stuttered. "Pardon me, did you say something?"

"I asked if you were going to hit me like you did that girl. That's a pretty mean right hook you have. Where did you learn to punch like that?"

"From my older brother, Junior. Who—who are you? I don't believe I've ever seen you around. Do you go to our school?"

"Sorry, I'm David Yarden. My parents just moved to a farm a couple miles south of here. What's your name?"

"Matilda—uh, Mattie. How come I've never seen you before?"

Caught off guard by the by the teen's good looks, Mattie was finding it difficult to speak. She knew she had to get her composure back, before she made a complete fool out of herself.

"I've been back east, staying with an aunt and uncle in New York. Anyway, would you like to dance?"

"What?"

"Dance? You know, move our feet in step with the music?"

"Um, yeah, I'd like that very much," Mattie answered, still flustered.

Keep it together, Mattie! the blonde chided herself.

Lydia Cochran escorted her daughter Dani back to their farm, about a fifteen-minute buggy ride from the town meeting hall, so that the teenager could change her dress.

"Is that the girl that's been giving you so much trouble at school?" she asked her daughter.

"Yes, ma'am!" the teen replied.

"Do you know why she's been causing trouble?"

"It's 'cause of Bobby Lee."

"Because of—you mean the Benson boy?"

"Yes, ma'am!"

"What about him?"

"Nelly's been…*sparking* with him."

"Danielle Marie Cochran!" Lydia exclaimed, shocked that her daughter said such a thing. "That's not a very nice thing to say about a young lady. It's also not a very Christian thing to say about anyone!"

"But, Mama, *everybody* at school says it. And Nelly doesn't deny it."

"That's still no reason to say such a mean thing about another young lady. And it doesn't explain why she's picking on you."

"She seen Bobby Lee talking to me—"

"She *saw* Bobby Lee…"

"She *saw* Bobby Lee talking to me and accused me of trying to steal her boyfriend—which I *wasn't*! I mean, Bobby Lee's okay, I guess. But all the girls know that he's only interested in them as long as they're willing to spark with him. Then he dumps them."

"I do declare, Girl, I believe you are getting a little too free with your speech! I don't like to hear my children talking about others that way. And if Bobby Lee is that kind of boy, I don't want you or your sisters to have *anything* to do with him. Now let's get back to that dance."

"Yes, Mama! And you don't have to worry about me and Bobby Lee or any other boy like him. Mattie, Cami, and I watch out for each other. And if we can't handle the situation, Junior steps in."

———∘∘❁∘∘———

"So who's this Junior you mentioned?" David Yarden asked Mattie as they took a breather between dances.

"Charles Cochran Junior. He's my older brother," the blonde teenager replied.

"Yeah, where is he?"

Mattie glanced around the hall until she spotted him.

"That's him over there," she said, pointing. "He's the blonde guy talking to the cute redhead."

Yarden looked in the direction the girl pointed and saw a tall blonde young man talking to a very attractive red-haired young woman. They both appeared to be in their late teens and more than just a little interested in each other.

While only an inch or two taller than the dark-haired Yarden, Junior was obviously wider in the shoulders and appeared to be much more muscular. David Yarden was a city boy while Junior Cochran had grown up on the farm. Yarden was neither a weakling nor a coward, but he knew instinctively that Mattie's older brother was not someone he wanted to mess with if it could be avoided.

A week after the Harvest Dance, David Yarden showed up at the Cochran farm and asked Charles's permission to begin courting Matilda. While her parents were a little leery of him at the beginning, they gradually began warming up to him; and by the time a year had gone by, they were willing to give the couple their blessing when David asked for their permission to propose to their daughter. It was clear that

David wasn't rich, but he did seem to have the means to provide for Mattie and himself.

On the surface, David Yarden was always the perfect gentleman, always treated Mattie with respect and courtesy. Mattie was utterly thrilled when he proposed and immediately said yes. But her two sisters weren't so sure.

It wasn't that Camille and Danielle were against their sister getting married or that it meant breaking up the trio. Rather, it was that they sensed that something wasn't exactly right with David. For the sake of their sister's happiness, they agreed to keep their opinion to themselves, but they were going to watch *very* carefully.

June 10, 1871

The couple was married in June of 1871 and moved into a house on the southern edge of Dewitt. The accompanying farm wasn't very big—only about a quarter of the size of the Cochrans'—but hard work should make it sufficient to provide for the couple's needs.

There's an axiom about people bringing their troubles with them. For David Yarden, it was more than just a saying. This was not David Yarden's first marriage, a fact he had failed to share with Mattie or anyone else in Iowa. His parents, of course, knew, but they had remained as tight lipped about it as their son had. However, not only had he been previously married; but his first wife was also dead, and the police in New York City very much wanted to question him about her death.

But New York City was hundreds of miles from Dewitt, Iowa, and years ahead in communications and policing methods. Consequently, no one in the Cochran family was aware of David's troubling situation. They also weren't aware of Mattie and David's marital problems, which began sometime in August.

Yarden's first outburst of anger culminated in a hard slap that stung his wife's face but did no physical damage. Half an hour later, he was on his knees, begging forgiveness and promising it wouldn't happen again. He blamed his outburst on his being tired and hungry, chastising his wife for not having dinner ready when he came in from the field. In other words, in his mind, it was actually Mattie's fault that he was angry. He claimed that he slapped her because she was talking back to him when, really, she was just trying to explain why dinner was late.

Over the course of the next month and a half, his outbursts became more frequent, and the physical abuse escalated. Even their lovemaking took on a more violent quality.

Early that October, Cami and Dani discovered the truth when they paid a surprise visit to their triplet sister. They were shocked to find her with a blackened eye and bruises on both arms. Further inquiry resulted in a discovery of more bruises beneath her dress. Mattie tried to pass it off as her being clumsy, but neither of her sisters believed that their normally solid sister could have suddenly turned so clumsy.

On the way back to their own farmhouse, the two young women stopped off at the Dewitt telegraph office and sent a message to their father's friend who lived in New York City. Two days later, they received a response that was both unbelievable yet still expected. The NY Police Department would not pursue their case against David because of the distance involved, but Cami and Dani decided to make their own plans.

October 1871

To the west of the Yarden farmstead was a long, wide swath of trees edging a very fertile plot of open ground. On the far side of the plot was a swiftly flowing stream marking the boundary between Yarden and his neighbor, Obadiah Hodkins. On the day that Camille, Danielle, and Matilda turned eighteen, David Yarden was plowing that particular field, preparing it for the winter crop he intended to plant.

Whether by chance or fate, it so happened that Hodkins was also plowing a field that was adjacent to David's. So he was able to observe two riders dressed completely in black emerge from the woods and approach Yarden. The two men, as Obadiah presumed them to be, were shielding their faces with wide-brimmed Stetsons that were pulled down low. Hodkins considered the situation suspicious but was not inclined to stick his nose in his neighbor's business, especially since he didn't particularly like David Yarden.

Obadiah tried to listen in on the conversation between Yarden and the two men but only heard some mumbling because of the distance. Nevertheless, he could tell that his neighbor wasn't happy about the interruption or about what was being talked about. Hodkins watched as David unhitched his plow horse and climb aboard. The three men then rode off into the woods. That was the last time anyone in Dewitt, Iowa, saw David Yarden.

It had been two days since Yarden's disappearance. Obadiah Hodkins was eating lunch at his kitchen table when his nine-year-old son, Trajen, came running into the house, yelling, "Rider comin', Pa!"

Obadiah grabbed his Springfield rifle as he walked out the front door of his log cabin; but he immediately set it against a porch post when he realized that his visitor was the town sheriff, Martin Crowley. Crowley had been elected sheriff back when Obadiah was a teenager in Georgia. He took Obadiah, along with his parents, two younger sisters, and young wife, in when they escaped from a plantation right at the beginning of the Civil War. It was September of 1861 when the family arrived in Dewitt and Sheriff Crowley and his wife welcomed them into their home, helping them to adjust to their new lives as free citizens.

When a group of gunmen—hired by southern plantation owners bent on getting back what they considered to be runaway slaves—showed up the following year, Crowley organized a "citizens' committee" to oppose the gunmen. A gun battle ensued, and all but two of the southerners were killed. These two men were hanged a week later after a very short trial in front of the regular circuit judge.

"Afternoon, Obadiah!" the sheriff greeted his thirty-year-old friend.

"G'noon, Martin! What brings you all the way out here?" Hodkins asked.

Obadiah's four children had been playing out in the yard when the lawman rode up, and now the youngest (a daughter) was clinging on to his left leg, halfway hidden behind it. The other three stood nearby gawking. Trajen was standing closest to his father, trying hard to look manly like his dad. Seeing the sheriff looking past him, Hodkins glanced back over his shoulder and saw his pretty wife standing in the doorway of the cabin.

"Mrs. Hodkins!" Crowley greeted.

"Sheriff!"

"Obadiah," the sheriff began, "when was the last time you saw David Yarden?"

"Le's see…Musta been two days ago. We's was both out plowing our fields down by the river. Is thar some kinda trouble, Martin?"

"Don't know yet. Did you see anything unusual down there?"

"Nows dat yous mention it, there was dem two black men dat rode up on him."

"Two black men?"

"Wells now, theys were dressed all in black. Buts I cunnant sees thems faces, sos I don't know if'n theys themselves were black."

"Martin, whys doncha comes in and haves some coffee. Obadiah canna answer alls your questions whiles yous relax," Mrs. Hodkins suggested.

"I thank you, Mrs. Hodkins. I believe I'd like to do just that."

The lawman dismounted and tied the reins to one of the porch posts before following the two adults inside. Their three-year-old daughter still clung to her daddy's leg, but the other three children quickly scampered away when their father threatened to find work for them if they couldn't find something else to do while he was talking to the sheriff.

Once inside, they were seated at the kitchen table with steaming mugs of coffee before them. Crowley then asked Obadiah to continue telling him about what he saw.

"Wells, these two young men—"

"I thought you said you couldn't see their faces. How do you know they were young men?"

"I's cunnant! But theys rode like theys were young men, sos I reckoned tha's whats they was."

"Okay, go on."

"Anyways, theys come outta dem trees nears where David was plowin' and rodes right up to him likes theys knows him. The threes of dem talked, and it looked like David was gettin' upset, yous know. Like, agitated. Thens he unhooks his plow hoss, jumps on, and all threes ride off inna the woods. I ne'er did sees if'n he come back, but the next day, da plow's gone."

"Anything else?"

"No, sir! Thas all I dun seen. Whas this all 'bout, Martin?"

"David Yarden didn't come home that night, and no one's seen hide nor hair of him since. Mrs. Yarden's pa came and got the plow yesterday, and the horse showed up on its own late yesterday afternoon. No one seems to know what has become of the young man. His wife is, understandably, worried sick."

"I'll go ove' thar tomarree and check up on her," Mrs. Hodkins offered. "My husban' and I dinna haves much use for the man, but the wife is a good woman."

"I think that's a fine idea, Mrs. Hodkins. I'm sure Mrs. Yarden will appreciate the company."

Sheriff Crowley spent the best part of a month investigating the disappearance of David Yarden, to no avail. He had some suspicions relating to the incident but no evidence to back up those suspicions, so he kept them to himself. Obadiah Hodkins was the only person who saw the two riders dressed in black but couldn't provide any more information than he'd already given Crowley. Eventually, more pressing matters pushed the event further to the back of the sheriff's list of priorities.

2

Deputies

Wichita, Kansas, January 18, 1875

THREE YOUNG WOMEN emerged from the lobby of a hotel onto a wide veranda. It had snowed overnight leaving a foot-deep covering on the street immediately in front of the inn. All three were wearing blue denim jeans and western cut shirts with pearled snap buttons down the front and on the pocket flaps. The shirts were identical except that one shirt was purple, one was green, and the third one was yellow. Over their shirts, the females wore leather vests and ankle-length sheepskin coats with heavy wool lining. Their leader (the one wearing purple) carried a Winchester rifle on her shoulder and a Colt six-shooter in a tied-down holster on her right hip.

One of her sisters, dressed in the green shirt, was wearing a pair of matching Smith and Wesson pistols with cherry wood handles. The other sister was armed with a six-shooter and a sawed-off double-barreled twelve-gauge shotgun. The shotgun was carried beneath her thick winter coat clipped to a special swivel device that allowed her to bring the weapon into a shooting position quickly. Her pistol was holstered on her left hip with the butt forward for a crossover draw.

Foot deep snow made them pause for a moment before they breathed a sigh of relief, noting that their destination this morning was on the same side of the street as the hotel. This meant that they wouldn't need to trudge through the accumulation in their freshly polished boots.

Wichita was not used to seeing heavily armed females walking along its boardwalk, and these three drew a large number of stares. Whispered comments ranged from distaste, mostly by the other womenfolk, to admiration, by the men who were paying attention mostly to the attractiveness of the armed girls. There were also those who made fun of Mattie, Cami, and Dani, accusing them of being dumb to dress the way they were.

Along the way to their intended destination, they passed the town's sheriff office. They saw him sitting behind his desk and it made them smile when he did a double take and then jump to his feet. A moment later he opened the office door and stepped out onto the boardwalk. If he meant to say anything he found out he was too late as Mattie was opening a door two buildings down. Above the door Mattie opened was a sign identifying it as the US Marshals Office.

"Hello, may I help you?" the female receptionist asked as the sisters stepped into a small lobby.

"We're here to see Supervisory Marshal Winters," Mattie replied pleasantly.

"Do you have an appointment?" The receptionist's tone was slightly on the snotty side.

Matilda Cochran removed a letter from her coat pocket and handed it to the woman, saying, "He invited us to stop in and see him when we came to Wichita."

"I see! Well, Marshal Winters is a very busy man. I'm sure that he meant he'd meet with you if he had the time, but right now is not a very good time. Why don't you come back in a week or so? Maybe he'll have time to see you then."

Keeping a smile on her face, Mattie said, "Why don't you show him that letter? I'm sure when he sees it he will make time to meet with us."

The receptionist's back stiffened as she retorted, "Why I never…"

"I'm sure you haven't," Dani interrupted. "Now, why don't you ask the man instead of making decisions for him." Then she gave the woman her brightest, sweetest smile.

Indignantly, the woman rose from her desk and marched down a narrow hallway behind her. Stopping at a door on her left, she knocked and opened the door. She entered the room and a moment later a tall man came out of the office, closely followed by the irritated receptionist, and walked out to the front counter. As his dark brown eyes sized up the three women facing him, Mattie spoke.

"Hi, I'm Mattie Cochran, and these are my sisters, Cami and Dani," the blue-eyed blonde said in introduction. "I'm the one who has been corresponding with you over the last few months."

"Yes, well I didn't realize that you were triplets. This could be interesting," he responded. "I'm Tobias Winters. Why don't we go back to my office, where we can talk.

"Katie, no interruptions unless it's an emergency," he instructed the receptionist.

Seated in the marshal's office, the Cochran sisters could barely contain their excitement. As they glanced around they noted that the room was about the size of their hotel room and was sparsely furnished. A wooden desk sat toward the back wall of the office and was badly scarred from abuse. Six ladder-back chairs were pushed up against one wall and there were a few documents that were framed and hung up on the wall behind the desk. There was also a large circular plaque bearing the seal of the United States Marshals Service affixed to the same wall.

Tobias Winters motioned for the three sisters to have a seat and then lowered himself into a high-backed, red leather chair behind the desk. As the chair appeared to be the newest piece of furniture in the office, the girls guessed that it was Winters's own personal property.

"So the three of you wish to become deputy US marshals?" he said, making the statement sound more like a question.

"For a little over three years," Mattie began to explain, "the three of us have spent our free time studying the law, practicing handling various firearms, learning how to defend ourselves, and learning how to live off the land. We investigated various law enforcement agencies and we have decided that the US Marshals Service is the best agency in the country. And we want to work for the best."

"After I got your first letter a couple of months ago, I contacted my superiors in Washington to get their opinion. I hafta tell you, their first reaction was that the whole idea was preposterous. However, they found out that the Pinkerton's had hired a couple of female agents and they decided that there was a political side to this issue. Consequently, they have given me some discretion and are willing to let me decide if you indeed are fit to be deputies.

"If you can prove to me that you're truly serious and that you have the necessary skills to 'make the cut,' I will give you a fair chance."

"What do we have to do?" Dani asked tentatively.

"First, you will have to take a written test on the law. The people in DC have devised the basic test, and I have added a few questions of my own based on my experiences. I will tell you flat out, it is not an easy test.

"Each of you will take the test by yourself. Anyone who doesn't pass the test doesn't get into the service. After the written test you will be tested on your gun skills. You will be asked to fire a number of different weapons as well as demonstrate the ability to break the weapons down, clean them, and put them back together. A dirty weapon is very dangerous, so we insist on making sure our deputies know what they are doing.

"Your third test will be an oral interview designed to ascertain whether or not you have the moral and mental capabilities we expect. The Marshals Service demands the highest standards of moral behavior. And the job is also mentally demanding, as I imagine you will find out very quickly if you are selected.

"Lastly, if you have successfully completed the first three tests, you will be given an assignment. Failure to pass any one of these four tests will disqualify you immediately. Any questions?"

"How does this compare with what the male officers go through?" Mattie asked.

"You're getting a fair shake, if that's what you want to know. Our male officers go through an academy where they spend several months of training. They are taught the law, learn how to handle firearms, and endure a rigorous physical regimen to ensure they can handle the vagaries of the job.

"You claimed in your letters that the three of you have already done these things on your own. I'm giving you a chance to prove what you've said. Our male cadets go through the same kind of testing I'm going to subject you to."

"When do we get this testing?" Cami asked.

"Right now!"

Marshal Winters led the three sisters from his office and to a room across the hall. There he introduced them to Chief Deputy Marshal Kyle Branch. Deputy Branch had set up the room with three desks, widely separated, and instructed the blondes to take seats behind them.

"This test is divided into two parts," Branch began once Winters left the room. "Each part is timed and is to be completed within one hour. You will be graded both on correctness of answers and on the number of questions you have answered during the allotted time. I suggest you answer the questions you know first and then go back and tackle the ones you are less sure about. I can help you if you are having difficulty understanding what the question is asking, so don't be afraid to ask me. However, you are not allowed to talk among yourselves. Doing so will automatically result in disqualification.

"I'm going to place the first part of the test face down on your desk. Do not turn it over until I tell you to begin. Are there any questions?"

After distributing the test, Deputy Branch looked at his watch and then said, "Begin!"

An hour passed before the deputy suddenly commanded the sisters to stop. He then quickly collected the three tests. Branch suggested to the young women that they take a half-hour break and go get a cup of coffee at the hotel. When they returned at the appointed time he gave them the second part of the written exam. This part only had five questions, but they each required a lengthy, detailed answer. Each question dealt with what was considered to be a "typical" scenario a deputy might face and required the applicant to describe how she would deal with it.

The hour they were given to complete the test wasn't sufficient and the three sisters were frustrated. This time Branch told them to take an hour-long break and grab something to eat. When they returned from their lunch they were told that there'd been a slight change of plans. Instead of displaying their firearm skills, they would now undergo an oral examination to determine their moral and mental acumen.

Camille was to be interviewed by the marshal himself while Danielle's interview would be conducted by Deputy Branch. Mattie would have to wait until those interviews were over as hers was to be handled by both Winters and the deputy.

Camille and Danielle spent just under an hour each with their respective interviewers and were clearly exhausted by the time their examinations were complete. However, they sat in the lobby and waited for their sister's interview to finish, nearly an hour and a half later. The three candidates were then told that it would be the next morning before they would learn the outcome of their trials. They proceeded to return to their hotel room where they promptly collapsed on their beds. It was more than three hours later before they could rouse themselves enough to get up and go secure some dinner.

Over a scarcely touched meal, Cami and Dani quizzed each other on the questions in both the written and oral exams. The lively conversation was in full swing when they suddenly realized that Mattie, usually the most talkative one of the group, hadn't once chimed in on the discussion. She was just quietly eating her meal, seemingly lost in thought and not answering any of her sister's questions. This caused the other two to quit talking themselves. Finally, Dani broke the silence around the table.

"What's wrong, Sis?"

"Nothing."

"Come on! You haven't said *two* words since Winters and Branch questioned you," Cami interjected. "Dani and I were also interviewed, and it wasn't *that* bad. This isn't like you, so what's going on?"

Mattie sat staring at her food for a couple of minutes before responding in a whisper, "They asked a lot of questions about David."

The two other sisters exchanged a worried glance. Mattie was obviously frightened.

Dani asked, "What kind of questions? What did they want to know?"

"Everything! They wanted to know every detail about our marriage, how we met, how we got along, what happened on the day he disappeared...They wanted to know where I was when he went missing. How did I feel about his disappearance? What have I done to help find him?...They also asked a lot of questions about the two of you. They thought you were the mystery riders who spoke to David that day."

"Wha—what did you tell them?" Cami asked, suddenly nervous.

"I told them that you were my sisters and that you would never do anything to hurt me. But they kept asking the same questions over and over, as if they believed I was involved in his disappearance and that I was hiding something."

After a long, uncomfortable silence, Mattie told her sisters about her fear.

"Cami...Dani...I think the marshal and his deputy think I murdered David."

3

DAKOTA SAM

Topeka, Kansas, September 15, 1874

A LONE RIDER reined-in out front of the First Mercantile Bank of Topeka, Kansas. He slowly dismounted, quickly checking around him to take mental note of who else was on the street. Removing his wide brimmed hat, he slapped it against his body. Puffs of road dust blossomed from his filthy clothing. He wore a red plaid flannel shirt and brown chaps over his blue denim jeans. The black boots on his feet were severely scuffed and looked like it had been years since they'd last seen any polishing.

Adjusting his gun belt until the Colt .45 on his right hip settled into the spot where it felt most comfortable, Dakota

Sam stepped up onto the bank's boardwalk, again scanning the streets and nearby businesses. The First Mercantile Bank was on a side street of the growing Kansas town, several blocks from the town's law enforcement offices.

Satisfied that no one was paying any attention to him, the half Sioux Indian brave pushed open the bank's doors and stepped inside. His Mexican spurs jangled as he walked across the hard, wooden floor toward one of the two teller windows. Those who turned to look at the dust encrusted half-breed quickly turned back to what they were doing. Sam's eyes registered the presence of five other people: two tellers, two customers, and a man he presumed was the bank manager as he was sitting at a desk off to the right. The manager's desk was fronted by a wooden fence with a gate in the middle of it allowing access to the manager.

In the center of the room was a waist-high table that customers would use to fill out their deposit or withdrawal slips. Sam used this table to pretend to be filling out one of these documents provided for the use of the bank's customers. As the half-breed wrote out his withdrawal, a second man entered the bank and exchanged a quick glance with him. Then the second man got into the leftmost customer line. Just as he was about to move to the front of the line, three masked men came rushing into the bank with guns drawn.

Dakota Sam and the second man pulled the bandanas they were wearing around their necks up over their noses and mouths and shouted that this was a stickup.

"Nobody do anything foolish and nobody will get hurt," Sam intoned. Passing through the small gate, Dakota commanded the manager, "Git up! Take me to the vault!"

One of the three newest men stood by the front door, keeping the two customers inside and watching out for any potential interference. The remaining three men went behind the teller's wall and collected all the cash they had in their drawers. Sam, led to the vault by the manager, stuffed canvas bags with all the money contained in the large safe. As he emerged from the vault he pointed his gun at the manager's head and pulled the trigger.

The five men jumped on their horses and, as townsfolk looked on their attention drawn to the gunshot, rode out of town to the south. One spectator drew his own six-shooter and fired at the fleeing men, but missed. His reward was a slug in the chest from one of the outlaw's pistols.

A barrage of gunfire chased the bandits out of town. However, only one bullet hit its mark, and that only resulted in a grazed arm.

Two days later, the same gang hit the bank in Lawrence, Kansas.

By the end of September, Dakota Sam and his gang had hit banks in Junction City and Manhattan, Kansas. By this time, six people had been killed, but none of them were members of the gang. Posses had chased the gang all over the eastern part of the state with no success.

The lawmen and their posses had not yet figured out the strategy Sam was using to evade capture. Just before they entered a town where they planned to rob a bank they would tether a string of four horses to a spot about a mile or so out of town. They were using older, worn out horses that were cheap to buy but could still give a good run for a few miles. As the outlaws raced from the town following a holdup, one of the gang members would grab the string of horses and ride off in one direction while the other members split up and rode off in various directions. Sometimes one of them would even ride back slowly toward the town, pretending to be nonchalantly headed there. One of them was arrogant enough to actually become part of a posse.

Meanwhile, the outlaw leading the old, worn out nags would release them one at a time. He would point the horse in a direction away from the trail and whip it so that it would run off. As the posse tried to catch up, they would have to allocate resources to following these phony trails. Eventually the outlaws themselves would meet up, divide the money among them, and then go off in separate directions until it was time to meet and pull off the next robbery.

This strategy was the brainchild of Dakota Sam, a twenty-five-year-old Sioux half-breed who didn't like being cooped up in a reservation. Sam wore white man's clothing and spoke English as good as, and maybe even better, than some white people. To further confuse the law he rode a shod horse and used a western saddle. His hair was cut short like a white man's and it amused him to think he was using the "white man's ways" to rob them.

———◦◦∘◦◦———

September turned into October, the leaves on the trees turning into a myriad of bright orange, red, and yellow colors. Sam and his gang continued to hit banks, including the ones in Salina, McPherson, and Emporia, in a two and a half week period. Right after the Emporia holdup, Sam informed the members of the gang that they were going to "lie low" until November.

During this "down" time, the gang members hid in plain sight. Instead of holing up in some ramshackle old house or cabin, they each went to a different town, got a hotel room, and then spent their time, and money, gambling and drinking at the local saloon. For over three weeks, the gang didn't pull off a single robbery. This caused many people to believe that they had either moved to another state or killed off each other in an argument over the money they'd stolen. But the town sheriff of El Dorado, Kansas was not one of those people.

Dakota Sam's gang met on November 13, 1874 at an abandoned farmhouse about two and a half miles northeast of El Dorado. A little after nine the next morning, Sam walked through the front door of the town's Farmers and Merchants Bank. Three minutes later, the rest of the gang was inside the bank, stuffing money into canvas bags and preparing to make their getaway. What they didn't know was that they were in for a big surprise.

The robbing spree had attracted the attention of every law enforcement officer in the state of Kansas. In the event that the desperados might actually come to his town, the local sheriff had called the town council together in early October and devised a plan to counteract the gang's activities. Each morning, the sheriff outlined, two men and two children would station themselves, one pair at each end of town. The watchers would rotate so everyone in town shared equally.

When a stranger rode into town and was soon followed by another stranger, the adult would send the child with him to the backdoor of the sheriff's office. Since nobody pays much attention to a child running down the street it was presumed that there was little danger to the child. The sheriff would check out the situation, and if he thought this was a holdup getting ready to happen, he would spread the news for all the men to get ready.

Caught off guard by the lawman's planning, Sam and his gang were outside the bank and starting to mount up when they were ordered to drop their weapons and raise their hands. The last outlaw to leave the bank rushed back in, expecting to escape out the backdoor. Instead, he was met by the blast from a twelve gauge shotgun, cutting him nearly in half.

The remainder of the gang began shooting it out with the townsfolk as they mounted their steeds and raced out the east end of El Dorado. One of the outlaws was hit twice, once in the left leg and then in his right shoulder forcing him to drop his weapon and fall off his horse. He was quickly jumped on by several men and arrested. Sam and the other two men with him barely got a hundred yards out of town when they saw a posse coming after them. Sam saw that there was no time to grab the string of horses they'd left at the farmhouse, so he signaled the other two men to split up and go in different directions.

When Dakota Sam met back up with his two remaining gang members over a week had gone by. The half-breed had learned that the one man that had gone back into the bank looking to escape was dead and that the one that had been captured had been tried and was sentenced to hang. He was mad that the town had come up with their plan and killed one of his men. Sam vowed to make them pay some day.

Despite being down to just three men, the gang hit two more banks—Hutchinson and Great Bend—before the end of November. However, they weren't the smooth robberies the gang had perpetrated back in September and October. Hutchinson and Great Bend had heard of the success El Dorado had had, and they adopted similar plans. The towns weren't as successful either, but both Sam and one of his men had earned themselves slugs during their robberies. Sam was shot in the left arm in Hutchinson, and the other man was shot in the leg in Great Bend. Neither wound was very serious, but they were painful.

Dakota wanted to hit two more banks—Dodge City and Garden City—before the December snows made an appearance and then leave Kansas. Sam's plans didn't always go according to plan.

Dodge City's bank happened to have a large copse of trees located right behind it, so Sam decided that he would camp out in the wooded area the night before their planned robbery. While the gang usually attacked the banks around nine in the morning, when they were first opening up, the leader changed and told the other outlaws that they would hit the bank at lunchtime.

Just before the bank was going to close for the noon hour, one of the outlaws walked in through the front door. At the same time, Dakota slipped in through the backdoor. The third gunman had arrived in town earlier in the morning and had been waiting in one of the town saloons, nursing a beer. He too entered the bank right behind his partner.

The heist went off without a hitch; and the three desperados managed to get out of town without any shooting, leaving the bank's two employees tied up. They had been so slick with this new approach, no one in the town knew the bank was robbed until people showed up at one o'clock. By this time, the outlaw gang had robbed *ten* banks, killed more than a dozen citizens and lawmen, and lost only the two men who didn't make it out of El Dorado.

According to Dakota Sam's plans the bank in Garden City would be the last one they'd rob until next spring, when the snows were gone. What he failed to tell the two men following him was that he also meant for this heist to be their *last* one.

When noontime came on the appointed day, Sam's two partners entered the bank on schedule, only to be greeted by four shotgun-wielding men. They were quickly relieved of their weapons, and marched off to jail. Unfortunately for them, Sam had gone into the bank earlier and informed the manager that he had overheard the details of a planned robbery. The manager arranged for the two outlaws to be intercepted.

After his gang members were escorted out of the bank, Dakota slipped in through the backdoor, tied up the teller and manager, and proceeded to loot the bank of the townspeople's hard-earned money. He then exited via the backdoor and took off, leaving town, knowing that the other two men would be tried and probably hanged for their part in the holdups. Meanwhile, Sam was headed for Pueblo, Colorado, where he planned on spending the remainder of the year.

4

DEPUTIZED

Wichita, Kansas, January 19, 1875

BRIGHT MORNING SUNLIGHT filtered around the edges of the heavy drapery covering the window of the hotel room the Cochran sisters were staying in. The three women were already up and dressed, ready to go down and have some breakfast in the inn's dining room. While Cami and Dani were well rested and excited about the day's planned events, Matilda's stomach felt twisted and knotted. She hadn't slept very well, her thoughts occupied by the questioning of the marshal and deputy on the previous day.

Mattie's husband had been missing for over three years, and was presumed dead. She had no clue as to why he'd suddenly disappeared one day and an investigation by the Henry County Sheriff had turned up more questions than answers. The day before, she'd undergone an intense interview by Supervisory Marshal Tobias Winters and Deputy Kyle Branch, an interview that lasted over an hour and a half. The questioning, part of her examination for the position of deputy marshal, was supposed to be, in Mattie's mind, about her qualifications for the job. Instead, the vast majority of the questions centered on her husband's disappearance and what she knew about it. By the end of the oral exam, she was convinced that the two men believed that she had murdered David Yarden and disposed of his body.

Knowing that you are innocent of wrongdoing doesn't mean that you will feel innocent when you are questioned. The stress of having those in authority grill you is bound to raise doubts in your own mind. No one on earth is ever completely innocent, and no matter how innocent you are, sometimes even the innocent are found guilty. She thought about Jesus Christ. Pontius Pilate declared Jesus innocent of all wrongdoing, yet he allowed the Jewish leaders to crucify Him as a political expedient.

Frightened by what might transpire when they returned to the marshal's office that morning, Mattie told her sisters to go on to breakfast, then she knelt down next to the hotel room bed.

"Lord," she prayed, "You know I had nothing to do with whatever happened to David. I don't know where he is or even if he is still alive. I answered Marshal Winters's questions as honestly as I could, to the best of my knowledge. Yet it seems, Lord, that they suspect me of having something to do with his disappearance. I think they might even believe that I killed him.

"Please, Jesus, open their eyes and their hearts to my innocence. And if it is according to Your will, I ask that you would direct them to accepting all three of us into the Marshals Service. In Jesus's name, amen."

After Matilda had joined her sisters and eaten breakfast, the three young women headed to Winters's office building. They noticed that a large portion of yesterday's snow had either melted or been trampled down by traffic. The roadway in front of the hotel was a muddy quagmire and the girls were glad that they didn't have to try and cross it.

Entering the office building they encountered the same receptionist from the day before sitting behind the counter that stretched across the width of the room. A small gate near the right hand end allowed access to the back area. A narrow hallway split the back office area into two.

"Have a seat. Marshal Winters will be with you shortly."

While the receptionist's tone wasn't antagonistic, it wasn't exactly friendly either. The sisters sensed an attitude of disapproval coming from the woman who appeared to be only slightly older than themselves. The feeling that she disliked them became even more evident when Winters stepped into the hallway and motioned for the three girls to come on back to his office. The receptionist glowered at them as they passed through the gate.

Having taken seats in his office, the marshal spoke. "I have good news, ladies. All three of you passed the written and oral exams yesterday, with flying colors." Directing his attention toward Mattie, he continued, "I apologize if Kyle and I seemed especially hard on you, Matilda. The situation with your husband has been of some concern to us. We had to be sure that we weren't looking at hiring a woman who'd killed her husband. You convinced us that you were not involved in his disappearance.

"Today, we will take you out to where we have a firing range set up and we'll test your skills with a variety of firearms. Presuming there are no concerns raised there, we will have a swearing in ceremony here in the office right after lunch.

"However, you need to understand that your acceptance into the Marshals Service is still contingent on your completing your first assignment successfully. After that, you will be subject to a six-month probationary period, during which you will be evaluated for your performance. A decision will then be made as to whether or not you will continue to be employed by us. Are there any questions?"

"I have one," Dani said. "What is the problem with that woman out at the front desk? She seems to really dislike us and she doesn't even know us."

Tobias laughed. "Katie will be okay. My sister was raised to believe that a woman's place is in the home, cooking, cleaning, and raising babies. You wouldn't believe how much trouble I had convincing her to come and work for me. Anyway, if she gives you too much trouble, let me know and I'll have a talk with her. But I think, in due time, she will come to be as impressed with the three of you as I am.

Pueblo, Colorado, same day

Dakota Sam sat at a table along the back wall of the "Come Git It Saloon" on Pueblo's Main Street. His back was to the wall so he could survey the whole room and see anyone who entered the beer hall. He nonchalantly stretched out his right leg when he saw the man wearing a star come through the batwing doors, giving him access to the six-shooter strapped on his right hip. He watched as the lawman stepped to one side, allowing his eyes to adjust to the dimmer lighting until he could locate the man he was looking for.

Sam's right hand fell off the table and came to rest on the butt of his pistol as he saw the sheriff head in his direction. The tall, broad-shouldered man greeted a few of the patrons as he moved steadily through the half-full saloon, yet he always kept Sam in his sight.

"Afternoon," he greeted Dakota when he reached the Indian's table. "How are you today" he asked pleasantly.

"Sometin' I can do fer ya, sherif'" the Indian replied.

The sheriff's left thumb was hooked behind his belt buckle, but his right hand was firmly planted on the pearl-handled butt of his six-shooter as he spoke, "You can start by removing your hand from your gun. I don't take too kindly to men who talk to me with one hand on a weapon."

Pueblo's sheriff was a big man, well muscled and solid looking. His dark-brown hair was cut short and graying at the temples. Dakota Sam guessed he was in his mid-forties. His light gray eyes were intense and gave the appearance of being able to stare through a brick wall.

From the corner of his left eye Sam caught movement over by the bar. A quick glance told the Indian that there was another man standing there, his left foot resting on the brass foot railing. A star was pinned to the front of his shirt and he was casually leaning on the bar. But a serious looking shotgun was held in his right hand, the stock resting on his hip.

Slowly lifting his hand off his gun and placing it back on the tabletop, Sam responded, "Sorry, Sheriff. I didn't mean ta make ya nervous."

"I'm Sheriff West. What's your name, mister?"

"Sam Barone," Dakota replied. "Do ya roust ever'one who comes to yer town?"

"I don't roust anyone who doesn't cause trouble, Mister Barone. But I do check out anyone who comes in wearing a tie-down holster and spends most of their time in a saloon. Are you gunslinger, Mister Barone?"

"No, suh!"

"Would you mind telling me what your business is here in Pueblo?"

"Jus' passin' thru. Thought I'd try some gamblin' and then on ta Denver."

"I see. Looks like all the poker games are back there," the lawman jerked his head back and to the left, indicating the tables where games were in progress. However, he never took his eyes off Sam, nor remove his hand from his six-shooter.

"Lookin' for the right game," Dakota informed him.

"Stay out of trouble, Mister Barone, and we'll get along fine."

West nodded to his deputy who immediately stood erect, the barrel of his rifle now ensconced in the palm of his left hand. The lawman then nodded at the Indian and then began exiting the drinking establishment. He stopped at one of the poker tables where a game was going on and spoke quietly to the men involved in the game. Then he headed to the exit, taking one last glance at Dakota Sam/Barone before he pushed out through the batwing doors.

Sam thought, "That man doesn't like me. If he gets in my way, I may have to kill him before I leave town."

Wichita, same day

The three Cochran sisters and Deputy Kyle Branch slogged through the mud and snow to get to the marshals' firing range. Two sets of targets had been set up, one target was set at ten yards (the effective range of most handguns) and the other target was set at one hundred yards (a rifle's effective range, for most people, was ten to twenty times that of a pistol).

Each of the girls had a rawhide thong tying back their heavy coats allowing them to be able to fast draw. Deputy Branch gave them instructions and then stood off to the side and watched as the triplets took turns firing at the targets, first with their six-shooters and then with their rifles. All of their weapons, other than the shotguns, were .45 so that they could easily exchange ammunition if conditions necessitated it.

After completing their qualifying tests, Branch led them back to the offices where he then watched them strip down all their weapons and clean them. Both the girls and the deputy knew that a properly cleaned weapon was essential to its serviceability and accuracy. Branch then sent them off to lunch and to get cleaned up.

That afternoon, Marshal Tobias Winters conducted a swearing in ceremony, making Matilda, Camille, and Danielle Cochran deputy US marshals. He then ordered them to return the next morning, ready to begin their careers as law enforcement officers.

Pueblo, same day

A half-hour after the sheriff had paid Dakota Sam a visit he watched as one of the poker players got up from the table, declaring in a loud voice that he was wiped out. The man who seemed to be the leader made a show of looking around the room before his eyes locked onto Sam.

"Hey, mister," he shouted across the room, "we got an open seat if you'd care to sit in."

In the two weeks Sam had been in Pueblo, hardly anyone (except the saloon girls looking to spend time with him for his money) had spoken to him. This was the first time anyone had invited him to join in a poker game, without his asking if he could sit in first. He was pretty sure that they'd only now invited him to join them because the sheriff had asked them to try and learn more about him. That meant that one of them (probably the one who'd just asked him to sit in) would be reporting everything they found out to the lawman.

"Shur," he replied, still faking a Southern drawl.

He ambled over to the table and sat in the seat recently vacated. After introducing himself as Sam Barone, the others introduced themselves (not that Sam actually cared).

The poker game lasted until almost midnight, by which time there were only three men left playing: Sam, Pete (the leader), and Clint. When Sam looked at his pocket watch and saw that it was five minutes until twelve, he stood up, yawning loudly, and said that it was time to call it a night. Pete and Clint remained at the table as Sam sauntered out of the bar. They watched through the window as the half-breed staggered across the muddy street toward the hotel where he'd been staying for the last two weeks.

At the front desk, he asked, slurring his words as if he were drunk, "Cou'd yew tell me wha' time is id? Ma wat's stopped."

The clerk gave Sam a disgusted look as he replied, "It is two minutes until midnight, sir."

"Than's! Any messes fer Sam Barone?"

"No, sir! No messages tonight," the clerk replied after checking.

Sam staggered up the stairs, still pretending that he had had too much to drink until he reached the third floor. When he had ascertained that no one was in the hallway or coming out of a room, he quickly straightened up and moved down the hallway to the back staircase. At the bottom of the stairwell, he quietly opened the hotel's backdoor and slipped outside, closing the door behind him as quietly as he could. Then he stealthily made his way down the back alley until he came to the opening between the hotel and the building next door. From a spot between the buildings at the front corner of the hotel, he watched the batwing doors of the saloon.

From the shadows, Sam saw Pete emerge from the beer hall and make his way across the same muddy street the Indian had crossed earlier. Halfway across the road, the cowboy stopped momentarily and glanced around. Sure that he was alone, he continued to walk straight toward the sheriff's office, just like Sam expected him too. Sam then drew his pistol and took aim at the unaware man. Though the distance was further than he'd like, he pulled the trigger anyway and watched as the poker player fell face first into a large mud puddle. There wasn't time to go and check to see if he was dead.

Dakota Sam hurried back to the hotel, reentering through the rear door. Once inside, he removed his boots so he wouldn't track any mud into the stairwell. Then he quickly ascended the stairs and slipped into his room. Because of the late hour, no one had come out of their rooms to investigate the sound of gunfire, so Sam was able to return to his room, get undressed, and climb into bed. He was planning on continuing his "drunk act" if the sheriff came by to question him.

Wichita, same day

While Dakota Sam was playing poker in Pueblo, Colorado, the Cochran sisters were preparing to celebrate their entry into the United States Marshals Service. Though they usually didn't drink alcoholic beverages, they decided that sharing a bottle of champagne for this very special occasion wasn't a bad thing.

To acquire the bottle of libation they went into one of Wichita's less seedy looking saloons. Still wearing blue jeans and form fitting western shirts, they drew the admiring stares of most of the male patrons, and even from some of the saloon girls who wished they could wear jeans to work. After ordering the champagne, they waited while the bartender went into the backroom to retrieve a bottle for them. Four cowboys, who'd already had a little too much to drink, came up to the bar and stood with the girls between them, two to Mattie's left and the other over on Cami's right.

"Wal, lookee har' boys," the one standing next to Cami drawled, "we's got us some little girls preten'ing to be real cowbo's."

"Actually, we are deputy US marshals. So why don't you boys mosey back to your table and mind your own business," Mattie suggested politely.

"Why, Merl, doncha see? Theys *real* US marshals!" interjected the cowboy furthest to the left.

The one called Merl reached across Cami and lifted the bottom of her badge with his right index finger. "Shur nuff, Dirk! Their play stars even look almost real."

Before Merl knew what was happening, Cami gripped his wrist with her left hand and twisted it, sending shooting pain up his arm. At the same time, she drew her six-shooter and jammed it's muzzle up under the cowpuncher's nose.

"Didn't your mama ever teach you not to touch a woman without her permission?" Cami asked softly. "And it's even more dangerous when she's a lawman with a gun strapped to her side."

The other three cowboys started to reach for their weapons but froze in mid-stride when they realized that Mattie and Dani were way ahead of them.

"What's goin' on here?" the bartender demanded as he walked back into the room. "Merl, you an' yer boys causin' trouble agin? I tol' you b'fore, I don' want no trouble in my s'loon. Not git outta here 'fore I git really mad."

Camille released Merl's wrist and the four cowboys slowly headed toward the door. Merl was massaging his abused joint and mumbled about how they were only having a little fun. The sisters holstered their six-shooters as soon as the four men were outside.

"Sorry 'bout that, Deputies. Merl and his friends don' mean no harm. They jest have trouble 'trolling their, um, energy."

"Oh, that's okay. I think Cami here helped Merl get things under control."

The three sisters laughed, and the bartender joined in.

Pueblo, January 20, 1875, early morning

Dakota Sam reacted slowly to the sudden pounding on his hotel room door. Pretending that he'd been sound asleep, he faked surprise at the sight of Sheriff West standing there when he opened the door.

"Sheriff, is there a problem?" he asked, innocently.

In his attempt to pretend he was half asleep, Sam forgot to use the phony accent he'd earlier employed. West noticed the faux pas, but decided to say nothing at the time.

"Where were you an hour ago?" the lawman asked gruffly.

"I guess I was right here. What time is it anyway?"

"It's a little after one. Can anyone verify you were here?" West questioned.

Running a hand through his hair, Sam answered, "Well, let me think now. There's the clerk downstairs. He saw me when I came in but there wasn't anyone else that I remember seeing. You wanna tell me what's going on?"

"Pete Warden was shot down an hour ago, right in front of this hotel. You know anything about that?"

"That's too bad, Sheriff. I was playing poker with him earlier tonight. Or I guess it was actually last night, huh? He seemed like a right nice fella too."

"Yes, he was! And I aim to catch his killer—"

"Sheriff! Come look at this!" The shout came from the back of the hotel, near the back stairwell.

"I'll be back," West told Sam. "Don't go wandering off anywhere."

The sheriff hurried over to the top of the stairs and peered down them. One of his deputies was standing on the landing between the third and second floors.

"Come take a look at this, Damien. Looks like someone went out the backdoor here."

The two lawmen went to the bottom of the stairs to look at what the deputy had found.

"I'm thinking," the deputy continued, "that he, or she, walked out the backdoor, down the alleyway, and up between the two buildings. They shot Pete and then came back into the hotel, taking off their muddy boots before going up the stairs.

"That's good work, Lem," the sheriff praised his deputy. "Let's go back upstairs and question that Barone fella some more. I don't think he's being up front with us. He's also lost that phony accent he had when we talked to him at the saloon earlier."

"You're right, sheriff. I thought he acted a little strange too," Lem replied.

As the two lawmen began to walk up the back stairs, the hotel clerk came rushing through the door that led to the front lobby.

"Sheriff, that Barone guy from room 312 just came running down the stairs and out the front door," the clerk yelled at them.

West and his deputy quickly changed directions, running through the lobby and out the hotel's front door. They spotted the man calling himself Sam Barone starting to mount a horse outside of the saloon. He had his left foot in the stirrup and was swinging his right leg up over the horse's rump. But the horse belonged to Pete, and it never allowed anyone other than Pete to ride it. Sam's right leg was in midair when the horse reared up on its hind legs, throwing the off balance Indian about ten feet through the air, right into the same large mud puddle Pete had ended up in. The two lawmen were promptly standing on either side of the puddle, their guns drawn and pointed at the half breed.

"Get up very slowly, with your hands up in the air," the sheriff commanded. "If we see your hands go anywhere near that gun of yours, we will shoot to kill.

Dakota Sam looked back and forth between the officers and decided he wasn't ready to die. He raised his hands as he sat up and then slowly rose to his feet. Lem quickly relieved him of his six-shooter and then, after holstering his own pistol, cuffed Sam's hands behind his back. The two led the half-breed to the jail house and placed him in an empty cell.

———∞❖∞———

Back in his office, Damien West began going through the saddlebags Sam had with him when they caught him. He was surprised to find almost a thousand dollars in cash in one of the saddlebags. But he was even more surprised when Lem came out from the cell area carrying something in his hands.

"Lookee here, Damien. Our friend was wearing this," he commented, holding up a money belt that was bulging.

"How much is in there?" West asked as his deputy dropped the weighty belt on the desk.

"Must be several thousand dollars in there, doncha think? Wonder if he migh'n be part of that thar gang was robbin' all dem banks in Kansas?"

"Good thinking, Lem. I'll send out some telegrams in the morning to some of the towns they hit and see if I can get a good description of the gang members. I'll also wire the US marshal in Wichita and see what information he has to offer. Why don't you go get some sleep and be back here first thing in the morning?"

As Lem started to leave the office he turned back and asked, "Ya think his name is real'y Sam Barone?"

"I doubt it. Refuse like him don't tell lawmen their real names. But we'll find it out when we get 'grams back from the Kansas towns."

5

Wichita, Kansas, January 28, 1875

THE FIRST NINE days as deputy US marshals were uneventful for the Cochran sisters. Supervisory Marshal Winters had not given them their initial assignment yet. Add to that the fact that the people of Wichita, the women in particular, had been less than friendly to the trio of armed females. Men tended to treat them as some type of joke or even with outright contempt while the women acted haughty. The sisters felt that they were being unjustly treated, but there wasn't much they could do about it.

So it was with great relief that they were summoned to the marshal's headquarters on the morning of January 28th. Katie Winters greeted them as they entered the offices.

"You can go on back. Tobey's expecting you."

"Thank you, Katie," Mattie replied for all of them.

While the slightly older woman still found it difficult to accept the sisters as deputy marshals, her attitude had become friendlier over the course of the last nine days. For their part, the sisters tried to appreciate Katie's hesitancy to completely accept them and graciously allowed her to come to terms with the situation in her own way and time. Because of their faith in Jesus they understood what grace really meant and were willing to wait for others to embrace them, just as Jesus waits for us to trust in Him.

"SIT!" Winters barked as they entered his office.

He was reading what looked like a telegram, so the three girls sat down and patiently waited. They were initially concerned that they had inadvertently done something wrong because of the tone of his voice. However, it soon became clear to them that the message he was reading was the source of his anger.

"I have an assignment for the three of you," he said after several minutes of silence. "It could be dangerous and I'm hesitant to put rookie deputies on this case, but I don't have much choice at the moment.

"There's a renegade Indian by the name of Dakota Sam who, along with four other men, robbed a number of banks here in Kansas. Sam was apprehended in Pueblo, Colorado by the local sheriff," he glanced at the telegram, "a Damien West, and is being held in the Pueblo jail. He needs to be transported to Topeka to stand trial on murder and armed robbery charges."

The sisters glanced at each other, their eyes giving away their eagerness.

"You can count on us, Marshal," Mattie said, speaking for the three of them.

"Not so fast, Mattie," he interjected. "There's a problem. Not all the gang members have been accounted for, which is what makes this job so dangerous. Three of the four robbers are dead, but the fourth one has disappeared. Also, the sheriff found sketches of the bank in Pueblo. He thinks Sam may have been planning to rob it. That means it's possible that Sam has already put together another gang and that they might try to set him free."

"When do we leave?" Dani asked, unfazed, as if she hadn't even heard Winters's warning.

Shaking his head at the young woman's zeal, he answered, "On tomorrow morning's train. We'll load your horses into a railroad car equipped to accommodate them. You'll take the train all the way to Pueblo. Sheriff West will meet you at the train station next Thursday evening. He'll provide you with a wagon you can use to confine Sam in while you take him to Topeka. I want you to telegraph me as soon as you arrive. The plan then is for you three to leave Sunday morning with Sam in the jail wagon. Any questions?"

"Church," Cami said simply.

"What about church?" Winters asked.

"We always go to church on Sundays, except when there isn't one to go to. It's very important to us."

Tobias Winters rubbed his chin thoughtfully before responding.

"Okay, go to church on Sunday. You can leave first thing Monday morning. However, you all need to realize that being deputy marshals means you're going to miss church services when duty calls. Are there any other questions or concerns?"

Seeing no further objections, he continued giving his instructions. "I want you to head straight for Great Bend. It's the first town you'll get to that's big enough to have a local law enforcement officer and a jail. I've already sent him a telegram informing him of your coming, so he will be expecting you.

"You'll need a couple of days to rest yourselves and the horses after the three hundred plus miles from Pueblo to Great Bend. The town marshal will keep Sam in his jail until you're ready to get back on the trail. Make sure you telegraph me when you arrive in the town.

"From Great Bend to Topeka is about half that distance, and there are a number of towns along the way where you can ask for help if you've run into any problems. I've marked them on this map here.

"Send me a final telegram when you get to Topeka and have turned Sam over to the federal authorities there. I want you to wait in Topeka until I contact you there. Any other questions?…No? Then go pack. You have a long train ride ahead of you.

"On your way out, stop and see Katie. She'll have vouchers for you so that you can purchase the supplies you'll need for the trip. You can buy some of them in Pueblo and then replenish your stock when you get to Great Bend."

The three women then stood up, but as they were headed for the door, Tobias stopped them in their tracks.

"One last thing, ladies. Don't try to be heroes—um, sorry, *heroines*. There is no outlaw worth getting yourselves killed over. If members of Sam's gang show up, it would be better to let him go than to get shot up. We can always catch him later if need be.

"Also, I value honesty from my deputies. I believe it is more important to be honest than to try and hide it if you've screwed up. If there is a problem, tell me. Don't sugarcoat it, don't hide it, and don't deny it exists. Chances are I'll find out about it eventually, so tell me up front so that we can deal with it. Now, get out of here—and be careful out there!"

—••oo•❦•oo••—

Early Friday morning, Cami supervised the loading of their horses into the special railroad car. Each of the sisters had specific duties they'd assigned to themselves based on their unique personalities. Because of her affinity for animals, Camille was in charge of caring for their mounts. Danielle was the best cook of the three and Mattie's main job was to set up camp and get the fire started, in addition to being the main planner and leader.

Thirty minutes after the horses were loaded, the train slowly began to pull away from the Wichita station. Mattie and Cami were involved in a lively conversation about the meaning of a particular passage of Scripture and didn't notice that Toby Winters wasn't there to see them off. But Dani noticed.

As her sisters got into the flow of their discussion, Dani wistfully looked out the window, staring at the platform in front of the train station as it slowly receded in the distance. Just before the platform was completely lost to view, the young deputy saw the tall marshal step into view. A satisfied smile crept across Dani's face before she turned and joined in her sisters' conversation.

Pueblo, Colorado, February 4, 1875

The train ride from Wichita to Pueblo was uneventful. Never having ridden a train before, there had been a great deal of excitement and enthusiasm on the part of the three sisters. However, the ensuing miles of endless prairie, coupled with the mind-numbing clacking of the train's wheels, had soon dulled the adventure. They were greatly relieved when the locomotive finally pulled into the Pueblo station late Thursday afternoon.

"You must be the Cochrans," a deep, mellifluous voice spoke from behind the young women as they stood on the train station's platform.

They turned to face a man they had to look up to because he was a full foot taller than they.

"I'm Sheriff Damien West, but my friends call me DW," he said, extending his hand for them to shake. "Do you have any luggage other than what you're carrying?" he asked politely.

"We decided to travel light so we only have one suitcase in the baggage car in addition to our carryon belongings," Mattie informed him after each of the girls introduced themselves. "Oh, and there's our horses, of course."

"Yes, one of my deputies is getting them unloaded right now. He'll take them over to the livery stable and get them settled in.

"If you'll excuse me, Sheriff," Cami responded, "I'll go help your deputy. Our horses tend to get skittish if I'm not there to handle them."

"Of course! My deputy's name is Lem. I'm sure he'll be glad for the help."

After Cami walked off, the sheriff commented. "I'd hate for her to get that pretty dress of hers messed up."

"Don't worry about her, DW. Cami would rather ruin a dress than have a horse get hurt. Besides, she really doesn't like wearing dresses anyway, so she'll be happy if it gets dirty and she doesn't have to wear it."

The sheriff had been subtly admiring the three young women and couldn't help commenting, "Marshal Winters didn't tell me you were triplets. He caught me by surprise when he informed me he was sending female deputies, but he also didn't tell me how lovely you are. Are you sure you're up to transporting a very dangerous man all the way across Kansas?"

Dani, miffed by the sheriff's insinuation, retorted, "Sheriff West, you provide us with the jail wagon and turn the prisoner over to us and we'll make sure he gets to Topeka in time to hang for his crimes."

"Sorry! I didn't mean to imply—"

"Yes, you did," Mattie interrupted him. "And my sister is right. Marshal Winters trusts us enough to give us this assignment, and that's all you need to know. Don't let our pretty dresses and looks deceive you.

"You may think we're three pretty little girls playing make-believe lawmen, but there's a lot more to us than you realize. We can outgun and outshoot any hombre out there, and any lawman too, for that matter."

The sheriff, who was taken aback by the two girls vitriolic remarks, huffily replied, "Everything will be ready for you Monday morning. In the meantime, I've made arrangements for you to stay at the Prince Hotel." With that, he walked off, leaving the two deputies to find their own way to the hotel.

"I don't like that man," Dani commented as they watched him walk away.

Her sister just nodded her agreement. They picked up their satchels, with Mattie grabbing up Cami's, and asked the porter to have their suitcases delivered to the hotel. Then the two of them went to check in.

Mattie and Dani had just sat down to dinner in the hotel's restaurant when Cami showed up with a skinny young man following close behind her. The blonde woman's pretty green dress was filthy from where the trio's horses had rubbed up against her, but she had a big smile on her face.

Rushing to her sisters' table, half dragging the man with her, the triplet blurted, "Mattie, Dani, this is Lem. He's the deputy sheriff here, and he's been helping me with our horses.

"Lem, these are my sisters, Mattie and Dani"—she gestured toward her sisters respectively. "I told Lem we'd buy him dinner because he helped me."

"I tried to tell your sister that it's not necessary," Lem said abashedly. "Truth is Sheriff West told me to take care of the horses. So really, you was help'n me. I shud be buyin' you dinner, 'cept I cant 'cause I ain'st got no money."

"Nonsense, Lem," Mattie broke in. "Cami invited you to dine with us and we expect you to join us."

"Well, if'n yer shur that you don' mind, I'd be right pleased to join you."

"We insist," Dani said, agreeing with her sisters. Then she exchanged a quick glance and a sly smile with Mattie.

After a pleasurable meal and some very informative conversation, Mattie and Dani excused themselves, bid Lem good-bye, and told Cami what room they were in. As soon as the two entered their hotel room and closed the door, they burst out laughing. Dani fell onto one of the beds she was laughing so hard and Mattie dropped into the room's only chair.

When Dani finally regained her composure, she commented, "It's a good thing our sister was raised on good, strong Christian values or we'd probably have to be out there pulling them apart. Did you see the way Lem was looking at her?"

"You've got a point there," Mattie replied, sobering up. "How long do you think we should allow them to be alone?"

"I don't know if we should interfere, do you?"

"It wouldn't be proper for them to be alone for a long period of time. We have enough problems getting people to respect our authority without giving them a scandal to gossip about."

"I suppose you're right. How about thirty minutes?"

"Yeah, I guess that sounds about right. That's not too much time, but it does give them some time alone."

Cami didn't need thirty minutes as she showed up less than twenty minutes later. However, she noticed both of her sisters staring at her strangely.

"What are you two looking at?" she asked gruffly.

"Oh, nothing in particular," Dani replied, and then snickered.

"So how's Lem?" Mattie asked, forcing herself not to smile or laugh.

"Lem's fine," their sister retorted. "What's gotten into you two anyway?"

"I'll just bet he's fine," Dani said before she could stop herself.

Dani and Mattie burst out laughing again.

"Wait a minute!" Cami yelled. "You two don't think… Lem and I…you guys don't think that I…" She could see by the looks on their faces that her thoughts were exactly what her sisters were thinking. "We didn't *do* anything! We just went over to the stables and checked that our horses were doing okay."

"Of course you did," Mattie responded, followed by another round of guffawing.

Cami's face turned a bright red before she ran out of the room, slamming the door behind her. A few minutes later she returned, anger still written all over her normally pretty face.

"Can you guys be serious for a moment?" she asked, obviously trying to control herself. Her two sisters calmed down so she could continue. "Lem and I really did just go over to the livery to check on the horses. I would never do anything to jeopardize our mission."

Mattie gave her sister a serious look and said, "Okay, we believe you, Cami." Then she couldn't stop herself from snickering again.

There was a moment of stunned silence as all three girls tensed for Cami's reaction, then she too burst into laughter.

6

Pueblo, Colorado, February 8, 1875

MONDAY MORNING AND the sky was without a cloud in
sight. Mattie, Cami, and Dani watched the sun coming up
in the east as Lem harnessed four sturdy horses to the front
of the jail wagon. Once the horses were in place, Sheriff
West and Lem would escort Dakota Sam out of his cell
and into the wagon, securing him inside. Then Mattie and
the sheriff would sign the paperwork officially transferring
the outlaw from the custody of the Pueblo County Sheriff
over to the US Marshals Service.

The sun had just cleared the horizon as the wagon and
its escort pulled away from the sheriff's office. Cami had

drawn the short straw and got the first shift of driving the wagon while her two sisters rode on either side of the conveyance. The trio had agreed to take turns so none of them would be stuck driving it the whole way to Topeka. By their estimation, it would take them nearly a month to make the almost five-hundred-mile trek across the Kansas prairie. And that was if the weather cooperated.

If they averaged fifteen to twenty miles a day they'd have to spend approximately ten to twelve hours on the trail. However, at this time of the year, daylight didn't last that long. Consequently, they figured they would have to get up before sunrise and drive on passed sunset.

At first things went smoothly and without incident. Except when Sam decided to serenade them one afternoon. Mattie, who was driving at the time, said it sounded like someone was standing on a cat's tail. Her sisters graciously began banging on the sides of the wagon with their rifle butts until the caterwauling stopped.

Colorado-Kansas Border, February 16, 1875

Midmorning of the eighth day they crossed the state line into Kansas and saw the first hint of real trouble. Other than a couple of short rain showers and some snow flurries one night, the trip was going very smoothly. So smoothly the girls were starting to get bored. For that reason, they almost didn't see the group of riders keeping pace with them. Only Cami's sharp eyes saved them from being completely surprised.

It was Camille's turn to drive the wagon, so she was perhaps a little more alert than her sisters. "Mattie," she called over her left shoulder, "riders to the north. They've been moving in and out of the trees, keeping up with us."

"How many?" she asked.

"I think there's five, but I can't be sure because they keep moving around."

"Dani, come around to this side of the wagon," Mattie shouted over the rumbling of the wagon. Maybe if they see there are three of us they'll ride off."

When Danielle was on the north side of the wagon they watched the riders continue to keep pace with them.

"Hold up, Cami," Mattie called. "Let's talk this over."

Her sister reined in the horses, set the brake, and jumped down from the driver's seat, a shotgun in her hands.

"How do you wanna handle this, Matilda?" Dani asked.

"Let's set here a spell and see if they move off or come toward us. If they come this way within rifle range, I'll fire a warning shot and tell them to move on."

"Shouldn't we spread out some?" Cami asked, suggestively.

"Good idea! Dani, why don't you get at the back of the wagon and Cami can go up by the horses. That way she can try to keep them calm if there's any shooting and they get skittish. We don't need the horses running off with the wagon."

A quick glance told Mattie the riders were moving. "Look alert! They're heading this way," she informed her fellow deputies.

Five rough looking men emerged from a stand of trees and rode abreast toward them. They were about two hundred yards away, the girls estimated, when they came out of the coppice. Mattie waited until they were only about a hundred yards away before she fired a shot over their heads.

"That's far enough," she yelled at them. "We're deputy US marshals. You men need to move on!"

The men came to a dead stop and exchanged glances. One of them raised his hands after a minute or so and slowly rode forward. Mattie let him get to within about fifty yards before she fired a second round, hitting the ground just a few feet in front of his horse.

"I told you men to move on," she said sternly. "You come any closer and I'll put the next one right between your eyes. And trust me, you don't want to test me on this."

Looking back briefly at his companions, the man smirked and asked, "Who ya got in that wagon, little lady?"

"None of your business! Now git, before I get angry."

"Why now, yore not bein' very neighborly. We here'd that ya'll were transportin' a dangerous crim'nal through the area and we jist wanted to git a looksee, ya know. Ain't no harm in that, now is thar?"

"Like I said, this is none of your business. So move on out of here, or someone might get hurt…real bad."

Yelling back over his shoulder to his friends, he said, "Their prisoner can't be too dangerous, they sent three little girls to guard him," he said, laughing.

Nudging his horse forward with his knees, he let his right hand drop to the butt of his pistol. With just a slight adjustment of her rifle, Mattie blew the man's six-shooter right out of its holster, wounding the man's hand in the process.

"Why you stupid—"

Cami took the man's hat off with a single shot from her rifle before yelling, "Watch your language, mister. Can't you see there are ladies present?"

The other four men started to ride forward, but Dani quickly fired off three shots that hit the ground right in front of them, causing the horses to rear up in fright. All four had to fight with their mounts to get them back under control.

"You men have been warned enough now!" Mattie yelled. "There will be no more warnings. Shuck on outta here, or we'll spill your blood on the ground. Your choice."

Getting off his horse, the apparent leader went to retrieve his six-shooter when they heard all three of the girl's rifles ratcheted.

"Leave it right there, mister," Mattie ordered. "Now git!"

The desperados took a long look at the three deputies and decided it was not the time or place to mess with them. Their leader climbed back onto the saddle and, after taking a last look at Mattie, turned his horse around and rejoined his companions. The five then rode back into the trees.

"Think they'll leave us alone?" Dani asked.

"Doubt it."

Realizing that Dakota Sam was laughing loudly inside the wagon, the three women started banging on the sides, telling him to shut up.

"You girls ain't gittin' nowheres near Topeka," he shouted back. "My gang's gonna put alls three ya's six feet under."

Grand Bend, Kansas, February 21, 1875

Marshal Billy Wilds stood on the boardwalk in front of his office and watched as the horse drawn jail wagon, along with its two outriders, slowly made its way up the town's Main Street and pulled up in front of him. Billy had been expecting the jail wagon for a couple of days, but was caught by surprise when he saw the deputies accompanying it were females.

"Billy Wilds, town marshal," he said by way of introduction.

"Deputy Marshal Mattie Cochran," the pretty blonde responded as she stepped down from the wagon and offered the plain-looking man her hand. "These are my sisters, Dani and Cami," she introduced, gesturing to them respectively.

"We were told that you could house our prisoner for a couple of days while we, and our horses, rest up," she continued.

"Tha's right, Mattie is it? I got a nice cozy cell jist awaitin' him. Rusty!" Wilds yelled over his shoulder. "Git on out her' and he'p these ladies wit' their horses."

A teenage boy scurried out of the office and began helping Cami unhitch the wagon's horses. Meanwhile, Mattie and Dani brought Sam out of the wagon and escorted him up the steps and into the lawman's office. Once he was safely locked up, and the proper paperwork was signed, the girls went back out front. Dani took the reins of their riding horses and headed for the livery stable where Cami was getting the wagon horses settled in. Mattie headed to the telegraph office to send Toby Winters a message saying they'd arrived in Great Bend.

After checking into the hotel, getting baths, and putting on clean clothes, the three women decided it was time to eat. Upon the recommendation of the hotel clerk, they headed for a restaurant that was reputedly the best in town.

Their steaks, potatoes, and asparagus spears had just arrived, steaming, at their table when they spotted Marshal Wilds entering the café. He looked around for a moment and then approached the table where they sat.

"Mind if I join you?" he asked politely.

"Please do," they responded in unison. That got a short laugh from all four people.

Billy Wilds was in his early thirties. Not exactly a handsome man he nevertheless exuded an air of confidence in who he is. At five-ten he was of average height and weight with a plain, unmarked face, his dark brown hair long and curly. Even his hazel eyes didn't seem all that remarkable. The girls noticed when he smiled that his teeth were yellowed with tobacco stains.

"Did you ladies have any trouble with Dakota Sam on your trip from Pueblo?" he asked.

"Not with Sam himself," Mattie answered for the group. "But we had an encounter with five men we think may be new members of his gang."

"What happened?" Wilds asked, surprised.

"Shortly after we crossed the state line into Kansas we noticed some men following us. We stopped and waited to see what their intentions were. After watching us for a few minutes they began riding toward us. I fired a warning shot and told them to stay away.

"While his partners held back, one man continued to come forward until I fired another round into the ground in front of him. He was about fifty yards away. He asked us about who our prisoner was. I told him it was none of his business and that he and his fellow riders should leave before someone got hurt.

"When he went for his gun I shot it out of the holster…"

"You did *what*?" The marshal asked incredulously.

"I had to stop him somehow. Then he started to cuss and call me a nasty name, so Cami here shot his hat off his head."

Billy Wilds just shook his head as he listened to Mattie's recount of the incident.

"When the other men tried to come forward to help their leader, Dani put it into their minds that doing so would be a bad idea. I told them to shuck outta there or lose some of their blood. I guess they decided that keeping all of their blood was healthier."

"I've got to hand it to you ladies, you're a lot more dangerous than you appear. So do you think they're gone?"

"We don't think so," Dani answered. "We were watching pretty close and we caught glimpses of riders several times. We're pretty sure it was them, but they stayed too far away to get a positive ID. They didn't try to approach us again and kept hidden as much as possible."

"We're not really sure what they're up to," Mattie filled in. "We posted a guard every night and kept a close watch on our back trail, but so far they haven't tried anything else."

"Are you sure they were part of Sam's gang?" Wilds asked.

"No, we're not," Dani said. "However, after our encounter with them Sam started telling us how it would be better for us if we just let him go. Otherwise, he said, he couldn't guarantee that his gang wouldn't try to have some 'fun' with us when they caught up."

"Frankly, I think Sam is just trying to get to us," Mattie opined. "He'd like nothing better than to get one of us to make a mistake, but we're being very careful around him, especially when he's outside of the wagon.

"As far as the men we encountered go, Sam may just have latched on to their existence as a way to get us rattled, thinking that they're there to help him escape. I didn't hear anything that would make me believe they knew who we were transporting."

"You let Dakota Sam out of the wagon along the way?" a surprised Marshal Wilds asked.

"We let him out during our twice a day water breaks and for breakfast and dinner," Cami informed him. "He's only out for fifteen to twenty minutes each time, and he sleeps inside the wagon at night."

"Well, I appreciate the information. I'll make sure he's closely guarded while you're in town. Those men may or may not have been accomplices of Sam's, but I'm not taking any chances. Everyone here in Kansas wants to see him hang for what he's done, so I don't want there to be any escapes from my jail.

"Ladies, I bid you a goodnight and a pleasant stay in our town. Rest up, the next part of the trip may not be as long as the first part, but I have a feeling it may be a lot more dangerous."

Having wished the sisters goodnight, Marshal Billy Wilds went off to tend to his "guest." Mattie, Cami, and Dani paid their restaurant bill and then took a stroll around town. Just as they had in Wichita and Pueblo, they suffered the stares and disapproval of a number of townsfolk, but they also saw that many looked on them with respect and even a bit of awe. They slept well that night.

February 24, 1875

They were supposed to leave Great Bend that Wednesday morning, but late Tuesday afternoon it started snowing and by the time they had planned to pull out more than a foot of snow lay on the ground with more falling. Mattie telegraphed Marshal Winters to say they were staying put until the snow had tapered off or stopped completely.

By noon Thursday the accumulation of snow equaled at least two feet with some drifts as high as six to seven feet. In the end, the delay cost Mattie and her sisters almost an entire week. Even then there was still a good deal of snow along the roadway leading out of town.

March 2, 1875

When the group of deputies decided it was clear enough to proceed everybody, with the possible exception of Dakota Sam, was glad to be getting back on the road again. Billy Wilds had been overly concerned that Sam's gang might attempt some type of jail break while they were in town, so he was especially anxious to see them go, although he had to admit that he would really miss having the three very beautiful deputies around. He urged them to return sometime in the future, perhaps in the spring or summer, under more favorable conditions. Toby Winters was glad to receive a telegram saying that they were leaving Great Bend heading to Topeka. And the women themselves were happy to be free from sitting around all day long doing nothing.

Dani, whose turn it was to drive the wagon that morning, wanted to put some distance between them and Great Bend, so she kept the horses at a steady canter for the first several miles. Consequently, their first break came a little earlier than usual.

With the horses watered and the women's canteens filled, Mattie climbed up on the driver's seat to take her turn. No sooner did she sit down than a shot rang out. She felt something hot and hard scrap against her left arm and was surprised to see blood starting to soak through her shirt when she looked at the spot where she'd felt pain. Momentarily confused, the young blonde was slow to react. More shots were being fired at them and Cami reached up and dragged her wounded sister from the high seat before another bullet could take her out completely.

The two girls tumbled to the ground as Dani returned fire at those who were shooting at them. Having saved her one sister, Cami now joined her other sister in fending off the attack. Mattie quickly regained her composure and assisted the other two in firing back. The barrage of bullets from the three blonde deputies was enough to convince the attackers that they would be better off elsewhere and they rapidly fled the area. While the battle lasted only one or two minutes, it had seemed much longer to the women.

Hearing their opponents ride off, the trio emerged from their places of cover and quickly discussed what happened. Mattie and Cami stealthily went to inspect the place the riders had been shooting from while Dani kept watch on their prisoner. As they approached the trees where the shots came from they spotted someone lying on the ground. Warily drawing closer they soon discovered that one of them had killed one of the outlaws.

"What should we do with him?" Cami asked after they had ascertained that he was indeed dead.

"Guess we'll leave him for the coyotes and buzzards to take care of," Mattie replied.

"Don't seem very Christian, Mat," Cami complained.

"No, it doesn't. But if we take time to bury him his pals might decide to come back and take some more pot shots at us. I don't relish the idea of another one of us getting a bullet in them.

"Besides, if they'd killed us I doubt they'd have given much thought to what happened to our remains."

"Guess you're right. Come on. Let's get back to the wagon so I can have a look at that arm. I'd forgotten that you were hit."

"That's okay! By the way, thanks for pulling me down off the wagon. You probably saved my life."

The two women made their way back to the jail wagon, rejoining their other sister, who was standing on the back platform and talking to Dakota Sam through the barred window. She stepped down when she saw her sisters approaching.

"What did you find?" Dani asked.

"A dead body," Cami answered. "We also found some blood on the ground in a different spot. Maybe another one of them was wounded."

"Dani, would you go check on the horses while Cami tends to my arm? And keep a sharp lookout. Those guys probably aren't finished with us yet. I have a feeling we're going to run up against them again maybe real soon."

Nodding her assent, Dani walked up to the front of the wagon while Cami pulled open Mattie's shirt so that she could tend to the wound. Both girls knew that Dani sometimes got squeamish at the sight of blood and was all too happy to leave the nursing duties to Cami.

Mattie sat down on the low platform her sister had been standing on a few minutes earlier. It was built on the back of the jail wagon to act as a stepping stool. On rare occasions, an officer might also ride on the back of the wagon by standing on the platform and holding on to a pair of handles attached to the back end.

"Now, let's have a look here." Cami gently peeled off the clothing. "It doesn't look too bad. I don't think I'll have to amputate it," she joked.

"Not funny, Sis," Matilda groused.

"Once I get it cleaned up, we'll probably see it's little more than a scratch. So quit being such a baby."

"It doesn't feel like it's only a scratch."

Cami poured water from one of their canteens onto a piece of cloth and began cleaning the gunshot wound. "Yeah, yeah! Suck it up, Sis," she retorted with a laugh when the other girl winced.

As Cami finished bandaging Mattie's arm, Dani yelled out, "Riders coming!"

The two young deputies quickly gathered up their rifles and ran toward the front of the carriage, checking, as they went, if the guns were fully loaded. Mattie quickly buttoned up her shirt before the riders were in view. At first, all they saw was a large cloud of dust about a hundred yards up the road.

"You think it's Sam's gang, Mat?" Dani asked worriedly.

"No, it looks like there's a lot of riders—too many for Sam's gang."

"Indians?" Cami questioned, concern in her voice.

"Guess it could be, but I doubt it. I think Indians wouldn't raise so much dust. But let's be ready just in case I'm wrong."

As the first rider crested the rise and saw the road ahead was blocked by the jail wagon, he raised his hand, signaling for those behind him to stop. He sat his mount and stared at the scene before him for several minutes.

Since the man had come forward peacefully, Mattie told her sisters to stay put and then walked forward until she was just a few feet away. She was impressed with how confident and strong willed the man appeared to be as he dismounted and removed a large glove from his right hand. As he extended his hand to her, he rested his left hand on the hilt of a saber.

"General George Custer at your service, ma'am," he introduced himself.

"Deputy US Marshal Matilda Cochran, sir," she replied as she shook his hand in a viselike grip. "These are my sisters"—she waved a hand in their general direction— "Camille and Danielle. They also are deputy marshals."

"My lands, woman! Female deputy marshals! What is this world coming to," he exclaimed, biting back his usual string of cuss words.

"A better world, we hope, sir." Mattie was nonplussed by the general's behavior.

"Of course," he said, rolling his bright blue eyes in disbelief. "And what, pray tell, are you, um deputies, doing out here in the middle of nowhere?"

"We're transporting a prisoner to Topeka," Mattie answered, pointing to the wagon.

"Who is it you have in there, may I ask?"

"His name is Dakota Sam. He's wanted for bank robbing and murdering."

"An injun?"

"He's a half-breed, sir."

The blonde woman was suddenly concerned with the general's apparent attitude, and wasn't surprised by his next demand.

"You will turn your prisoner over to me immediately," he commanded.

Mattie stiffened up. "No, sir! We have orders from the marshal's office in Wichita to deliver Sam to the federal court in Topeka for trial. We aim to do what we've been assigned to do."

"Young lady, I am responsible for keeping the Indians in this part of the country under control. That includes any who leave the reservation, especially those who prey on white people. You will hand him over to me, or I will take him by force."

"You will have to kill my sisters and me first." She brought her rifle up across her chest to show that she meant what she was saying.

Incredulous, Custer countered, "I have a hundred and fifty highly trained troopers on the road behind me. You think a little slip of a woman scares me?"

"Sir, I doubt that there's very much—if anything—that scares you. But if you try to take our prisoner from us, they will leave here with fewer troopers. And they'll be short one general. *Sir.*"

The general's eyes turned ice-cold blue as he stared into Mattie's equally cold eyes. The general and the twenty-one-year-old rookie deputy stood face-to-face for what seemed to those present an eternity. Suddenly, the army officer burst out laughing, relieving all the tension from the impasse.

"I do declare, Miss Cochran, you do have some gumption. All right, have it your way. You can take your prisoner to Topeka. If you'll pull your wagon off to the side a bit, my troopers and I will be on our way.

"But before I go, let me warn you. There've been reports of a large band of Indians running around and causing trouble. If you like—and it doesn't violate your sensibilities—I can have some of my troops escort you as far as Fort Riley. After that, you'll be on your own, though, as I can't afford to let them go all the way to the capital."

"That's a very generous offer, General. However, this assignment is also part of our final testing process. I'm not sure if Marshal Winters would approve of our accepting help."

"Marshal Winters? Would that be Marshal *Tobias* Winters?"

"Yes, sir! Do you know him?"

"If that young—if Winters gives you any trouble, you tell him I insisted on sending along the troops because of the Indian problem. He won't have anything to say after that."

Cami jumped into the driver's seat and pulled the wagon off to the side. As the troopers filed out, General Custer detailed ten of his men to accompany the women to Fort Riley and ordered them to remain there until he returned. The corporal assigned to lead the detail ordered one of the soldiers to drive the wagon because of the wound on Mattie's arm. Consequently, Mattie was able to sit next to the young private and not have to drive.

Two days later, they arrived at Fort Riley.

7

DAVID YARDEN

Cheyenne, Wyoming, March 2, 1875

DAVID YARDEN COULD, despite his alcohol addled brain, see himself flying through the air, only to land in a large, muddy puddle in the middle of Cheyenne's Main Street.

"And stay out!" shouted the burly bartender of the Three Barrels Saloon before returning to the raucous crowd inside.

Shaking muddy water from his face, David tried to clear his mind from its drunken stupor. Pulling his knees up under his torso, he tried to stand up, but his feet slipped out from under him and he again landed face down in the mud left over from the recent snowstorm. The sudden blizzard had caused him to be stranded in the Wyoming cowboy town.

It took several more attempts at standing before Yarden was able to gain his feet without falling back into the miry soup. Gingerly, and not too steadily, he made his way across the street and onto the boardwalk, where he promptly fell on his rear end with a loud, hard thump.

Talking to himself, David observed, "That's the third saloon I've been thrown out of in this dismal town, and I've only been in Cheyenne for a couple of weeks. Well, I'll show them they can't treat me this way. I'm going to get on my horse and ride out of here."

After looking around for his horse, it dawned on him that he'd lost the critter in a poker game, trying to raise money to buy more whiskey. "Guess I'll have to buy me a horse, 'cept, I don't have any money," he mused. "What's a man to do? Gotta have me a horse if I'm gonna ride outta here," he said aloud, scratching his head in puzzlement.

Surveying the street, David spied three horses tied up in front of the saloon he'd just been evicted from. Without considering the potential consequences of his idea, including the fact that horse thieving was a hanging offense, Yarden struggled back to his feet. Staggering like a drunken sailor, he crossed back across the street and approached the three horses.

Using the porch post to keep his balance, David loosened the reins of the first horse from the hitching post, stuck his left foot in the stirrup, and tried to swing himself up into the saddle. Partly because he was falling down drunk and partly because the horse he was trying to mount was not familiar with him, the horse shied, causing David to do a 360-degree turn before falling flat on his face again. In the mud. Again.

To make matters worse, three cowpunchers emerged from the saloon just as he took his nosedive.

"Hey, look, Ralf!" one of them exclaimed. "Some idjit just tried to steal yore hoss!"

"Les' string 'im up!" Ralf's second friend suggested.

Hearing a train whistle in the near distance, Ralf responded, "I's gots a better ide'er. Give me a hand fellers."

The three men yanked the sottish young man to his feet. Ralf told one of his friends to bring a rope while he and the other man half dragged Yarden toward the train station.

"C'mon, pard, I'll buy you a drink," Ralf lied to David.

"Tha's right neigh...neigh...nice of ya," Yarden slurred in response.

The foursome arrived at the train station just as the locomotive came to a complete stop. Leaving David in the care of his two pals, Ralf went to talk to the engineer. Seeing the cow puncher walk away confused Yarden.

"I thou...thought we ware goin' fou' drinks?" he questioned the two men with him.

"We are buddy," one of them replied. "Jes' keep yore shirt on! On second thought, take yore shirt off."

David was too drunk and too confused to understand what was happening. Believing that the men were befriending him, he quickly complied, removing his shirt. When they insisted he remove his trousers and boots also he began to realize that this was not going well, but they were too strong and too many for him to fight them. Stripped to his long johns and socks, Yarden was led to the front of the train where the men forced him up against the cow catcher and tied him there.

"Engineer says he'll cut 'im loose 'bout ten miles from town," Ralf informed his friends.

Sobering up more quickly than usual, David started yelling at the men. "This isn't funny, guys. Cut me loose right now!"

However, David's complaints were drowned out by the train's whistle as the engineer signaled that they were leaving the station. As the train slowly pulled away, David started screaming, but no one could hear him above the tremendous noise of the engine beginning to build up its speed. David had thought that the men were only trying to scare him, but as the iron horse left Cheyenne, Wyoming in its dust he became so frightened he lost consciousness.

8

TOPEKA, KANSAS

Fort Riley, Kansas, March 9, 1875

TOPEKA WAS ONLY a three-day ride from the army fort located right outside Junction City, Kansas. The acting commanding officer, a Brigadier General filling in for the patrolling General Custer, offered the three female deputies an escort all the way to the state capital, but was politely turned down. Since the current Indian problems mainly affected areas west and north of the garrison, the girls felt that they could manage the remainder of the trip on their own. They left early that Tuesday morning.

What the sisters did anticipate was more trouble from the group of white men that had been shadowing them earlier. They hoped that the military escort and the stay at the fort would have discouraged any further interference on their part, but were aware that some men were not so easily dissuaded. The routine army patrols reported no sightings of Dakota Sam's friends, but that didn't mean they weren't out there waiting, as Mattie pointed out the night before.

The plan they'd come up with was for them to take turns, one of them riding ahead about a mile, scouting for possible places of ambush. It was a risky plan. However, an early warning as to where an attack might take place could give them the opportunity to turn the tables on their pursuers.

At mid-morning on Thursday, Dani, who'd been riding scout, came racing back to the wagon. Mattie was driving at the time and quickly reined in the team of horses. Cami, who had been outriding to the south, joined her sisters. Mattie set the wagon's brake, jumped onto the back of Cami's mount and the duo met their sister about twenty yards away from the rolling jailhouse. They had discussed earlier that they needed to keep strategy discussions out of Sam's earshot.

"What's going on?" Mattie asked Dani when they'd dismounted.

"I found them! They're about a mile and a half up the road," the young deputy breathlessly informed the others. "There's a place where the trees are pretty thick and come right up to the edge of the roadway. I found two of them hiding in the trees on the north side and I suspect the other two are in the south side trees.

"I was able to sneak up on the two I saw. They had all four horses tied up there, but only two of the men were hiding in the trees."

"Did they see you?" Mattie asked nervously.

"No! I was very careful. I circled around to the north and tied up Rebel," her gray Appaloosa, "to a tree before proceeding on foot. I got up close enough to see that it was just the two of them and then was very quiet as I snuck back out."

"Okay, here's the plan then. Dani, you go back in the way you did before and sneak up on them. Cami, you circle around to the south and sneak up on the two guys that are probably hiding there.

"Dani, could you see the road from where you were amongst the trees? Would you be able to see the wagon as I drove up?"

"Yes, I'd have no problem seeing the wagon coming up the road long before you got there."

"Okay! Just before I get to the trees, I'll rein in. That'll be the cue for both of you to announce yourselves."

All three sisters nodded in agreement to the plan. Dani and Cami remounted and headed out to their assigned tasks. Meanwhile, Mattie walked back to the wagon and stepped around to the backdoor. Looking inside, she spoke to Sam.

"How's it going, Sam?" she asked the Indian.

"Wha' yew up to, Missy?" he responded, sensing that something was about to happen.

"We're about to capture the rest of your gang, Sam."

"Zat so? Wa'll I guess we'll see who captures who, won't we?"

Dakota laughed uproariously. Mattie was smiling as she went back to the front and climbed up into the driver's seat. She was confident that her and her sisters would prevail, and have the last laugh. The twenty-one year old blonde had faith in her sisters and her own abilities. Nevertheless, she still took a couple of minutes to pray to God for their safety and success.

Fifteen minutes later, Mattie pulled the wagon to a halt about thirty yards shy of the trees Dani had told her about. She set the brake and jumped down to the ground, pulling her double-barreled shotgun from its place under the driver's perch. She heard Dani shout, "US marshals, drop your weapons," followed immediately by Cami shouting the same thing on her side of the road. Then there was a plethora of gunfire.

---•००‑◉‑००•---

Gun battles like this one are usually over in just a few seconds of time, but they seem to be longer. Then there is the deafening silence that follows.

"Dani? Cami? Are you guys okay?" Mattie shouted. Getting no immediate response, she shouted again. "Talk to me ladies! Are you okay?" The silence scared her.

Then she heard Dani yell, "Cami, you okay?"

"I'm good," came her sister's reply.

Mattie breathed a big sigh of relief. When she saw her sisters emerge from the trees, she rushed forward to meet them. "Are either of you hurt?" she asked, concerned.

They shook their heads no.

"What about the gang members?"

"The two on my side of the road are dead," Dani informed her sisters.

"I've got one dead and one with a bullet in his shoulder. He's tied up back in the trees."

They spent the next half-hour getting the dead outlaws tied down onto their horses so they could bring them into Topeka the next day. The wounded desperado was treated and then placed into the jail wagon with Dakota Sam. As Mattie slammed the rear door shut a smile crossed her face as she thought about Sam's earlier comments. She really wanted to "rub" it in his face, but knew that wasn't a Christian attitude, so she refrained from doing so.

Topeka, Kansas, March 12, 1875

Mattie, Cami, and Dani were relieved to have finally arrived at the Kansas state capital late Friday morning. They turned their two prisoners over to the deputy federal marshal in charge of the Topeka office and the three dead outlaws to the mortician. They were surprised, however, to find Marshal Winters waiting for them.

"Congratulations, ladies!" he said effusively. "You did an excellent job. You even brought in the rest of Sam's gang. Go get yourselves checked in at the hotel. You'll probably want to get cleaned up and have something to eat. Come see me at the office here first thing in the morning. I'll give you the paperwork fully authorizing you to be deputies in the marshal service. And I'll give you your next assignment."

Without another word, he turned and walked away.

———◦◦•◦◦———

Ninety minutes later, the three sisters came out, freshly bathed and clothed in pretty dresses. Then the trio of beautiful young women entered a restaurant in the middle of Topeka's main business district. Their badges and pistols were in the reticules each of them had hanging from their lovely arms.

After taking their seats and placing their orders, Cami asked, "What kind of assignment do you think Tobias will give us next?"

"Hopefully something that won't take over a month to resolve. I wouldn't mind a little bit of a break right now," Mattie groused.

"I hope it's something in Wichita," Dani said, putting in her two cents.

"I think our sister is lovesick," Cami said teasingly.

"You guys saw where that got me," Mattie bitterly remarked.

Dani defensively bit back. "Tobias is not like David, Mattie! He's kind and he cares about people."

"I thought the same about David. Until I married him and found out what a monster he was."

"You're not being fair, Mattie," Cami interjected. "Dani's right. Tobias isn't anything like David. Besides, David got what he deserved."

Mattie's back stiffened. Then she asked suspiciously, "What's that supposed to mean?"

"Nothing, Sis," Dani quickly said, shooting Cami a stern look. "Let's just drop this and have a nice dinner. Let's celebrate a job well done and our now being full-fledged deputies."

"Look, here come our dinners!" Cami chimed in.

Mattie didn't pursue the discussion at the dinner table anymore but was ready to do battle the minute they get back to their hotel room. That's when she turned on Cami, fiery anger blazing in her eyes.

"Camille Erin Cochran, what exactly did you mean by that comment you made at dinner tonight!"

9

DAVID

Wyoming, March 4, 1875

MATTIE'S FORMER HUSBAND woke with a start. The last thing he remembered was passing out, tied to the front of a train's locomotive. Something heavy lay on top of him. He twisted to see what it was, and realized he was naked. The good news though was he was no longer tied up, and he was covered with a thick hide of some kind.

Slowly sitting up, David looked around him at his surroundings. It appeared that he was in a cave and that his covering was a buffalo skin. A cooking fire was burning to his right, making him sweat beneath the animal hide. He started to cast off the hairy covering when he heard a female softly giggle.

"Who's there?" he demanded loudly, hastily pulling the covering back over his body, holding it up to his chin.

Focusing his eyes beyond the burning fire, he spied a young Indian girl sitting against the cave wall. "Who are you?" he asked.

The girl did not respond, but just stared at him. Yarden's eyes searched for his clothes but could not find them. "Where are my clothes?" he yelled at the young female. But again she remained mute. David's yells and demands were only serving to scare the girl, but he could not tell that because her face was mostly in shadows.

Summer Wind was scared. She had inadvertently giggled when the strange white man began to uncover himself from the buffalo hide her father had thrown over him. She had never seen a naked man before, let alone a naked white man, and she had let a small laugh escape her lips. Now she was scared. Scared by the man's shouts and yelling with words she'd never heard before and did not understand.

Only twelve summers old, the young Indian girl had never seen a white man close up. She was curious why this man's skin was so pale and why the tribe she and her father belonged to had told her that the white man was full of evil spirits. But that wasn't what her father had taught her. He said that it is true that there are evil white men, but that is also true of the Indian. However, he taught her that there are good white men just like there are good Indians and that she should learn to tell the difference.

Summer Wind was already convinced that the white man on the other side of the fire from her must be one of the evil white men. At least his words, the ones she could not understand, sounded evil to her ears.

Staring at one another through the bright fire, neither one could move, David because he had no clothes and the girl because she was scared.

"What is your name?" Yarden asked, modulating his tone in an effort to try to make her less fearful. "Name?" he asked again when he didn't get a response. He realized that the girl didn't understand, so he tried a different tactic.

Pointing to his chest, he simply said, "David!" Then he sounded it out slowly, "Day...vid!" This he repeated several times, pointing to himself as he spoke his name.

Sensing that the white man was trying to communicate with her, Summer Wind attempted to sound out the strange word he was repeating, "Day...vid!" Then she pointed to her own chest and repeated the word, "Day...vid!"

It was Yarden's turn to laugh, finding humor in the girl's misunderstanding. He pointed again at his chest and said his name. Then he pointed at the girl, shook his head, and said, "No, David!" Finally, after several more attempts to get the girl to understand, she pointed at him and said, "Day... vid!" He nodded his assent and said yes.

As David's eyes adjusted to the dimness of the cave and looking through the glowing fire, he began to see that the girl was quite beautiful. However, he did not know that she was Pawnee, nor did he know that her mother had died giving birth to her and she had been raised by her father. The truth is she knew more about men in general than most girls her age, but knew nothing about the white man. Summer Wind had been told by her father to come and get him when the white man awoke, but she was so intrigued by this strange-looking man that she could only sit and watch him through the firelight.

Is this white man crazy? Summer Wind wondered. He had kept pointing to himself and saying a strange word, "Day...vid!" Or maybe that was his name and he was trying to tell her that. When she finally pointed at him and said the strange word, he seemed pleased. So she decided that she would tell him her name. But she spoke in Pawnee, the only language she knew. And when he tried to say it out loud, it sounded very funny, so she laughed. And that made the white man mad. Maybe he really was crazy.

Then he stood up, holding the buffalo blanket in front of himself. She quickly stood also, but when he took a step toward her, she ran. Right into her father.

Man Who Eats Bear spoke to his daughter in their native tongue. After they spoke for a couple of minutes, she stepped off to the side and watched as her father approached the crazy white man. Yes, she was sure he must be crazy.

The Native American man wasn't any taller or wider than David Yarden, but his bulging muscles attested to the fact that he was in far better shape than the other man.

"Hello, my name is Man Who Eats Bear," he said, speaking English, "and this is my daughter, Summer Wind. She says your name is Day…vid, so I assume she means it is David."

Shaking the Indian's hand, David replied, "Yes! It is nice to meet you. You speak very good English."

"I have traveled many miles with the white man as an army scout. They have taught me your language."

"Your daughter wouldn't speak to me in English though."

"That is simple. She doesn't know your language. She will one day marry a Pawnee brave and bear him Pawnee children. For that, she does not need the white man's tongue."

David suddenly felt a cold draft, bringing him back to the realization that he was still naked.

"Um, can I have my clothes back?" he asked sheepishly.

"I apologize. Your clothes were badly damaged, so I had to burn them. I have brought you new clothes."

Man Who Eats Bear tossed a parcel at David, and it landed at his feet. He then spoke to his daughter, and they quickly left the cave together. After dressing, David walked outside and spoke to his benefactor.

"How is it I came to be here with you two?"

"Two days ago, Summer Wind and I were hunting over near where the Iron Horse passes through the country. We were camping there when we heard it approaching. Then it did something we had never seen or heard it do. It *stopped*. We carefully snuck up and watched from behind the trees as two men freed you from the front of the big locomotive. Then they tossed you off to the side, got back on the train, and left.

"After the train was out of sight, I went and saw that you were badly injured. Together, we managed to get you to our campsite for the night. The next day, we brought you here to our home. Summer Wind has tended to your injuries as best she could."

"Why would you help a white man?"

"White men are no more evil than some Indians. Many summers ago, when I was still a young brave, a couple came to our village and told us of a Great Spirit whom they called God and how He allowed some evil men to kill His only Son, a man called Jesus. This was because all men are born evil, and only those who believe in Jesus can be made right in God's eyes. Jesus taught that we should treat other people the way we wish to be treated.[1] When a person believes in Jesus and what He did, God forgives them for their wrongdoing[2] and gives them eternal life.[3]"

"Yeah, well, I gotta tell ya, I'm not into all that holy roller, religious stuff. My wife and her sisters were constantly harping on me to go to church and believe all that nonsense. But when we were home alone, my wife didn't have any problem talkin' back to me and refusing to do the things a wife is supposed to do. Where was her religion then?"

---

[1]   Matthew 22:39 (author's paraphrase)

[2]   Romans 10:9–10 (author's paraphrase)

[3]   John 3:16 (author's paraphrase)

"I don't know your wife, so I can't answer your question. However, I do know Jesus, and I can promise you, He has never let anyone down.

"Even when my wife got sick and died and I was left with a newborn baby to care for, God was right there with me. He helped me deal with all of it."

"But your wife died. If God is so good, why didn't He heal her instead, so she could help raise your child?"

Man Who Eats Bear laughed generously, "David, we will all die eventually. Dying is just another part of living. What is important is where we will spend eternity. How we deal with the death of someone we love determines the quality of our life here on earth. How we prepare for our own death determines the quality of our life in the hereafter.

"There are only two places to spend eternity—heaven or hell. Frankly, I've had enough of hell here on earth, and I'm looking forward to spending my eternity in heaven."

"Well, I don't choose either!" David declared.

"David, to make no choice is to choose."

"How do you figure that?"

"Suppose I had a twenty-dollar gold piece and I told you that you could choose to receive it or receive nothing. If you told me you weren't going to choose either option, what do you suppose you would receive?"

"Nothing, I guess."

"So then, haven't you, in essence, made a choice?"

10

TRUTH COMES OUT

Topeka, March 12, 1875

"WHAT EXACTLY DID you mean by that comment you made at dinner, Camille Erin?" Mattie demanded. One look into her eyes told her triplet sister that Mattie was furious.

The three women were identical physically, but uniquely different in their personalities. Camille tended to be shy, introverted, and consistently avoided confrontations, except when it came to outlaws. Danielle was the steadying influence among the three. She was most often the peacemaker. She rarely got into an argument with either of the other two and often ended up "refereeing" their fights. Usually she was the one who would get them to stop and settle their differences.

Mattie was the most dominant one, sometimes to the point of being overbearing. Headstrong and sure of herself, she never hesitated to let everyone around her know how she felt, particularly when she was displeased about something, as she was now. Some said that you could see lightning in her pretty blue eyes, and smoke coming from her ears, when she was mad. Camille knew that the use of her middle name meant that she was in serious trouble with Mattie.

"Com'n, Mat, she didn't mean anything by it," Dani said, trying to calm her sister.

"Yes she did! And you stay outta this! What did you mean, Cami?"

Her voice weak with fright and full of tears, Cami tried to talk, "I'm sorry, Mattie...it's... it's...just...David was just so mean to you. Wha...whatever, you know, whatever happened to him, well...we just thought, you know...it was...it was what he deserved."

Mattie's angry eyes pierced through the tear-filled eyes of her sister. She'd always been good at "reading" her sisters, especially Camille, and knew that there was something more going on here than Cami was telling her. She heard Dani take a deep breath and knew that she was getting ready to put in her two cents worth, but one glance at her and the other blonde quickly decided to swallow her comment.

"You're lying to me, Cami," Mattie accused, her voice low and menacing.

"Dani?" the blonde girl squeaked a plea of help.

Turning on Danielle with her fiery blue eyes, Mattie glared, "What do you have to say to this?"

Dani took a deep breath and let it out slowly before she spoke, "Sit down, Mattie. I'm not going to talk to you until you calm down."

The two sisters locked stares at each other for what seemed like a dozen minutes, though it was really only ten seconds. The tension in the room was palatable until Mattie finally sat down on the edge of one of the beds, took a deep breath of her own, and let it out. Dani sat down beside her and took her sister's hands into her own. They sat looking into each other's eyes for a minute before Dani spoke.

"Camille and I love you very much, Mattie, and we couldn't just stand by and watch as David continued to beat you and abuse you just to make himself feel better. After discussing it for a couple of months, we decided we had to do something about the situation. So we disguised ourselves as men and rode out to where he was working. We ordered him to ride into the woods where we had a noose waiting for him.

"After tying his hands behind his back and placing the noose around his neck, making like we were going to hang him, we gave him a choice. He was so scared he wet himself.

"We weren't trying to embarrass him and I was ready to call our plan off, but he started crying and begging for his life. He swore that he would do whatever we asked if we would let him go, so we told him to leave Iowa and never come back.

"I cut off his bonds and Cami took the noose off his neck. We told him to not even go back to the cabin or stop and talk to anyone. We said if we ever caught him in Iowa again, we'd finish the job. David rode off as fast as he could and we haven't seen him since." Dani paused in her story, but when her sister didn't say anything, she continued, "We only did what we did because we love you and didn't want to see you hurt anymore. David didn't love you, Mat. Please forgive us."

Tears were running like a river down the young woman's face as she tried to deal with the story Dani had just told. Cami sat down on the other side of Mattie and took her sister's right hand into hers. Interminable minutes passed before any of the trio could speak. Cami and Dani could sense that their sister's anger had diminished, replaced by an overwhelming emotion of grief and sadness. When Mattie finally spoke, her voice trembled and her speech was tentative.

"Why didn't you tell me?" she asked them.

"Because," Cami answered, "we thought you'd be more believable when you were questioned by others if you truly didn't know what had happened to David."

"So what you're saying is, you didn't trust me to keep my mouth shut!" The anger was back in her voice, and her eyes.

"Be fair, Mattie!" Dani complained.

"Be fair?" the young woman shouted as she pulled herself free from her sisters' embrace. Quickly standing and turning to face them, she continued to yell, "Be fair? The two of you contrive to scare and run off my husband, my husband, without even considering how I might feel, and you tell me to be fair. I…I…" Mattie looked like she wanted to say more, but couldn't get the words out of her mouth. Instead, she stomped out of the room, slamming the door behind her.

"Guess that didn't go too well," Cami commented.

A quick exchange of glances was Dani's only response.

Wyoming, March 12, 1875

David Yarden had spent more than a week with Man Who Eats Bear and his daughter Summer Wind, recovering from the injuries he'd suffered as a result of being tied to the front of a locomotive. While he'd been allowed to learn some of the Pawnee language he was not allowed to teach Summer Wind any English, except for his name. But now it was time for him to move on.

On a bright Friday morning, he left the Indian's campsite and began walking westward. Man Who Eats Bear had told him about a town called Laramie that could be reached by following the train tracks. He had also graciously provided David with a bundle containing enough provisions to see him through several days of travel, if he was careful with it. After that he would have to provide for himself.

No money, no horse, no gun, and no idea where to go or what to do when he got there didn't leave David with many options.

Topeka, March 13, 1875

Cami and Dani were lying on one of the beds, fully clothed but sound asleep, when Mattie slipped back into their room just before dawn on that Saturday. She'd been gone all night and her sisters had spent a good portion of those dark hours searching for her. Finally, totally exhausted, they'd returned to the hotel room in hopes that Mattie would be there waiting, only to be disappointed. They had fallen asleep less than an hour before the triplet returned.

It wasn't hard for Mattie to figure out what her sisters had done, considering the fact that she would have done the same thing if one of them was gone all night. She quietly undressed and slipped into the other bed, leaving her sisters alone so they could sleep. It was mid-morning when the two finally woke and found Mattie was back in the room.

Dani woke up Mattie and demanded, "Where were you all night? We searched all over town for you."

"I was praying," she softly replied.

"Praying?" Cami asked, skeptically.

"Yes, praying. I do pray, you know, though not as often as I probably should," a small smile creased her face.

"But where were you?" Dani repeated her question. "We searched most of the night for you."

Mattie sat up and hugged her sisters. "I'm sure you did, and I apologize for worrying you. But I needed to be alone, to deal with what you told me. And to spend some time alone with God.

"I found the door at the Baptist church was unlocked, so I went in and knelt at the altar, and just started praying. The minister was there, in a back room apparently, and heard me crying. He came out to see if he could be of any help. When I told him I just needed to be alone and pray, he told me to take all the time I needed.

"I couldn't say how long I actually prayed, long enough to lay it all at Jesus's feet, but eventually I fell asleep. I woke up just before sunrise and came back here."

Cami and Dani stared at Mattie, the unasked question evident in their eyes. Mattie saw what they were thinking and laughed.

"No, I'm not still mad at you two. I know you were only trying to do what you thought was best for me. However, if there is ever a next time, which I doubt will happen, please come and talk to me *before* you run off my husband."

Turning serious, she continued, "I know David didn't really love me, I knew that after the first month of our marriage. But I did love him, and I was determined to win him over and save our marriage. I prayed all the time that he would change.

"Unfortunately, you can't change people. Only God can do that, and only if they want to be changed in the first place. David had no desire to change, nor did he want to become a better Christian. I'm not even sure if he is a Christian to start with. He talked about God and Jesus, but there was nothing in his life beyond the talk. And talk is cheap.

"I know all that now, but at the time, I was still naive and immature and believed him when he blamed me for all our problems. While I don't necessarily approve of what the two of you did, you probably ended up saving my life. David would have eventually killed me, accidently, before he would admit that he has serious problems.

"Looking back on it, ladies, I realize that if you allow a man to hit you once, and get away with it, you have trained him to abuse you whenever he wants to. If a man ever hits either of you, other than in self-defense, do something about it. Don't let him think that it is okay or that saying he's sorry is enough. If he hits you, he has a problem."

Cami and Dani sat there, listening soberly as their sister poured out her wisdom from experience. Then Mattie shouted, "Group hug!"

The three young blonde deputies threw their arms around each other, laughing and giggling like they had when they were children. All was forgiven.

11

NEW ASSIGNMENTS

Topeka, Kansas, March 15, 1875

US MARSHAL TOBIAS Winters met his three newest deputies for breakfast on Monday morning. After the obligatory greetings and placing of food orders, the trio's boss got down to business.

"I've got your new assignments. You did an excellent job on transporting Dakota Sam from Pueblo to here, so I'm confident the three of you are ready for what I have for you. Unfortunately, I'm going to have to split you up as I have three different jobs that need to be done."

The looks on their faces told him immediately that they weren't happy about this. Before they could voice their protests, he raised his hand and said, "I never promised you that you would always work together on every assignment. Right now, I need three deputies in three different places. Since you three are what I have to work with at the present, it means you each will have to work alone.

"One of you will be going undercover in Chanute, Kansas. The second one will be escorting a man from Colorado to San Francisco to stand trial. He is not considered to be dangerous and is cooperating with the investigation. However, for his protection, we have decided that someone from the marshal's services needs to accompany him. The last one will stay here and audit the trial of Dakota Sam. I don't expect that she will have to testify, but needs to be prepared to if the need arises."

"So who is assigned to which job?" Mattie asked what they were all wondering.

"I'm going to leave that decision up to the three of you, subject to my approval, of course. Let me explain the assignments so you can make the best decision.

"Chanute, Kansas is an undercover assignment. Someone in Chanute is running a clandestine organization that has been systematically harassing and terrorizing blacks who have settled in the county, Neosho, and surrounding area. Recently they killed a black man there.

"The Chanute Town Sheriff, a man named Blanchard, has asked for our help. The blacks don't know who is behind this, and the whites are either too scared or too involved to say anything. The plan is for one of you to go there as a nurse and 'hire' on with the local doctor in an effort to blend in with the people and, hopefully, get them to trust you enough to tell you who is the leader of the group. Any questions?"

When none of them spoke up, he continued, "The Colorado man is one Ridley Adams, He's wanted in San Francisco on attempted murder charges."

"I thought you said he wasn't dangerous?" Dani interjected. All three girls had concerned looks on their faces.

"He isn't. The story is, Adams was helping an old army buddy of his rescue the man's wife and daughter, who'd been kidnapped several years ago. They were being held captive while the woman was forced into slave labor at a jeans factory. The girl was 'insurance' that the mother would cooperate.

"Assisting Adams and the former army First Sergeant was a former Confederate Army officer, who happens to be friends with a Brigadier General, the Executive Officer at Fort Riley, Kansas. General Beauregard is the one making the request, which is why we are involved rather than someone from Colorado or California. Incidentally, the Confederate officer is also Beauregard's son-in-law, a man named Hancock."

"Brody Hancock?" Mattie asked, surprise in her voice.

"You know this man?" Winters asked.

"No, I only know him by reputation. He was a hero for the rebels. He supposedly saved General Lee's life the day before he surrendered."

"I hadn't heard that story. Anyway, General Beauregard says that Adams is willing to go to San Francisco to clear his name. However, the general wants an unbiased witness to insure that the proceedings are fair and impartial. He is also concerned that this may be a setup in order to kill Adams.

"Finally, the last assignment is pretty simple. I want one of you to stay here and watch the proceedings at Sam's trial. Watch the trial, testify if necessary, and then watch them hang him."

The marshal waited to see if there were any questions regarding the assignments. Nothing of any real significance was asked; so after a few minutes, the marshal excused himself, saying, "Discuss it among yourselves and let me know by suppertime which one of you is going where."

The three young deputies sat in silence, each contemplating which assignment most appealed to them before discussing the options out loud. To say they weren't happy about splitting up would be an understatement. However, they each came up with a proposal in their minds as to which one should take which assignment.

As usual, Mattie took the lead, proposing that Cami would stay in Topeka, Dani would go on the escort trip to San Francisco, and she would go undercover in Chanute.

Dani, on the other hand, was convinced that Cami should go undercover and Mattie, who Dani sometimes felt was overbearing, should go to San Francisco. She herself would stay in Topeka, hoping that Tobias Winters would also be staying around for an extended period of time.

Not to be outdone by her sisters, usually shy Camille told them that she thought she should be the one to go to San Francisco while Dani went undercover in Chanute and Mattie stayed in Topeka to attend Dakota Sam's trial. Over an hour later they were still discussing it, each woman championing her own plan.

The sometimes heated discussion prompted the café owner to request that they take their meeting elsewhere. Dani then suggested that they go their separate ways so they could each spend time considering all the various arguments. They could meet up in their hotel room in an hour or so and try to come to a resolution. Her two sisters agreed to the idea.

Mattie was the first to arrive back at the room, much to her surprise, with a changed attitude. She felt certain that she'd come up with the right solution and was looking forward to explaining her thoughts to the other girls. She also had found something while shopping that she was excited about and wanted to share with Cami and Dani.

Cami was the next to arrive, about ten minutes after Mattie, and she was carrying a bag. She was obviously excited about something and blurted out, "Oh, Mat, wait until you see what I found!"

Before she could show her sister what was in the bag, Dani came rushing into the room, carrying a bag of her own, and declared, "Wait 'til you two see what I found while shopping!"

Without hesitation, the three young women simultaneously reached into their shopping bags and pulled out an article of clothing, shouting in unison, "Women's jeans!"

There was several seconds of stunned silence as the three deputies looked from one to the other in disbelief, then they all burst into raucous laughter. It was apparent that all three of them had used shopping as a means of "cooling off." By some trick of time, they had each gone shopping at the same general store, but at different times, and had each discovered the same jeans.

"You know ladies," Mattie said, after she had recovered from her bout of laughter, "God worked this out so we'd have something to bring us back together. Let's not argue anymore. We can either draw straws or present our three plans to Toby and let him decide."

"I say we draw straws," Cami voted.

"Why don't we pray together and let God decide who should go where?" Dani suggested.

The three knelt down next to one of the beds and took a turn praying for God's wisdom in the situation. Though they only spent roughly ten minutes praying, they stood up and yelled, "Cami's, Dani's, Mattie's" as they each called out one of the plans. However, they each called out someone else's plan this time instead of their own. This brought more laughter from the three sisters.

Finally, Mattie called for her sister's attention. "I think we should go with Dani's plan, as it makes the most sense. It actually utilizes each of our strengths.

"Cami is the best 'nurse' amongst us. She is the most caring and sensitive to others feelings. Dani, on the other hand, doesn't like the sight of blood, yet is definitely the most patient one of us. Cami or I would go stir crazy sitting around here waiting for the trial to begin and then having to sit through it. Besides, if one of us has to testify, Dani is the best at staying calm and getting the truth out. I doubt even the best defense lawyer could rattle her. As for San Francisco, you both know that I'm the one who travels best."

Mattie's sisters looked at one another and shook their heads in agreement with her assessment. When they saw Marshal Winters at lunch they told him of their decision. Interestingly, he told them that their choice was the same one he would have made.

March 17, 1875

Mattie was the first one to leave Topeka, taking the noon train to Pueblo, Colorado. By horseback, the approximately 475-mile trip would have taken at least four weeks. However, by train, she was going to be able to be in Pueblo on the twenty-ninth. From there, she would borrow a horse from

Sheriff West and ride the seventy-five miles to the Double H ranch where Ridley Adams was living with friends.

It was a good thing that Dani was a patient person, and one who was comfortable being alone, as the Kansas Attorney General's office notified her that Dakota Sam's trial wouldn't begin until the week of April 5th.

Meanwhile, Cami stayed in town until the following Monday morning, March 22nd, meeting with Marshal Winters daily so that he could go over strategy and instructions with her. At first, Dani was upset that Cami was spending so much time with Tobias, but then she joined them, using her sister's meetings as an excuse to spend time with the marshal.

The splitting up of the trio was emotional for each of them since they'd hardly ever been apart before. Even when Mattie was married, they saw each other every couple of days. Now they wouldn't see each other for what was probably several months.

---o0o—|O|—o0o---

Life is strange sometimes. Those who seem strongest when they are in a group are often the first to feel the pain of separation. So it was with Mattie. She had always been the one to take care of her sisters, to stand up for them when they were in jeopardy. Yet as the train pulled out of the

Topeka station headed westward, it was Mattie who was wiping tears from her eyes.

The pretty blonde's mind went back to a day when they were ten years old. School was boring for Mattie and she found it hard to concentrate on her studies. But one day, a boy forced Cami to kiss him. Mattie stepped right in and set matters straight. She was sent home with a ripped dress and bloody lip, but the boy had a busted nose, cracked ribs, and a lot to live down. The other schoolchildren laughed at the boy because he'd been "whupped by a gurl." In Mattie's mind, it was the best school day she'd ever had.

Cami wasn't the only one who'd been rescued by her sister. Dani, the peacemaker she was, had tried to break up a fight when she was fourteen. The older boys had turned on her and had had her pinned to the ground when Mattie arrived on the scene. Grabbing a fallen tree limb, the blonde weighed into the fracas, beating the boys on the back. When the older of the two boys tried to take the stick away, he ended up with a concussion while the other one ended up with a broken leg and arm.

Mattie's tears turned to a satisfied smile as she recalled these events. It also occurred to her that her sisters had returned the favor when they scared off David Yarden. As she fell asleep listening to the rumble and clickety-clack of the train's wheels, she wondered where her former husband had gone and if he was still alive.

12

DAVID

West of Laramie, Wyoming, March 20, 1875

TWENTY-FOUR-YEAR-OLD DAVID YARDEN rode a horse down the bank of another dry creek bed. It was nearly two weeks since he had left Man Who Eats Bear and Summer Wind. In Laramie, he had found some work, mucking out the livery stalls, and had a little bit of money. Like most people who have an addiction, his resolve to no longer drink lasted only until he received his first pay from the stable master.

After two days of mucking stalls, David had acquired a certain "air" about him. However, he decided that he'd rather drink his new found "wealth" than using it to take a bath and clean himself up. Consequently, he had stood at the bar in one of Laramie's drinking establishments, nursing his way through a beer.

"Hey, Howie, what's that awful smell?" David heard from behind him.

Looking up into the mirror on the wall behind the bar, David saw two cowpokes sitting at the table directly behind him. He intended to just ignore them, but they had different intentions.

"Why, Rusty, I believe it's the backside of a horse you smell," the one called Howie responded.

Making a show of sniffing the air, Rusty said, "No, Howie, I think it smells more like what comes out of the back end of a horse. What do you suppose a horse is doing in our saloon, Howie?" Rusty asked.

"I don't know, Rusty. Maybe it got loose from the stables. Think we should take it back and put it in one of the stalls?"

Both men had been watching David's back, waiting to see what kind of response they would get from their comments. When Yarden didn't react, Howie tapped Rusty on the arm and motioned toward the stranger at the bar. They stood up together and moved into position on either side of David.

"Hey, barkeep, I want a pitcher of beer, and make sure it's really cold," Howie ordered.

With a fresh pitcher of beer in front of him, Howie asked, "Hey, mister, can I buy you a drink?"

"No, thank you! I have plenty," David answered. He wasn't trying to be impolite but was just hoping that the men would return to their table without further trouble.

"Well," Rusty began, "If you're not gonna have a drink on us, how 'bout we have a drink on you?"

Before Yarden could respond, Rusty reached across, picked up the pitcher, and dumped its entire contents on David's head. Both men broke out in raucous laughter as the cold beer ran down the side of Yarden's face, soaking his hair and the shoulders of his plaid flannel shirt. Rusty set the pitcher down on the bar top and he and his partner started to walk away.

An unamused David Yarden picked up the now empty pitcher and swung around, smashing the glass vessel on the side of Rusty's head. The pitcher shattered on impact and Rusty dropped to the floor, blood flowing from a cut just above his left ear. He was unconscious before he hit the wooden plank floor.

Howie was struck dumb by the sudden attack on his friend and didn't see the right fist that was headed toward his face. The connection of David's fist to Howie's face made a loud splat sound in the saloon that was stunned into silence. However, David failed to take into account that there were a number of cowpunchers in the beer hall, most of them friends of Rusty and Howie. They took exception to the treatment of their fellow cowboys who were, in their minds, just having a little fun, albeit at the expense of a stranger.

David felt his arms being grabbed from behind. He struggled to free himself and managed to pull his left arm loose when a big, burly man stepped in front of him and smashed a fist into his stomach, doubling him over in pain. The big man used his left hand to raise David's chin and then caught him on the side of his head with a vicious right. David crumpled to the ground and was quickly surrounded by half a dozen cowboys who continued to inflict damage on his body with the hard pointed tips of their boots.

Mattie's former husband would probably have suffered considerably more injuries if it hadn't been for the intervention of Laramie's town marshal. He had walked into the saloon just as the men begin kicking the downed Yarden. After pausing a few seconds to appraise the situation, he pulled his six-shooter and fired a single round into the air.

The 'punchers stopped what they were doing and glared at the lawman, who said, "I think that's enough, boys. Why doncha all return to your seats now and let me handle this?"

As the cowboys filed back toward their tables, two of them decided to give David parting kicks. The marshal figured it would serve them right to carry Yarden up to the doctor's office as punishment for the two kicks. When the doctor finished treating David's cuts and bruises, the lawman questioned him.

"Wha's yer name, boy?" the fifty-year-old marshal asked.

"David Yarden," came back the answer, between deep breathes of pain.

"Wanna tell me wha' happened back thar'?"

"I was standing at the bar, drinking a beer and minding my own business, when those two cowboys started harassing me. I tried to ignore them, but they weren't about to let it drop. They came up on either side of me, ordered a pitcher of beer, and dumped it on my head. I fought back, defending myself. That's when the rest of those maniacs jumped in and started beating on me."

"Ya hit one of 'em wit' a pitcher?" the lawman made the statement into a question.

"Yes, sir. The one who poured the beer on me set the pitcher down on the counter. So I picked it up and hit him with it."

"Wal, ya hit 'im pretty bad. Doc says he might die. Guess I'm gonna hafta lock you up 'til the judge comes to town."

The marshal had figured David to be just another drifter and wasn't prepared for the fast move the young man made. As the lawman took hold of David's left arm with his right hand, Yarden pulled the marshal's gun from his holster and eared back the hammer in one smooth move.

"Now, tha's not too smart, Son," the marshal drawled. "Yer already in 'nough trouble wit'out addin' the killin' of a lawman."

"I'm not planning on killing you marshal," David informed him. He raised the pistol over his head and brought it butt first down on the other man's head, knocking him unconscious.

David had been in a back room of the doctor's office. Carefully, he opened the door just enough to peek out. No one was in the outer office, so Yarden slipped out of the room, quietly closing the door behind him. From a window overlooking the Main Street, David could see that it had turned dark outside, so he silently exited the doctor's office and faded into the shadows from the nearby buildings.

Main Street was virtually empty. A couple was walking along the boardwalk across the street, hand-in-hand. An old man was dozing in a rocking chair on the porch in front of the hotel. A horse was tied to the hitching post in front of the marshal's office, saddled and ready to ride, and several other horses were hitched in front of the saloon down the street a little ways. David moved to the back of the buildings he was between and looked left and right. Seeing no one, he returned to the front of the buildings. The only change he observed was the absence of the couple who had been out for a stroll.

Despite his last experience trying to steal a horse, David knew he would have to get out of town quickly, before the marshal came to. He went over to the marshal's palomino and began softly talking to it. The big gelding didn't seem bothered by David, maybe because he smelled like other horses, and allowed the young man to climb up into the saddle. It would be risky riding past the doc's office, but he would have to take that risk in order to head east out of town. His plan was to go a couple of miles eastward and then double back, avoiding the town completely as he continued to head west.

March 22, 1875

Two days after leaving the cow town of Laramie, Wyoming, David found himself out on the plains with no food, no money, a stolen horse, and nowhere to go. His hunger and thirst was exacerbated by the knowledge that he was in the middle of Indian country. While he had heard that the Cheyenne were sometimes friendly, especially if you had something to trade, he knew that the Sioux were on the warpath and would just as soon scalp a white man as look at him.

Later that afternoon, David spotted a sage hen in some nearby brush. The marshal's Henry rifle had been conveniently left in its saddle scabbard, so Yarden used it to shoot the bird. Riding further west with his prize, he soon came across a copse of trees with a babbling brook running through it. David made camp, got a small fire going, skinned the prairie hen, and had himself a small feast. For the first time in, well he honestly couldn't remember when, he felt full and satisfied.

He slept well that night, like a newborn baby he thought, but woke to a surprise that nearly gave him a heart attack. David woke to find himself surrounded by a half dozen Indians. One of them was kneeling close to his right side and was holding a big knife in his right hand, with some of David's long hair in his left hand and a big smile on his face.

13

CAMI

Chanute, Kansas, March 30, 1875

CAMILLE'S STAGE ARRIVED in the wet, cold, windy town of
Chanute just before the noon hour on a Tuesday. The trip
from Topeka had been long and arduous, the last couple of
days had been very rainy in Kansas. She had wanted to ride
Ginger, her red-blonde quarter horse, but Marshal Winters
thought that would betray her character, a nurse.

As she alighted from the stagecoach the wind whipped
her nurse's cap off her head and tore at her white dress.
Cami hated the stupid cap and wondered why nurses wore
them. She turned to see where the cap went and bumped

into a man holding an umbrella in one hand and her cap in the other.

"I believe this belongs to you, miss," he said, holding the cap out to her.

Cami quickly looked the man over. He was an older man. *At least in his late fifties*, she thought. *But quite distinguished looking.* He was wearing a dark gray suit, white shirt, and a black bowtie.

"Doctor Norman Holliday at your service," he intoned, extending his now empty hand.

"Camille Sanders," the young deputy replied, using the pseudonym she and Winters had agreed upon. Toby had told her it was best to use her real first name as that was the name she was used to responding to. "My friends call me Cami," she informed the doctor as she shook his hand.

"It would be best if I called you Nurse Camille and you called me Doctor or Doctor Holliday. I encourage my patients to keep things on a strictly professional level.

The doctor was not what Cami would call handsome, but he carried himself as one used to being in charge.

"I took the liberty of securing you a room at Miss Edna's boarding house. It is not much to look at, but it is infinitely better than the Chanute Hotel and Saloon. And quieter too."

"I'm sure it'll be fine. Thank you, doctor."

"I've told the stage driver to deliver your baggage to the boarding house. I presume you will wish to rest and clean up after the long ride down here. I will expect you to report to work promptly at eight o'clock tomorrow morning. Good day!"

Before Cami could respond, the good doctor turned on his heel and walked briskly away, leaving the pretty blonde standing there in the rain. Stunned by his abrupt dismissal, Cami stood there momentarily until she felt someone gently take hold of her elbow.

"Let's get out of the rain," a man said, leading her to the boardwalk in front of the stage office. "I'm Sheriff Blanchard," he told her once they were up under the building's over-hanging front. "Don't let Doc there scare you. He tries to put on a curmudgeon façade, but we all know that he's a softy when it comes right down to it."

"'Curmudgeon façade?' That doesn't exactly sound like a Kansan to me."

Blanchard laughed. "No, I guess it doesn't, does it? Actually, I was born in North Carolina and raised in New York City. I learned my law enforcement skills working for the police department there. But I got a yearning for the wild west and its wide open spaces.

"Why don't we go to my office where we can talk more openly?" he suggested.

The Cochran girl looked over the big, handsome law man, thinking that she wouldn't mind spending some time getting to know him, before asking, "Do you always invite women that have just come in on the stage to your office?"

"No," he answered, unsure of her point. Blanchard was surprised how beautiful the deputy marshal was. When he'd been told that the undercover agent coming to help him was a female, he imagined an older woman who probably would be significantly overweight.

"Then it might raise suspicions if we go there now. Let me go to the rooming house for now and you can 'just happen' to come by at the right time to join me for supper, unless your wife would object," she snuck the last bit in to see if he was married.

"That makes sense. I'll carry your bag and escort you to Miss Edna's, since you're very attractive that shouldn't raise too many questions, and then I will meet with you at suppertime. Miss Edna's Café is pretty good, and it's right next to the boarding house."

Grabbing an umbrella from the stagecoach office, the sheriff led Cami across the muddy street and down the far side boardwalk until they reached the boarding house where she'd be staying.

"I'll see you later," he said as Cami started to enter the two story building. "Oh, and I'm not married," he tossed over his shoulder as he walked away.

Cami smiled as she undressed and dried herself off. The good doctor may have a "curmudgeon façade," but the sheriff...now that was a whole different story. In his late twenties or early thirties, she guessed, he stood six feet tall, give or take an inch, and was solidly built. Ruggedly handsome with dark brown hair and electric blue eyes he had the aura of a man not to be trifled with. She had tried to talk her sisters into letting her go to San Francisco on the escort assignment, but now she was glad that she'd lost that argument. Regardless of how this assignment turned out, meeting Blanchard would make it all worth missing the trip to the west coast.

While Cami was musing about her encounter with the sheriff, the selfsame lawman was sitting at his desk, whistling to himself, a huge smile on his normally placid face. Just then, Kurt Smathers, his parttime deputy, came bursting in through the door.

"Sheriff, have you seen the new girl in town?" he blurted out.

"What new girl is that?" Blanchard asked nonchalantly.

"The one that come in to be Doc's nurse."

"Ummm! What about her?"

"Why, Bat, she's mighty purrty, doncha think?"

"Is she now? I guess I hadn't really noticed," Bailey "Bat" Blanchard commented, lying through his teeth.

"Wal, she's just 'bout the purrtiest gal I seen this side of the Atlantic Ocean, doncha know. She's so pretty all 'em boys gonna be getting''emselfs hert jes so's she's gotta pa'ch 'em up."

The sheriff hadn't considered that possibility before now. He made a mental note to pay close attention to the situation. It had already occurred to him that he would have competition for her attention, but he couldn't let guys deliberately go around getting hurt, though he wasn't sure how he could stop them from doing so.

Maybe he could convince Camille to wear an ugly nurse's uniform. He continued to dwell on the matter after Smathers left the office. The ugly uniform idea wouldn't work, he decided, as there wasn't any clothing she could wear that would make her unattractive. He would just have to take his chances. As they say, let the best man—him—win.

The object of Blanchard's interest skipped lunch, much to his dismay when he'd hoped to "accidently run into her" and put away her things before laying down for a nice nap. When she awoke near suppertime, she was starving. She headed for the café the sheriff had told her about, hoping that he would join her as he'd promised. Little did she know that the handsome lawman was looking forward to the meal as much, if not more, than she did.

Cami placed her meal order with Miss Edna's daughter, who ran the café and was its primary waitress, when the sheriff came walking in. She immediately sat up straighter, and then mentally admonished herself for doing so. Their meeting was supposed to be by chance and her actions suggested that she'd been expecting him. Besides, it wasn't a good idea for a young woman to let a man know that his presence caused her heart to pirouette in her chest. The increased palpitations caused a sheen of perspiration to form on her forehead just above her eyebrows. She quickly wiped it off with her napkin as she watched Blanchard look around the dining area, as if he was unsure where to sit.

Her first instinct was to worry that he had forgotten that he was supposed to have dinner with her. *Or what if*, she thought, *his only interest in me is because of the job I'm here to do?*

"This is crazy!" she said to herself. "You're thinking like a lovestruck schoolgirl rather than a professional law enforcement officer!" By the time the sheriff arrived at her table, Cami had suppressed her excitement at seeing him and put on an air of nonchalance and solemn demeanor.

"May I join you?" Blanchard asked, a little too loudly and stiffly.

What is wrong with me? I'm acting like a silly schoolboy, he thought.

"I guess that would be okay," Cami answered him, her tone cool but not too cold, she hoped.

"I, uh—I didn't, uh, get a chance to, um, properly introduce myself earlier. I'm Bailey Blanchard, but most people call me Bat."

"Pleased to meet you, Bailey—er, Bat. I'm Camille Sanders, but my friends and family call me Cami."

Blanchard couldn't believe how lame he sounded. He couldn't remember the last time he was this nervous around a woman, nor could he remember ever being with one who was quite so beautiful. He smiled as he surveyed the pretty blonde in the mint-green, off-shoulder dress with the short, puffy sleeves. It was much better looking than the plain white nurse's uniform she'd been wearing when she'd arrived in town.

"Have you ordered yet?" he asked.

"Yes. I ordered a small steak, baked potato, and peas."

"Sounds good, except for the peas." He signaled to the waitress and ordered. "Please bring me a medium-sized steak, baked potato, and broccoli."

"Sure thing, Bat," Edna's daughter, Vanessa, answered.

Bat was finding it difficult to keep his eyes off the gorgeous deputy sitting across from him. Her sweet, subtle perfume wafted across the open space, tantalizing him. What had seemed like a "cool" reception when he first sat down was slowly turning into a warm, generous conversation. He liked the way her eyes smiled when she laughed and the bright blue orbs seemed to sparkle whenever their glances met.

Camille had tried to maintain a cool, professional, real lawman demeanor with the more experienced sheriff, but quickly found it impossible. Bat Blanchard was a warm, humorous man and his stories of life in "the middle-of-nowhere Kansas" had her laughing so hard at times that she could scarcely eat. They spent over an hour at a meal that would ordinarily have taken less than half that time.

At one point, the conversation lagged for a few minutes; and as Cami chewed on a piece of steak, she closed her eyes. She spent the interlude wondering what it would be like to be held by this tall, strong man, with his lips firmly pressed against hers. She'd never been kissed—really kissed—by a man.

She laughed, not realizing she did so out loud, as she recalled her first "kiss." Only ten years old at the time, she was suddenly grabbed by Bobby Keslowski, a twelve-year-old, who tried to press his mouth against hers, getting more chin than lips. Mattie had practically obliterated the boy, breaking his nose in the process. Cami had been mad at her sister for interfering, but never said anything. A couple of months later she caught up with Bobby out by the privies, with the intention of completing the act, but he was so scared of Mattie that he just ran away. The pretty blonde hadn't had any opportunities since then to find out what it would be like to kiss someone.

"What's so funny?" Blanchard asked.

"Excuse me?" Cami responded, not understanding his question.

"You laughed—well, I guess it was more like a giggle. I was wondering what you found funny."

Did I really giggle? she wondered. "I just had a thought about something that happened a long time ago."

"Care to share it with me?"

"Umm, I think I'll keep it to myself, at least for the time being."

Having finished their dinner, the two went their separate ways. They had paid for their own meals so it wouldn't seem like they were really together, in case anybody was watching. Cami then waited in her room until well after dark before slipping out the backdoor of the boarding house. She surreptitiously made her way down the alley to the backdoor of the sheriff's office and slipped inside. Blanchard, who was expecting her, met her in the back room where the cells are. Sitting in one of the unoccupied cells, both cells were currently empty, they talked for over an hour.

Most of their time was spent discussing the case that had brought Camille to Chanute. Bat explained that several black families had recently been harassed by a group, most likely all men, wearing white robes and hoods to hide their identities. The sheriff had learned that this was part of a larger organization, calling itself the Ku Klux Klan.

"From what I've been able to discern, they started up in the south a few years after the War Between the States. However, it seems that some of them have filtered northward, starting new groups up."

"Marshal Winters told me that one black man was killed," Cami said.

"That's right. Ezekial Hawkins was his name. No one knows for sure what happened, but it appears Zeke tried to fight them off and was hit over the head with something heavy. According to Doc, it killed him instantly."

"How many men are in this group?"

"Based upon what witnesses have told me, I believe there are at least ten. However, since they're wearing these robes and hoods, getting an accurate number is difficult. I also fear that the group may be growing. Witnesses to the first encounter told me there were only five of them, but the last time they appeared there were ten. They could be varying their number, however, in order to confuse us."

"Is there any pattern to when or where they're hitting?"

"'fraid not! I'm thinking that their leader is someone who is pretty smart and who knows his way around the area. He probably also knows me and knows how I operate, so he knows when is the best time to strike.

"I've been trying to vary my patrols and those of my deputies, but they always seem to know where we are and strike where we're not."

"Any idea who the leader is?"

"Maybe. The most likely suspect is a man by the name of Drake Mosley. He owns a big cattle ranch about four miles south of town. I'm sure he'd like nothing better than for a lot of these small time farmers to sell off their land to him.

"I've talked to him a couple of times and he's become plenty incensed that I would even think that he could be the leader, but I don't put a lot of stock in his tantrums. He's fairly convincing in his denials, so either he's innocent of wrongdoing or he's a very good actor. I'm currently betting on the later.

"Another suspect—believe it or not—is the very man you are here to 'work' for. Doctor Holliday."

"The doctor! Really? Why him?" the deputy marshal asked.

"Doc came here about four years ago from Georgia, just outside of Atlanta. When all of this started, I sent a letter to the Cobb County Sheriff Office asking about the doctor. I was concerned because I'd heard rumors that he resented treating the blacks.

"The sheriff down there sent me back a letter stating that the doctor was approved by the Georgia Medical Board to practice medicine. However, he couldn't find any indication that he'd actually treated anyone, black or white. He also couldn't come up with a description of the doctor so I could compare it to the man here.

"I contacted some of the other counties in Georgia, Fulton, DeKalb, Gwinnet, and got the same results. I just don't know if Holliday is the same doctor approved in Georgia or an imposter.

"To top it all off, he came busting in here one day, yelling and cussing at me, telling me I had no right to be checking up on him and to mind my own business. I don't know if it has anything to do with anything, but two days later

Hawkins was killed. I've wondered ever since then if I was partly responsible."

Without thinking, Cami took the lawman's hand in her own and said, "Bat, you can't blame yourself like that. There's no way you can know if there is any connection between the two events. I mean, why would there be? You don't even know if Holliday is involved in this or not. Besides, why would he agree to allow me to work undercover if he was the leader of this group?"

"He doesn't know who you really are. But you're right, of course," he said, standing up. He began pacing back and forth in the small cell. "It's just that, every time another family gets attacked, I feel like I've let them down. I feel like I should be doing more to protect them. I just don't know what."

"Doc doesn't know I'm a deputy marshal?"

"No. I'm the only person who knows your true identity. When I telegraphed Winters for help three months ago, he sent back a message telling me he would set something up. Then he sent me a telegram a couple of weeks ago saying that Doc was getting a nurse who was really one of his deputies. I didn't even know he was sending a woman until I saw you get off the stage. Come to think of it, I don't even know your real last name."

"So the telegraph operator also knows I'm a deputy marshal?"

"No. Whenever someone is sending me a private telegram, he comes and gets me and I go get the message myself. I learned Morse code when I first came out west because I knew it would come in handy for police work."

Blanchard tried to turn the conversation to more personal matters, asking Cami again about her last name, but Camille quickly begged off, saying she needed to get to the rooming house before someone noticed she was gone. However, once she was back in her room she found she couldn't stop thinking about Bailey Blanchard. She laid on the bed, daydreaming that she was still in the jail cell with him when he suddenly pulled her into his arms and gave her a long, passionate kiss. Her last thought, before falling into a deep, dreamless sleep, was what a "passionate" kiss would be like.

14

MATTIE

Pueblo, Colorado, March 29, 1875

DEPUTY US MARSHAL Matilda Cochran arrived in Pueblo, Colorado on the Topeka Santa Fe train at eight o'clock in the morning of March 29th. After stopping in to see Sheriff Damien West, Mattie got a room at the Dew Drop Inn. A week and a half of bone-jarring, sleep-depriving bouncing in a train car left her wearier than the recent trek across Kansas escorting Dakota Sam to the Kansas capital in Topeka.

She ate a quick breakfast in the hotel dining room and then headed off to bed. The pretty blonde, blue-eyed triplet didn't wake up until after six that evening. She was eating a late supper in the same dining room when Sheriff West came in. After a brief glance around, he headed directly for Mattie's table.

"Damien," she greeted him.

"Mattie. May I join you?" he asked her.

"Please do!"

Mattie had been impressed with the older man when she'd met him on her earlier visit to his town, despite his standoffish attitude when she and her sisters had first arrived. In his early fifties, the tall, muscular man didn't seem like someone you'd want to go up against. On the other hand, she was sure he was someone you could trust and could count on when needed.

"How are you, Damien?" she asked politely.

"I'm doing well. How was your trip to Topeka with Mister Sam?"

"It had its moments, that's for sure. His gang, at least five members of it, attacked us a couple of different times. Four of them are discussing their ineptness in a very, very hot place."

West laughed. "And what about Sam?"

"Sam is awaiting trial in Topeka, along with the fifth man."

"So where are your sisters, I was surprised when they didn't get off the train with you."

"Danielle is still in Topeka, waiting for the trial, and Cami is on another assignment for the marshal's service."

West nodded. "I see! Well, I thought I'd come and talk to you about the assignment you have. What do you know about the situation in San Francisco?"

"Just that this guy Adams killed somebody in Frisco while helping a friend."

"Okay! Let me fill in the details as I understand them. Starting with the fact that he didn't kill the man but only *wounded* him. The man is confined to a wheelchair. The problem is the man wasn't part of the criminal gang.

"Ridley Adams was a Buck Sergeant at Fort Riley, Kansas when the family of his first sergeant, Lonnie Harrelson, was kidnapped by some desperados. They were out on a patrol together, looking for some white men who'd been dressing up as Indians and causing havoc. These same men raided Harrelson's house and took his wife, daughter, and son.

"When the two men returned to the fort and learned about the kidnapping they took leave and began searching for Lonnie's family. I don't know how long their search lasted, but eventually they were forced to give up the search. The only thing they had been able to discover was that the boy had been sold to some slavers.

"Eventually, Lonnie was asked by an officer he knew, who'd been promoted to colonel and been given the command at Fort Sill, Oklahoma, to accompany him there and be his First Sergeant. Meanwhile, Adams decided he was tired of the army and wanted to try his hand at prospecting. When that didn't pan out, no pun intended, he drifted around.

"Several years passed and Adams ended up in San Francisco, where he accidently saw Lonnie's wife, Katherine, working in a sweatshop."

Seeing Mattie's blank look, West explained, "That's a shop, or factory, where the employees, usually women and/or children, are kept either in slavery or near slavery. They're worked long, hard hours, are paid very little, and are often punished in some way if they don't produce the quantity, or quality, demanded.

"This particular sweatshop was making jeans and holding the women's daughters as hostages. If a woman didn't perform as expected, the daughter would be made to suffer. Apparently, some of the girls were sold into prostitution.

"Harrelson, along with a friend of his, a Brody Hancock, went to San Francisco, met up with Adams, and launched a rescue of Harrelson's wife and daughter, along with all the other women and girls. Now Adams works for Hancock and Harrelson at their ranch, the Double H, about sixty miles from here.

"One more player you need to know about. Miranda Hancock, Brody's wife, is the daughter of Brigadier General Beauregard from Fort Riley. She is—how can I say this?—a woman one should not mess with. She can outdraw, outshoot, outtalk, and out *anything* any man she meets, including—I suspect—her husband if she puts a mind to it. She is not, rest assured, your ordinary, run-of-the-mill housewife."

"Do you think they are going to give me trouble?"

"Not at all! They are very law-abiding, decent people. I've visited their ranch a couple of times and they come up to Pueblo every other month for supplies and to sell their horses that they've raised. I think you'll find them very cooperative. Frankly, the only reason you're escorting Adams to San Francisco instead of me is Colorado is not a state yet, so our governor won't allow me to. Besides, General Beauregard specifically asked for a US marshal.

"All I'm saying is, when you go down to get Adams, don't act superior just because you're a deputy marshal. These are good Christian people and deserve your respect and consideration."

"How far did you say it was to the ranch?"

"It's just about sixty miles, so you're looking at least three days down there and three days back. Barring any bad weather or trouble, you should be back here in time to catch the train on Monday, the fifth."

March 30, 1875

Mattie set out at first light the next morning. Sheriff West had lent her a stout pinto that was a little shorter than her quarter horse mare, Miss Molly, but was very energetic and had, according to West, great stamina. Mattie planned on arriving at the Double H ranch by sundown Thursday and would need such a horse. Because she wouldn't be on the trail for more than two nights, she didn't take a packhorse, opting to carry everything she'd need in her saddlebags or rolled up in her bedroll.

April 1, 1875

Shortly after noon, the young female deputy came to a white fence that ran along the right side of the road. She followed the fencing until she came to a break in it, about two miles further south. Over the break was a large archway with the words "Double H Ranch" carved artistically into the wood.

Mattie turned her horse up the pathway and passed under the archway. Both sides of the path were lined with groves of magnificent pine trees casting a faint shadow over the roadway. The young blonde woman felt a peacefulness come over her as she slowly walked the pinto along. Two and a half days of riding through unfamiliar territory had made her slightly tense and the sudden relief of the beautiful greenery reminded her of home, bringing a smile to her face.

Without warning, two masked men rode out from the trees, one on either side of the path. Brandishing rifles, one of them ordered, "Reach for the sky lady!"

Hearing the speaker's voice crack halfway through his demand, Mattie took a second look before reacting. She was glad she did.

"A couple of desperadoes, huh?" she quipped.

"That's right, lady! Now, hand over yer jew'ls and money and we mite let yew live."

Mattie had already noticed that the "rifles" were carved pieces of wood and that the two "gunmen" were boys.

"You outlaws don't know who you're up against," she said, making her voice low and tough. "I'm a deputy US marshal, and I aim to take you ruffians in. We don't allow desperados like you two to waylay innocent travelers," she said, playing along with their game.

"Yer a gurl," the second boy complained. "A gurl can't be no marshal."

"Yeah! And gurls can't shoot nohow," the first boy said, concurring with his young friend.

"Really?" Mattie said as a smile creased her lovely face. "See that pine cone hanging from that limb?" she asked, pointing to a nearby tree behind the boys.

Both boys looked over their shoulders and asked, in unison, "Which one?"

They heard an explosion and saw a pine cone shatter as the young deputy said, "That one!"

When they looked back at her in amazement, they noted that her pistol was already back in its holster.

"Wow!" they exclaimed together.

"You're as good as my ma," said the boy who had been the spokesman of the two.

"Now, you boys drop them rifles and put up your hands. I'm arresting you for assaulting a federal lawman. You boys are in a heap of trouble."

"I'll say they are," came a deep voice from the trees off to the right. A big man on a tall Appaloosa slowly rode out onto the dirt pathway.

"Pa!" the boy to Mattie's right gulped. "We was jist playin', Pa," he quickly tried to explain.

"And your playing around like that could have gotten you both killed. Not only that, you both know how to speak properly. Robert Lee, your mother is going to skin you alive when she finds out what you've been up to."

"Please don't tell ma, Pa. We was only playacting…"

The big man held up his hand to stave off any further comments by the boys.

"We'll discuss this further, later." Turning toward Mattie, he said, "You must be Marshal Cochran?" he asked.

"Mattie Cochran," she replied. "And you are?"

"Brody Hancock. The boy to your right is my son, Robert Lee, and the one to your left is Zackery Tyler, son of my head wrangler."

Mattie nodded her head in greeting to both boys and then Brody spoke again. "You boys go on ahead. Robert Lee, you tell your ma that our guest has arrived, then you put up your horses proper like. When you are done with that, you wait on the stoop for me." The boys turned their horses back up the pathway and started to ride away before Brody gave them one last instruction. "And don't you boys go racing those horses."

The blonde deputy couldn't help but notice the crestfallen looks on the faces of the two boys when Robert Lee's dad mentioned the word "stoop." It didn't take much to figure out that they were facing a punishment when Brody got back to the house.

"I hope you're not going to be too hard on them," she sympathized.

"I'm not going to whip them, if that's what you mean. I don't do that unless it's a really serious offense. But I can't allow them to get away with what they did.

"I don't mind they're playing around like that with their friends, or people they know, but when it comes to strangers, it's just too dangerous. Sooner or later, they'll encounter someone who doesn't know they are playacting and doesn't take the time to see they are only boys with make-believe guns.

"I appreciate the fact that you didn't shoot first and that you played along with them. However, when I heard you shoot, I knew it wasn't one of them and I was afraid I'd find one of them dead."

"I see your point. I apologize if I did anything to encourage them the wrong way."

"Don't worry about that. A week or two mucking out stalls under my wife's steady eye, will be a good lesson for them.

"Marshal Winters didn't tell me he was sending a female deputy. Matter of fact, I didn't even know the Marshals Service had female deputies. How long have you been a deputy?"

"We've been deputies since January. As far as I know we are the first, and only, females in the service at this time."

"'We'? How many of you are there?"

Brody had turned his horse back toward the ranch house and they were riding along the path slowly, enjoying the spring weather.

"There are three of us," Mattie answered, "my two sisters and I."

"Are they older than you?"

Mattie was amused by Brody's inability to fathom her being a deputy marshal. "Actually, we're triplets… identical triplets."

Hancock stopped dead in his tracks. "There's three of you!" he blurted out. Realizing his mistake, he tried to back track. "I'm sorry, that came out the wrong way."

The blonde woman laughed, "That's okay. Lots of men have the same problem accepting that we are females and deputies."

Brody decided to drop that issue before he put his foot in his mouth again. "It will be interesting to see what my wife thinks about there being female marshals now."

"I've heard some stories about your wife. It sounds like she'd make a good marshal."

"Please don't tell her that!" Brody grimaced at the thought. "It's hard enough keeping her at home."

A slight smile played across Matilda's lips as she asked, "Is it true that your wife single-handedly wiped out an entire band of renegade Indians?"

"Wha…What?" Brody sputtered. "Are they saying she did that by herself. Do people really believe…" Brody saw the smile spreading across the blonde woman's face.

"Gotcha!" Mattie bragged.

They both burst out laughing.

When they had both regained their composure, Mattie asked, "What kind of trees are these?" pointing toward the side of the pathway.

"These are blue spruce. We also have an area of aspens and some oak."

"How long have you lived here?"

"We moved to Colorado shortly after we got married. That would have been back in '66. At the time, it was just Miranda, Lonnie, Katherine, Jamima, and Ridley. And, of course, me," he threw in as an aside. "Miranda is my wife, Lonnie and Katherine are good friends of ours, Jamima is their daughter, and Ridley is the man you're here to escort to San Francisco."

Mattie didn't respond right away because she was in awe of the beautiful trees. After what seemed like hours, she finally asked, "How large is your ranch?"

"We started off with about five hundred acres and now have over five thousand. We're looking at some land on our western border but haven't decided yet if we want to purchase it. It would add another one thousand acres to our property."

"And you raise horses, right?"

"Yes. We have an Appaloosa/Morgan mix that we sell primarily to the army. Lonnie and I are both ex-army, he was with the Union Army and I was with the Confederate during the war."

The two riders emerged from between the rows of spruce into a wide open area where the ranch's main buildings were. Mattie looked on in wonder at the size of the main house, a sprawling two-story abode painted white with dark blue shutters and a bright blue front door. A deep veranda spread across the front of the house with a number of rocking chairs scattered about and a two-seater swing at the left end. The two boys were sitting glumly on the steps leading up to the veranda.

Off to the left of the house, there was a large building that Mattie guessed was the bunkhouse, and next to it was a large barn. Mattie could see there was a corral behind the barn as well as a rather large paddock further off to the left. There were trees scattered around the yard area as well as those surrounding the main campus.

"It's idyllic," Mattie commented dreamily.

"I'm glad you like it," Brody responded. "Come inside and I'll introduce you to the rest of the gang."

———•○○◦▶◀◦○○•———

Thursday night at the Double H was a real treat for Mattie. In addition to Brody and Robert Lee, she met Miranda, Emily Janine (Brody's four-year-old daughter), Lonnie and Katherine, Frank Tyler, Jamima Harrelson Tyler (Frank's wife and Lonnie's daughter), Zackery Tyler (their son whom she'd met earlier), and Ridley Adams.

When Mattie heard that Zackery had been born the same year that Jamima and her mother had been rescued, an explanation seemed in order. Frank provided the story.

"I was raised in Gettysburg, Pennsylvania. When I was old enough, I moved to a town called Altoona. There I met a woman named Evelyn, from Harrisburg, and we got married. When Zack was born, Evie got sick, dying a year later, having never fully recovered.

"Both of our families lost a number of lives, not to mention property and fortunes, during the war, and when Evie died, I was left alone to raise my son.

"In 1869, I decided to pull up stakes and head west, wanting to start over. Zack was three at the time, so we traveled slowly. I met Brody in Pueblo in '70. We talked and he ended up offering me a job as a wrangler on his ranch. That led to me meeting the Harrelsons, and their beautiful daughter Jamima. A couple of years later, it became obvious to me—as it already had to everyone else in this house— that I couldn't live the rest of my life without Jamima, so I asked her to marry me. She took pity on me and agreed to save me from myself. We got married in '73."

"If I'm not being too nosy, how come you're not married?" Jamima asked the young deputy. "I would think—as pretty as you are—that men would be falling all over themselves anytime you walked by."

Mattie had already come to like the young woman and her sweet Christian spirit and wasn't offended by the question though she suddenly found it difficult to think about the answer. Other than Adams and a couple of the other hands, everyone at the ranch were Christians, so Mattie'd been told. She felt more at home here than she had anywhere else in a very long time. She even found herself dreading having to leave the next morning.

After a moment of reflection, the blonde woman answered, "I was married once. It was five years ago and I was too young, and too foolish, to know better."

Leaving out the specific reasons behind David's disappearance, Mattie explained, "The man I married, David Yarden, was from New York City. I lived in the small town of Dewitt, Iowa, where my family has a fair-sized farm. I met David at the annual dance, and he swept me off my feet. He was handsome, intelligent, and charming.

"After we got married, we lived on a farm of our own. One day, David went out to till one of the fields…and never came back. Later we learned that he was wanted in New York."

"What was he wanted for?" Lonnie asked.

"At first they just said they wanted to talk to him about the murder of his wife. Eventually, they told us that they were sure he had killed her. He was tried in absentia and found guilty. To the best of my knowledge, he has not been caught, yet."

The group was stunned by Mattie's story and Miranda asked, "Is there any indication of what happened to him?"

The blonde deputy liked the brown-haired, blue-eyed wife of Brody Hancock from the moment she met her. Miranda, just a few years older than Mattie, exuded a warmth and friendliness that made those who came in contact with her love her immediately. The blonde found herself a little envious that Miranda and Jamima were both pregnant, Miranda with her third child and Jamima with her first. Wistfully, she wondered if she'd ever have a chance of having her own baby.

"The sheriff in Dewitt investigated, so he says, but it seemed like he was more interested in investigating me. I'm sure he thought I had killed David and buried him somewhere. But I didn't."

"Just like a man," Katherine Harrelson interjected. "Always blaming the woman."

Knowing that Katherine was being facetious, everyone laughed. Mattie joined in.

The remainder of the meal was consumed while enjoying a casual, lighthearted conversation that covered everything from the weather to politics to life in general. Mattie regaled them with stories of her and her sisters, and everyone was astounded by the fact that the three girls were all deputies. Brody bragged about the exploits of his lovely wife, and everyone shared stories about the rambunctious kids. No one spoke about the real reason Mattie was there, treating her instead like a relative they hadn't seen in a long time.

When the meal was over, Brody, Lonnie, Ridley, and Mattie retired to Brody's den to discuss the upcoming trip to San Francisco. Brody and Lonnie informed the young deputy that they would like to also accompany her and Ridley. At first, Mattie was a little leery of the idea, but she eventually agreed.

15

DAVID

Western Wyoming, March 23, 1875

THE SIX CHEYENNE braves laughed uproariously when they saw the look of abject fear on David Yarden's face. The one who squatted next to him with a knife in his hand stood up.

"We no kill you, white man," he said in broken English. "We trade for big horse." He motioned toward the palomino.

Swallowing the bile that had risen to his throat when he thought he was about to die, David considered the Indian's offer to trade. It stood to reason that every lawman in Wyoming was probably on the lookout for the tall, cream colored gelding. If he could unload it on these redskins in exchange for a pony and some food, he'd come out much better. Then let the savages try to explain it to the law.

David stood up, along with the rest of the braves, and looked over at the Indians' horses. He spoke to the group's obvious leader.

"The palomino for a pony and some food?" he asked suggesting.

"Big horse and rifle for small horse and food," the Cheyenne countered.

David knew he was getting the raw end of the deal, the small horse the Indian indicated being no more than thirteen hands tall compared to the sixteen hands of the marshal's horse. He would still have the marshal's pistol, which was tucked into the back of his jean waistband, and some .45 ammunition in the saddlebag, so he tried a counteroffer of his own.

"The big horse and rifle for that horse," he pointed to a medium-sized pony, "some food, and I get to keep the bullets for my pistol."

The Cheyenne made some motions with his hands and one of the other braves brought over the horse to which David had pointed at. Yarden transferred the saddle, minus the rifle, and saddlebags to the mare he'd just traded for. He removed a box of .30–06 cartridges for the Henry rifle and handed them to the Indian before stuffing the food they'd given him into the saddlebags. The six Indians promptly jumped onto their horses and rode off, yipping and yelling as they headed away from David.

David made a breakfast of the remainder of the sage hen he'd shot and cooked the previous day. As he mounted the mare, it occurred to him that now would probably be a good time to get out of Wyoming as fast as he could. He knew that southward lay Colorado, with a town called Grand Junction near its western border. He would head southwest, hoping that if there was still any pursuit, they would follow the trail of the palomino and its Indian owner.

Somewhere northwest of Denver, March 29, 1875

It was almost a week since David had made the trade with the Cheyenne Indians that had netted him a different horse and some food, which was completely gone now. Armed with only the pistol he'd relieved from the marshal, he had been unable to kill any game to eat. He was getting hungry, was broke, and wasn't interested in working to get money to buy food.

As he approached the small town of Wormwood, Colorado he decided to hide in the heavily wooded area on the northern edge of town and assess the situation. It was midafternoon when he arrived and there didn't seem to be much activity on the Main Street.

Just before the sun starting setting, a single rider came into the quiet town and hitched up his horse in front of the lone saloon. The man was riding a big gray horse and his saddlebags looked awfully full from where Yarden looked out. There hadn't been much in the way of activity throughout the day, and didn't appear to be increasing. David decided he would try to quietly slip into the town, steal the man's horse, and hightail it out of there. He was hoping that the saddlebags were full of food. He could also see a rifle sticking out of a saddle sheath on the horse's right side. Since he hadn't seen any other horses all day, he figured if he also took the gray with him, at least until he was a significant distance out of town where he could turn it loose, the man wouldn't have any means of chasing him anytime soon.

Yarden waited until the sun was fully set and it was very dark, hoping too that the rider he'd seen was getting very drunk, before he quietly and stealthily entered Wormwood. Executing his plan flawlessly, for a change, David led the bigger horse westward about three miles before turning south. Riding at night was risky, but David knew he had to put some distance between him and the town, in case someone did have a horse and was pursuing him. Finally, judging that he'd ridden some additional five miles since turning southward, David pulled up and came to a halt. He transferred the saddlebags and rifle from the gray to his mare. He thought that if he let the gray loose there would be no reason for anyone to try to track him, the horse being the only thing of value.

David noticed that the saddlebags were quite heavy as he lifted them off the gray and draped them across his own horse in front of his saddle. He was going to eat good tonight, he thought. The rifle, a Winchester, was a .40-.45 he noted before sliding it into his scabbard. Then he turned the big gray horse loose, letting it find its own way home.

Turning the gray toward the north, he wrapped its reins around the saddle horn, gave it a big slap on the rump, and watched it take off like a bolt of lightning. Once the horse was out of sight, David turned his mare southwestward and took off at a mild canter.

David rode until the first rays of dawn peeked over the horizon, turning the sky a vibrant hue of pink with streaks of orange racing westward. Tired beyond anything he's ever experienced before, the young man rode among the trees, seeking a spot where he could camp out in relative safety. Beside a stream of clear, cool water, Yarden unsaddled the pony he'd been riding. Having led it to the stream to drink, he then picketed it up under the trees in a patch of new grass.

He was so tired, he hadn't noticed that there was new growth on the trees and that some of them were starting to fill out with leaves. The snow which had been so deep less than a month ago was rapidly disappearing and even the air was starting to feel warmer as spring replaced winter.

Thinking he would rest for a few minutes before fixing a breakfast, David laid down and promptly fell asleep. When he woke up several hours later, the sun was past its zenith and his stomach was complaining loudly. He built a small fire and then dug into one of the overstuffed saddlebags looking for food. He found a small coffeepot, a small skillet, a plate and cup, and some eating utensils. There was also coffee, flour, and some beef jerky.

He set the pot on the fire to brew some coffee while he chewed on a piece of the beef jerky. Not being much of a cook, he wasn't quite ready to try his hand at using the flour to make biscuits.

Hoping to find additional food in the other bag, he opened it and began rummaging through its contents, still chewing on the jerky, until he suddenly stopped, his mouth agape. Like most people who have unexpectedly come across something, David quickly glanced around, searching for someone who might be watching him, or someone who could confirm what he'd found. He sat back hard on the ground, and alternated staring into the bag and looking around for several minutes. He simply could not get his brain wrapped around what he was seeing.

Not able to stand it any longer, he finally reached into the bag and withdrew a handful of paper scrip. As he held the money in front of his face, a low, soft whistle escaped his dry, chapped lips. Everything in his hand was either a fifty- or a hundred-dollar bill, and from what he saw in the bag, there must have been several thousands of dollars. After pulling out all of the paper money and carefully stacking it up into several piles, he peered back into the bag and saw a substantial amount of various gold and silver pieces in the bottom.

David just had to have a drink of coffee, he actually would have preferred whiskey, but beggars can't be choosy he thought. After pouring himself a cup of the rich, dark brew, he sat back down and began separating the fifties from the hundreds. Then he separated out all the coins into piles based on their value. Then he counted his findings. The total shocked him again. There was $6,700 in bills and another $53 in coins.

David had never been what he would consider to be a lucky person. Therefore, his first fear was that the money was Confederate scrip, left over from the War Between the States. That concern was quickly disavowed. Next, he thought that it might be counterfeit. However, despite the fact he knew he was no expert on the subject, he determined that the money was real, at least as far as he knew.

Having stuffed the money back into the saddlebag, except for a small amount that he'd shoved into his jean pocket, David took his cup of coffee and beef jerky and sat back against one of the big pine trees to ponder on what might be the source of this windfall. Of course, he was concerned that the previous owner of the saddlebags might feel it necessary to track David down and relieve him of the cash—as well as his life, probably. This caused David to get up and search around his campsite, making sure that there was really no one preparing to jump out at him. It now became imperative that he be more watchful and that he use great care in concealing his trail from anyone who might try to follow him.

With the day waning and darkness starting to settle in, David decided to spend the night alongside the stream. He fell back to sleep with thoughts of all that money flitting about in his mind.

16

Topeka, Kansas, March 26, 1875

DANIELLE WAS FEELING the first pangs of loneliness. Mattie had left over a week ago and her sister Camille was now gone for four days. While she had been looking forward to being on her own, the reality of sitting by herself at lunch made her realize that being alone was not always as much fun as one thought it would be. To make matters worse, Toby Winters, the man she was hoping to get to know better, had informed her at breakfast that morning that he would be leaving the next day for St. Louis to tend to some matters there.

Tears came unbidden to her eyes as the thought of being truly alone for the first time in her life struck home. An unfamiliar town and a trial that was still at least a week and a half away, Dani was suddenly homesick, wishing she could just ride back to Dewitt, Iowa. Not usually given to self-pity, Dani felt the first tear slide down the side of her pretty face.

"May I join you?" the soft, obviously accented female voice asked.

Dani looked up into the face of a young Asian woman.

"Um, yes, sure! Please have a seat," the young deputy answered, motioning to the empty chair across from her.

Dani thought that the woman who sat down was younger than the twenty-one-year-old blonde. *Maybe eighteen or nineteen.* And, well, Dani wasn't sure if she could say that the girl was pretty or not. There was a plainness about her face, and yet, there was a certain…aura, maybe… that made Dani reevaluate her first impression. Her visitor had very long, dark brown, almost black, hair that Dani thought might be waist length, and golden brown, almond shaped eyes. Though the deputy had never met an Oriental before, she knew that this woman was definitely from one of the Asian countries.

"I am Ming Le," the dark haired woman said, extending her hand in greeting.

"Please to meet you. My name's Dani, short for Danielle. Danielle Cochran, but everybody calls me Dani," she responded, rattling on.

"Danny? But isn't that a boy's name?" Ming Le asked, confused.

"Well, yes, sometimes it is. But I spell my name with an *I*, as in D-A-N-I. That makes it a girl's name…Ming Le. That's a pretty name. Where are you from?"

"I am from China. I am on my way to New York City. We had to stop here because our wagon's axle broke."

"You speak very good English," Dani complimented her. The deputy noted that Ming Le spoke very formally, but that her accent caused some of her words to sound strange.

"Yes, thank you! I have worked very hard, learning from the missionaries that came to our village. They are the ones who are taking me, and my friends, to New York City to work. We will make lots of money, they say, and will send it back home so our families can come to America too."

"Oh, what kind of work will you do there?" Dani had a sudden feeling. It was both surprising and…frightening… to her. Something didn't seem quite right. For some reason, Dani was suddenly frightened for this lovely young woman sitting across from her.

"I do not know, yet. They have only told me that there is plenty of work and that they believe I will be very good at it."

While Dani couldn't exactly put her finger on what was wrong, she knew instinctively that Ming Le should not go to New York with these people. She decided to finish her lunch with the Asian woman and then speak to Marshal Winters about the situation. She was sure that he would be able to either relieve her fears or come up with a way to resolve whatever it was that was wrong.

———··∘✵∘··———

Dani and Ming Le spent the next half-hour eating their lunch and trading stories about their homelands. Dani found Ming Le to be articulate and intelligent and really enjoyed the young woman's company. So much so that she elicited a promise from the Asian girl that she would join Dani for dinner, if the missionaries would allow her to. As she watched her new friend walk away, Dani was determined to find Toby Winters immediately and get to the bottom of this situation. She found him in the marshal's office located in the federal courthouse.

"I met this Chinese woman at lunch today," she informed him, "and I have this feeling that something isn't quite right in her story."

"What's her story?" Winters asked, only mildly interested.

She proceeded to tell the marshal how two missionaries had come to Ming Le's village and taught the children how to speak English and how to act like an American.

"What's wrong with that?"

"Ming Le doesn't know anything about Jesus! She never even heard of him until I asked her a couple of questions."

Not understanding the significance, Toby shrugged his shoulders and asked, "So?"

"Toby, these are supposed to be Christian missionaries. Wouldn't you think they'd teach the children about Jesus, in addition to the English lessons?"

"What do you think they're up to?" Winters asked, starting to see his deputy's point.

Now it was Dani's turn to look confused. "I don't know, but my intuition tells me that there is something very wrong here. Am I being too suspicious?"

"Perhaps. But I always tell my deputies, 'If you think something doesn't look right, check it out.'"

"How do I do that?"

"You just started to. I'll send a telegram to a friend of mine in New York City and see if he knows anything about this missionary group. What did you say the name of the group is?"

"The Final Times Missionary Alliance. Clyde and Henrietta Morton are the missionaries."

"Is this Ming Le the only girl with them?"

"No, there are five other girls, aged sixteen to eighteen. Ming Le, it turns out, is seventeen."

"Okay, here's what I want you to do. Where are they staying?'

"At the Holladay House."

"Good! Across the street from the hotel is a dry goods store owned by a Mister Tibblets. I want you to go to him, identify yourself and show him your badge. Tell him that you are working on an assignment and that you need to watch the hotel from inside his store for a little while.

"Watch out the front window. If you see this couple leaving the hotel with their baggage and the girls, come and get me right away. I'll get the Topeka Police chief to have one of his men watch the backdoor, just in case they try to slip out that way.

"Be careful! And by the way, good job! Even if it turns out that everything is legitimate, you have done the right thing by bringing this to my attention so we can check into it and make sure it really is okay."

Danielle left Marshal Winters's office and headed for the dry goods store where he directed her. Mister Tibblets agreed to let her watch from his store and even provided her with a chair to sit in. Two hours later, Marshal Winters came to the store to talk to Dani.

"I heard back from my friend in New York. He's checking out this Final Times Missionary Alliance with some law enforcement people he knows. He said that he has heard of a group that has been 'importing' Chinese girls. Some of them are put to work in sweatshops while the more attractive ones are forced into prostitution. He isn't sure this is the same group, but he will look into it.

"He said he would try to let me know something today, but it might not be until tomorrow before he has an answer. In the meantime, I've postponed my trip to St. Louis and I've asked Chief Wilson of the Topeka Police Department to post surveillance on the hotel until we're able to resolve this situation."

"Thank you for believing in me," Dani said sincerely.

"No, thank you for believing in yourself and coming to me with your suspicions. I would rather my deputies tell me when they sense something's not right, and be proven wrong, then not tell me and find out they should have. You, and your sisters, should come to me anytime your intuition tells you to."

A Topeka police officer showed up to relieve Dani and Winters sent her back to her hotel room to rest up and prepare to meet Ming Le for dinner.

—•oo◖◗oo•—

Dani met the young Chinese woman at six o'clock and they had dinner together. The blonde deputy kept the conversation away from the missionaries and her suspicions regarding them. Instead, they talked about China and Iowa and their families back there. Marshal Winters had asked Dani not to tell Ming Le that she was a deputy marshal or anything about her sisters, so she complied with his instructions.

Consequently, Dani was surprised when Marshal Winters came into the restaurant where they were eating and approached their table.

"Deputy Cochran," he greeted her, and then turned to the Chinese girl, "and you must be Ming Le. I'm US Marshal Tobias Winters. May I join you ladies?"

Both women weren't sure how to react. Ming Le had never officially met a lawman before, and didn't understand why she was meeting one now. She was also confused about why he called her new friend "deputy."

On the other hand, Dani was caught off guard by Toby's sudden appearance and by the fact he was wearing his badge prominently on the outside of his shirt. She realized she'd never seen him wear the badge, or his six-shooter, before.

As he took his seat, Winters addressed the seventeen-year-old. "Ming Le, I'd like to ask you a few questions about Clyde and Henrietta Morton."

"I do not understand. Have I done something wrong?" Both Winters and Danielle could see the fear in Ming Le's eyes. They did not understand the fear that Chinese 'police' put into their subjects lives.

The blonde deputy reached across the table and placed her hand on top of Ming Le's. "It will be okay, Ming Le. You are not in any trouble. Marshal Winters just wants to ask you a few questions," she said, soothingly.

When Ming Le regained her composure, the marshal asked, "How old were you when the Morton's came to your village?"

"Fourteen," she answered.

"Do you know, did the Morton's pay your family any money, any yuan, so they would let you come to America?"

"I think so, but I don't know how much it was."

"What kind of work did they say you would be doing in New York?"

It was obvious to Tobias and Danielle that Ming Le was becoming very agitated by the questions. Her English, which had been nearly flawless, was becoming increasingly accented and they could see her eyes were tearing up.

"Please, tell me what is wrong. What did I do bad?" she pleaded with them.

"You haven't done anything bad, Ming Le," Winters replied. Speaking softly, trying to calm the young woman's fears, he continued, "We have reason to believe that the Morton's aren't real missionaries and that the Final Times Missionary Alliance is a front for illegal activities."

"I don't understand. What do you mean 'front'?"

"They are using the organization to cover up what they are actually doing," Dani said, trying to explain it to the seventeen-year-old.

"What are they doing?" Ming Le asked, her face etched with worry.

Toby answered, "A friend of mine in New York City tells me that some of the girls being brought in from China are being sent to sweatshops, factories where the girls work up to eighteen hours a day for as little as a dollar or less. With that, they have to pay for all of their meals and their lodging.

"Meanwhile, other girls are forced into prostitution, selling their bodies to men for sex. Still other girls are being sent back to China. They are transported back and forth, smuggling opium into the United States.

"We need your help Ming Le. We have to stop these people from ruining the lives of more young women, such as yourself. Dani and I believe they intend on forcing you into being a prostitute. Will you help us?"

"But what can I do? I am just one girl."

Marshal Winters outlined the plan he had, telling Ming Le and Dani what their roles would be. After he was sure they understood and agreed to his plan, he left them to finish their meal. A half-hour later, the two young women walked slowly along the boardwalk, talking quietly.

"I am scared, Dani," Ming Le informed her new friend. "One of the other girls with us did something wrong last night. Mister Clyde hit her with his belt several times. I am afraid…if he finds out I am helping you…he will hit me too."

"You have every right to be afraid, Ming Le," Dani responded. "But Marshal Winters told you we will be very close by, and if anything goes wrong and either of the Mortons try to hurt you or any of the other girls, we will step in and arrest them."

March 28, 1875

As the missionary's wagon, fixed and loaded with the Chinese girls, slowly made its way out of Topeka heading eastward, Marshal Winters and Deputy Marshal Cochran watched from a small knoll, using binoculars to track its movement. They would follow the slow moving vehicle for the next two days, staying far enough behind that they wouldn't be spotted.

Late at night, Dani would meet Ming Le in the woods away from the missionaries' campsite. Tobias was convinced that the one girl that had been beaten may have been carrying opium and something had happened to it. It stood to reason that at least a couple of the Chinese girls were transporting the narcotic, and Winters aimed to discover exactly how. Ming Le had already told them that she had not seen any opium and did not know how it was being transported. The first clue came two nights later.

It was nearly midnight on the thirtieth when Dani and Ming Le met in a wooded patch about a hundred yards from the campfire. Dani could immediately tell that her young friend was anxious about something.

"One of the girls, Sung Hi, is very sick," the Asian girl informed the deputy. "She is coughing up blood. We are afraid she will die." Dani assured her that she would tell the marshal and he would take action now.

After his deputy told him what Ming Le said, Toby Winters declared, "It is what I have been waiting for. I wasn't sure, but this seems to confirm my suspicions.

"Smugglers often fill balloons with drugs and then make someone swallow them," he told the blonde. "They can then recover the drugs when the person passes the balloon through their system. I suspect that the one girl Morton beat passed her balloon, but failed to tell Clyde until it was too late to recover it.

"One of the problems with this method of smuggling drugs is, the balloon can burst after it has been swallowed. This usually results in a huge overdose and, most often, death. I think it's time we made an arrest here. What do you think?"

Dani liked that idea very much. The two lawmen mounted up and headed to where the Morton's were encamped with their charges. A short ways from the camp, they split up and approached from different angles.

Just as she drew near, Dani heard a woman cry out in pain. Dismounting, she tied Rebel's reins to a nearby tree and slowly moved in on foot. At the edge of a clearing, Dani saw a man she presumed was Clyde Morton raise a riding crop above his head. Lying at his feet on the ground was a Chinese girl the deputy recognized was Ming Le. It only took a fraction of a second for her to deduce what was about to happen.

Quickly drawing her pistol, Dani shouted, "I wouldn't do that if I were you!"

Morton looked around in confusion before he spotted Dani emerging from the trees where she'd been hiding. "I'm Deputy US Marshal Cochran," she loudly proclaimed. "Throw down the whip, and raise your hands. You're under arrest!"

As the man complied with the first part of her instructions, tossing the riding crop onto the ground, Dani heard the distinctive click of a gun's hammer being pulled back. A stern woman's voice commanded, "Drop that pistol, Missy, or I'll blow ya to kingdom come."

Dani turned her head to the left and saw a woman holding a double barreled shotgun pointed at her.

"Missus Morton, I'm Deputy—"

"I don't care even if yer Jesus Christ Hisself," she interrupted. "You don drop that pea shooter, yew'll be meetin' Him in person."

Mrs. Morton suddenly dropped the shotgun as the clearing was filled by the sound of a rifle shot and a crimson spot appeared on the front of her dress. Clyde took a step toward his wife as she fell to the ground, but stopped when Marshal Winters commanded him to.

"Danielle, go pick up the shotgun. I've got Morton covered from here," he yelled across the clearing.

The matronly woman was gasping for breath as the blonde deputy picked up the shotgun and carefully released the twin hammers. Cracking it open, she removed the two buckshot shells and slipped them into her coat pocket. Dani heard the woman gasped as her final breath escaped her body.

Marshal Winters went over and picked up Mrs. Morton and carried her dead body over to her husband. After setting her down, he instructed Dani to watch Mr. Morton while he dug a grave for the deceased woman. Meanwhile, Ming Le began talking to the other Chinese girls in their own language, explaining to them who Dani and Winters were and what was happening.

When Tobias had completed the digging, he carried Mrs. Morton's body over to the hole and carefully dropped it in. Then he and Mr. Morton shoveled in the dirt with Dani standing watch, holding her Winchester in her arms in case Clyde tried anything. Toby then allowed Clyde to say a few words over his wife's grave.

When Henrietta was finally buried and eulogized, the marshal turned toward her husband. "Clyde Morton, you are under arrested for drug smuggling and for attempting to enslave these young ladies."

"You can't prove nothing," Clyde blustered. "I'm gonna sue you and that female deputy of yours for killing my wife."

"When the remaining girls pass the opium filled balloons you made them swallow, I'll have all the evidence

I need to get a drug smuggling conviction. And if Sung Hi dies, I'm going to add murder to the list of your charges.

"As to the slavery charges, when we get to St Louis, we'll be met by marshals from New York. They will escort you, and the girls, to the city, where I understand they have substantial evidence against you and the other leaders of this Final Times Missionary Alliance. It seems they've been investigating your organization for some time now, and were just waiting for you to arrive with the latest group of girls. They are looking forward to having a nice long talk with you."

Marshal Winters secured Mr. Morton and placed him in the wagon for transport to St. Louis. Then he met with the Asian girls and, through Ming Le's interpretation, filled them in on anything Ming Le may have left out and answered their questions. Finally, he then took a look at Sung Hi. Since she hadn't died yet, and had vomited a great deal, he was convinced that she was probably going to be okay, though not feeling well for at least a couple of days.

While the marshal talked to the girls, Dani fetched their horses, rode back to their campsite and gathered their belongings, and returned to set up their own bedding. It was nearly three o'clock in the morning when they both laid down, pulling their heavy wool blankets over themselves.

"I have a question," Dani said quietly.

"Mmm. What would that be?" Toby asked, unsure if he wanted to know what her question was.

"Am I going to Saint Louis with you?" she asked, hopefully.

"No. There are two deputies who are supposed to meet up with us tomorrow or the next day. We'll camp here until they arrive and then you can head back to Topeka for the trial."

Dani was very disappointed.

April 1, 1875

The arrest of Clyde Morton took place during the early morning hours of March 31st, but the deputies from St. Louis didn't arrive until the afternoon of April 1st. Toby Winters and the deputies left the next morning, heading eastward, while Danielle headed back westward toward Kansas.

Topeka, Kansas, April 3, 1875

Dani rode into Topeka late in the afternoon of the 3rd. She was tired and dirty after spending seven days out on the trail and was looking forward to a bath and a good meal. After taking Rebel to the livery stable and making sure the Appaloosa gelding was well tended, she wasted no time. Back at the hotel, she grabbed some clean clothes and headed to the bath room, where she spent over a half-hour soaking in the hot, perfumed waters.

Following that, she headed for her favorite Topeka café and was enjoying a nice, hot full meal when she was approached by a uniformed member of the Topeka Police Department. She recognized him as the officer who had helped with the surveillance of the Mortons.

"Good evening, Officer Toomey. How are you this evening?" she greeted him pleasantly, and with a wide smile.

"I'm doing fine deputy. However, we've been trying to find Marshal Winters. Would you know where he is?"

"He's on his way to Saint Louis, if he isn't already there. What do you need him for?"

"I see! Did you go after that couple with all them Chinese girls?"

"Yes, we did. We caught them and arrested Mr. Clyde Morton. Mrs. Morton was killed however. He's going to be taken to New York City where he'll face charges of drug smuggling and forcing the girls into slavery. I'm afraid the marshal won't be back for several weeks."

Dani paused, but the officer seemed hesitant to speak. "Do you have some news for us? I can send the marshal a telegram if you need me to."

The look on the officer's face told the young deputy that this was going to be bad news. She immediately became concerned for the safety of her sisters. "Has something happened to one of my sisters?" she asked, worriedly.

"Uh, no ma'am! It's, um, it's not your sisters. I regret to inform you that Dakota Sam has escaped and we've been unable to recapture him," the officer's face had turned red with embarrassment.

"When did this happen?" Dani stood, nearly shouting at the policeman.

"Yesterday afternoon, ma'am."

"How did he escape?"

"I don't know the details, ma'am. I was told he overcame a guard as he was being led outside for his exercise time. Captain Greco could give you more details, I'm sure, ma'am."

"Do you have any idea which direction Sam went after his escape?"

"They finally found tracks that led north out of town. They followed them for a little ways, but lost them when he rode in a stream bed for a while."

"All right. I'll change my clothes and saddle up. Give me thirty minutes, and then I want whoever was tracking him to show me the spot where they lost his trail. And quit calling me ma'am!"

"Yes, ma'am."

17

Chanute, Kansas, April 11, 1875

IT'D BEEN ALMOST two weeks since Camille Cochran arrived in Chanute to investigate the harassment and murder of black farmers, and she still had no clue who was behind these vicious attacks. There had been a significant increase in the number of "patients" visiting the doctor's office, most of them young males with minor problems that would have ordinarily gone untended, if it weren't for the pretty blonde "nurse." This had limited Cami's opportunities to investigate.

Another limitation confronting her was the young sheriff, "Bat" Blanchard, who was sitting beside her in church, beaming like a sunbeam stabbing through thick clouds. The two had been secretly meeting at night to discuss the investigation and taking their meals together in public. However, this was the first time they'd attended church together and Cami was still trying to determine if that was a good thing, or not. One thing for sure, it had the old ladies' tongues a wagging faster than a dog's tail.

Over lunch, the two young adults discussed the preacher's sermon and their views on what it meant to be a Christian.

"I've heard some people say that this Ku Klux Klan thing is just God's way of punishing the Negroes for running away from their owners," Bat commented.

"You don't believe that, do you?" Cami asked.

"I'm not really sure. I've always been taught that if you don't obey God then He'll punish you. Didn't Paul send a runaway slave back to his owner?"

"Okay, did God forgive you of your sins?"

"Well, yeah."

"And didn't He separate you from your sins 'as far as the east is from the west'?"[1]

"Yes."

"Then how could God punish you for something He has already forgiven you for? When Jesus died on the cross, He took upon Himself the guilt of all our sins and paid the punishment we deserve—death.

---

[1]   Psalm 103:12 (NLT)

"Imagine that you have arrested a vicious criminal. He's tried and convicted and sentenced to hang. Then along comes someone who volunteers to take the convicted man's place. The judge agrees to allow it and you hang the volunteer. Would it be right to now go and arrest and hang the first man?"

"Of course not!"

"Then why would you think God would punish us for a 'crime' His Son has already paid for in our stead?"

Pondering her question, the sheriff responded, "I guess I never thought of it that way. But what about punishment for the new sins we commit?"

"John talks about that in his first letter. He says that we shouldn't sin, but if we do, Jesus pleads our case with His Father. We are covered by Jesus's righteousness, and John says that He is the propitiation for our sins. That's a fancy way of saying that Jesus is the means by which we regain favor, or right standing, with God.[2]

"In other words, when we do sin, Jesus leans over and, in essence, says, 'I've already died for that one, Father.' His blood covers all our sins—past, present, *and* future.

"Paul gives us further information in Colossians when he says that the written requirements of the law, that is, death as punishment for our sins, was removed from us and nailed with Jesus on the cross."[3]

---

[2] I John 2:1–2 (KJV)

[3] Colossians 2:14 (author's paraphrase)

"How come you know all this?" Blanchard asked.

"It's what our dad taught my sisters and me. One of the reasons we became deputies was to help others know what Jesus has done for them."

"Sisters? You haven't told me about any sisters. And you're saying they are deputies also? Are they as pretty as you?"

"Oh, no. They're ugly as witches!"

"Now, surely you're exaggerating. Your sisters aren't that ugly, now are they?"

Cami laughed.

"What's so funny?" Bat asked, feeling like he was missing something.

"My sisters and I are identical triplets!"

"Wha? Triplets? There's three of you?"

Cami burst into laughter again.

The residents of Miss Edna's boarding house were all inside due to the cold and blustery weather. Cami knew that there were seven other women staying there, not counting Miss Edna or her daughter, but she only saw two sitting in the parlor, reading, as she entered the domicile. She assumed the others were cozily ensconced in their rooms. Consequently, she was startled when she opened the door to her room and discovered a red-haired woman sitting in her chair.

"Good afternoon, Miss Sanders," the woman greeted her. "Or should I say *Deputy* Sanders?"

Upon seeing Camille's perplexed reaction, she added, "No, I guess your last name probably isn't Sanders either, is it?"

After a momentary pause, Cami responded, her voice tinged with anger, "Who are you, and what are you doing in my room?"

"Very good!" the redhead said, laughing slightly. "A nice touch of anger and a hint of denial without coming right out and lying.

"My name is Kathy Irish, Kat to my friends, and though he wouldn't admit it, Toby Winters told me that he'd sent a deputy here to investigate the attacks on the negroes. It took me a couple of days, but I finally figured out you must be the deputy. Frankly, I'm surprised."

"Slow down, Miss Irish. I'm sure I don't know who or what you are talking about. I don't know any, what was his name, Toby something. Nor do I understand how or why you are in my room. I demand that you leave this instant."

"As to the how, that's easy. I simply picked the lock, a trick taught to me by my employers. And as for the why… well…Marshal Winters hinted to me that he had sent someone here because he didn't want me to come here also."

"Yet you apparently disregarded this Marshal Winters's request and came here anyway, is that it? You seem to be inferring that I should, for some reason, trust what you're telling me."

"Touché! Okay dep…Miss Sanders, here's the truth. As I said, my name is Kathy Irish. I am currently employed by the Pinkerton's Detective Agency as an undercover operative. I've been assigned to solve the problem here in Chanute."

"Let's say I believe your story a little bit, why would Pinkerton's be interested in what is happening here?"

"Toby said you were smart. The railroad is planning on building a line coming from the east that would run past Fort Davidson, Missouri and then through Wichita. That means it would most likely come right through Chanute. Having a gang of vigilantes, or Ku Klux Klanners, running around causing trouble would not please the railroad people."

"Okay. And how is it you know this Marshal Winters fella?"

"My boss introduced us about a month ago when I was in Wichita on business. He told us that he had a couple of deputies escorting a bank robber and murderer to Topeka and that he was planning on sending one of them here as soon as he could, if things weren't resolved by the sheriff before then. Which, of course, was before Mr. Hawkins was killed and things escalated."

"And you think I'm that deputy?"

"Darn, I was hoping we were beyond that." Kathy breathed a deep sigh, then said, "Yes, I believe you are that deputy. I am a bit surprised that you are a woman, and young, but I have watched you closely. You've had several late night visits with Sheriff Blanchard. I've been following you," she added when she saw the disbelief on Cami's face. "And you've been asking a lot of questions of the locals.

"Don't worry!" she said, trying to allay the sudden concern evident in the blonde deputy's eyes. "I don't think anyone else will find your questions, nor your visits with the very handsome sheriff, suspicious. I was expecting someone and was listening for very specific questions being asked. When I heard you asking them I started following you to see if I was right."

"But I never saw you following me," Cami protested, ashamed she'd been so easily discovered.

"Actually, you did. Do you remember an old drunk guy Thursday night? You gave him two bits."

"What about him?"

"That was me."

"You!" Cami said, incredulous.

"I'm very good at disguises. I'm really a very good operative and I've had a lot of experience doing this."

The young deputy took a moment to study the red-haired woman a little closer. She'd initially thought the woman was in her mid to late twenties, but now realized Kathy Irish was probably more like forty.

Pacing the floor of her room while trying to figure out what to do with the detective, Cami threw out the question, "So what's next?"

"Well, I thought you could tell me what you have found out and I could tell you what I've found out and then maybe we could put our heads together and figure out who's behind these attacks."

"That sounds good, except…"

"Except what?" Irish asked when it seemed like Cami wasn't going to finish her sentence.

"Except, I'm a federal officer, and this is a federal investigation. I'm not at liberty to discuss my findings with anyone other than Marshal Winters or Sheriff Blanchard, especially not any civilians. I'm sorry, Miss Irish, but I was given very precise instructions."

Cami's statement was essentially true, but her reluctance to share information with the Pinkerton operative went further. She had a feeling that Miss Irish's motivation was based on something other than the safety of the blacks in the community. Cami sensed a more personal interest in her desire to solve the case.

Meanwhile, Kat could only nod her head a couple of times. So far she'd been outsmarted by this young deputy. But she knew from experience that the game wasn't over yet, and she still had some tricks up her sleeve. Kathy Irish wasn't about to concede defeat to some "wet behind the ears" deputy fifteen years her junior.

18

IKE STURGIS

Rooks County, Kansas, March 30, 1875

IKE STURGIS AND his gang hid behind the large boulders that formed outcrops on either side of the east-west road between Denver, Colorado and Fort Riley, Kansas. They were about one hundred forty miles west of the fort and were awaiting the arrival of two special wagons bound for the military compound. The wagons carried a load of ammunition as well as the monthly payroll coming from the Denver mint.

Ike had been told that the wagons would be guarded by some twenty cavalry troopers, which should be easy for him and his gang to pick off from their position among the large rocks. The outcropping was about a quarter mile long, essentially forming a long, open-roofed tunnel. They would wait until the convoy was completely between the rocks before opening fire.

The gang leader assigned one man to shoot the two mules on the lead wagon and another man to shoot the two on the following wagon. That would prevent the wagons from trying to escape the ambush. Then his men could systematically eliminate the troopers, though he hoped he'd be able to capture a couple of them as he had a special plan for any who surrendered.

Sturgis's gang waited a little over an hour before they heard the sound of horse hoofs and creaking wagon wheels. As Ike expected, ten of the troopers led the convoy along with a lieutenant and a sergeant. The remaining eight troopers were riding behind the second wagon.

The two men assigned to take out the mules opened fire on Ike's signal. Once they opened the dance, it took all of about thirty seconds to end it. Only two troopers remained alive as they were at the very back and had raised their hands in surrender as soon as they saw they were in a no-win situation.

Ike's "special" plan was to make it look like Indians had attacked the wagons and made off with the ammunition and money. Therefore, he had instructed his men to tie heavy burlap bags over the horse's hoofs to make the tracks appear to be from unshod horses. Then he had the men scalp the troopers. Any who they found still alive were to be killed with tomahawks first. Finally, he had the two soldiers that surrendered staked out over a mound full of fire ants. Their mouths were stuffed with clothing so that they would not be able to yell for help.

With everything having gone according to plan, Ike took the time to divvy up the ammunition, supplies, and money from the wagons. He then told his men to scatter in different directions and to meet up with him at a certain place and time.

One thing Ike didn't plan on was a farmer and his daughter coming along about an hour later. They released the two troopers and took them to their farmhouse where they treated the men's wounds. A few days later, the two soldiers rode on to Fort Riley and reported the attack to their commanding officer. Ike Sturgis and his gang would become the most wanted men in Kansas, and soon, the United States.

19

MATTIE

Grand Junction, Colorado, April 7, 1875

THEIR TRAIN LEFT Pueblo early in the morning on April 6th. Mattie, Brody, Lonnie, and Ridley sat on facing benches with Brody and Lonnie across from the deputy and her charge. With Adams showing every intention of cooperating, Mattie had decided not to handcuff or shackle him. It was shortly before noon on the seventh when the train pulled into the Grand Junction station.

The conductor informed the passengers that there would be a thirty minute stop, so Brody offered to go into the town and get sandwiches for the four of them. He returned just as the train whistle sounded, announcing its imminent departure.

Mattie had taken the sandwich Brody brought her and was unwrapping the wax paper when movement outside the train's window caught her peripheral vision. At first, she thought she must be mistaken, but twisting around in her seat for a second look, she knew she wasn't.

"Is something wrong, Mattie?" Lonnie Harrelson asked, seeing her sudden agitation.

"No! I mean…yes…I mean…well, I'm not sure what I mean," she answered confusedly. Turning back to face the men, she continued, "I think I just saw a dead man. At least, a man I thought was dead."

There was an extended pause while the young deputy gathered her thoughts. "I think I just saw my husband…I mean, my ex-husband."

"If he's dead, then you couldn't have seen him," Brody said reasonably.

"That's part of the problem. We don't know that he's dead, we just assumed that he was."

"Well, is there some reason why he might be in Grand Junction?" Lonnie asked.

"None that I know of, but it's been years since he disappeared, so I don't know what he would be doing now."

"Perhaps it was just somebody who looked like your husband," Ridley offered.

Mattie thought about that possibility before shaking her head. "No, I don't think so. I'm pretty sure that the man I just saw was David. But what is he doing in Grand

Junction? And where has he been for the last five years? And was it an accident that I saw him, or is he trailing me?"

All of her questions were rhetorical and none of the three men attempted to answer her, nor could they even if they'd tried. For now, Mattie could only sit there and get lost in her own thoughts.

With San Francisco still more than three days away, a hearing for Mr. Adams once they arrived, and then three to four days for a return trip to Colorado, the blonde was looking at around two weeks before she could get back to Grand Junction and try to find David. But should she try to find him? What would she say if she did find him? Where had he been for the last five years? Did she still love him? No! she answered herself quickly. Yet she felt something. Was it guilt for what her sisters did? Or was it guilt because she was glad he had disappeared and was out of her life? Something gnawed at her conscience, but she couldn't put a finger on it.

"A penny for your thoughts," Brody said quietly after about an hour of watching her struggle with her thoughts.

"Pardon me?" Mattie replied, looking up.

"It's something Miranda says to me whenever she sees me lost in thought. I presume you're thinking about your husband, ex-husband, and wondering if you should go back and try to find him."

"You're very perceptive, Mister Hancock."

"Please, call me Brody, and it isn't hard to guess what you're thinking. You keep glancing back over your shoulder, almost like you expect to see him riding alongside the train,"

"Really! I wasn't aware I was looking back."

"Only about a thousand times in the last hour," Ridley chimed in.

"Why don't you tell us what happened to him and why you thought he was dead. Maybe we can help you sort out your questions," Lonnie suggested.

Should she tell them, she asked herself? And if she did, should she tell them the truth or the sanitized version her sisters allowed everyone to believe. Mattie decided on the truth.

The blonde deputy took a deep breath and then started. "Before we got married, David was the sweetest, kindest, gentlest man you'd ever met. About a month after the wedding he beat me for the first time."

Shocked, Brody couldn't help but blurt out, "What for?"

"He came into the house all upset because the mule had kicked him in his…backend. I laughed and he backhanded me. That made me mad and I yelled at him. So he hit me again, knocking me to the ground. He stood over me, pointing his finger at my face and told me to never talk back to him again.

"Later, he came to me crying, telling me that he was sorry and that he'd never hit me again if I would just forgive him. I'd been telling myself that it was all my fault because I'd laughed at him. But it was all a lie.

"A month or so went by and everything seemed to be all right, but then I ruined a meal and he got mad and hit me.

Then a couple of months later he got mad about something else and hit me. This went on for almost a year."

"Didn't you tell anybody?" Brody asked quietly.

"Who could I tell? Everybody, including my parents, thought I'd married the perfect man. I tried to hint about it, but nobody caught on. I felt trapped, unsure what to do."

"So what finally happened?" Lonnie inquired.

"My sisters, Camille and Danielle, decided to intervene, without telling me about their plan. It seems that they found out that David was wanted in New York for questioning about the death of his former wife, whom I didn't know about, and for stealing a horse.

"The girls dressed up like men, all in black clothing and masked, and rode up on David when he was in one of our fields plowing. They forced him at gunpoint into the nearby woods and put a noose around his neck. I don't know what they said to him, but they told me he started crying and begging for his life. They finally agreed to let him go when he promised to leave the area and never come back. He didn't even come by to tell me that he was leaving."

Lonnie mused, "It sounds like he's one of those people with a split personality. He can be charming and sensitive one minute and meaner than a rattler the next."

"Did you try to find him?" Brody asked.

"Yes, but I didn't know what my sisters had done and I didn't know where to begin to look for him. I only learned this part of the story a few weeks ago when my sisters confessed to what happened. And to be honest, I wasn't all that unhappy that he was gone. If it wasn't for my faith in Jesus, I probably would have tried to kill him. I don't believe in divorce usually, but I couldn't continue to let him beat me whenever his temper flared. It was to the point where one of us was probably going to have to die.

"Your 'faith in Jesus,' you said. I presume that means you are a Christian?" Brody asked.

"Yes. Everyone in my family believes in Jesus. My parents were saved before they got married. Cami, Dani, and I were saved at the same time. A traveling preacher named Whiteman held a series of revival meetings there in Dewitt about eight years ago. Dani accepted the Lord the first night, and Cami and I went forward the second night."

"Did you say Whiteman?" Lonnie queried. "That wouldn't happen to be Reverend Keith Whiteman would it?"

Mattie thought for a moment, "Why yes, I think that was his name. Do you know him?"

The three men laughed. "All three of us know him," Lonnie answered. "Brody and I met him a couple of times several years ago and he also helped us rescue Katherine and Jamima."

For the next hour, Brody, Lonnie, and Ridley took turns telling Mattie the details of the daring rescue of Lonnie's family. After that, they all fell silent, each lost in their own thoughts. Mattie fell asleep thinking, and wondering, about her sisters and what they were up to.

20

DANI

Topeka, Kansas, April 1, 1875

WHAT CHOICE DID she have? Toby Winters was en route to St. Louis with the Morton and the Chinese girls while Deputy Branch was down in Wichita. By the time she wired either of them and they arrived in Topeka, Dakota Sam would have too much of a head start. No, the only choice Dani could see was for her to set out immediately to track down Sam and bring him back. She really missed her sisters.

It was nearly noon by the time Deputy Marshal Danielle Cochran rode out of Topeka in search of the escaped outlaw. In addition to Rebel, her gray Appaloosa gelding, she had a chestnut gelding she was using as a packhorse. She'd sent telegrams to both Winters and Branch letting them know that Sam had escaped and that she was pursuing him. In an effort to make up for lost time, she decided to ride well into the night.

Southern Nebraska, April 5, 1875

Dani was tired. She spent four days alone on the trail but still had not caught up to Dakota Sam. Twice she'd had to dodge war parties of Lakota Sioux. Fortunately, Sam's trail wasn't hard to follow.

Despite the fact that she hadn't seen Sam yet, she was pretty sure she was gaining on him, so she decided to continue to ride past sundown. The early spring days were getting longer and she knew she'd either have to catch him soon or give up the chase. If he got much further north she'd find it nearly impossible to continue to avoid the Indians.

Just as she reined in Rebel and looked around for a place to bed down for the night, she smelled smoke coming from a campfire. She sat still on the Appaloosa, trying to get a sense of what direction the smoke was coming from. There was a slight breeze coming from the west and she deduced that the smoke was being carried on the breeze. She urged her horse off the pathway and into a grove of woods where she dismounted and tethered the big gelding to one of the trees.

Proceeding on foot, she'd gone about twenty yards when she caught a glimpse of firelight through the budding oaks. Moving as stealthily as she could, she inched closer to the campsite until she could see Dakota Sam sitting calmly on the ground. He was just to the right of the fire and Dani could only see him in profile, but she knew she had finally caught up with the outlaw. He was drinking from a tin cup and had a spit of meat roasting over the open flames.

"Yew mite's well com on in," he invited, his voice conversational. "I know yer out thar."

Caught off guard, she squatted where she was for a couple of minutes before he spoke again. "Don know who yew is, but I herd yew when yews were a gud fifty yards way. Yew mite's well com closer. I've got coffee and grub iffen yew're hungry."

Dani emerged from the trees, her Winchester pointed straight at the renegade Indian. "I'm Deputy US Marshal Cochran, and you're under arrest. I want you to very carefully shuck your rifle over to your left, followed slowly by your six gun. Don't try anything stupid as I am an excellent shot and I'm not afraid to shoot you if I have to."

"Well now, iffen it isn't one of dem purtty gurl deputies that ran me in for Marshal Winters." He tossed his rifle off to his left as Dani had instructed. A moment later he tossed his pistol over by the rifle. "Hadda I'd knew it was yew followin' me dem last cuppa days, I mighta jest waited for ya." Sam was starting to really lay it on with his "aww shucks" routine, and Dani wasn't impressed.

Moving slowly to her left and closer to the campfire, she came to where Sam's guns lay on the ground. She smoothly squatted down and picked up the pistol, sticking it into her waistband. Her Winchester rifle never wavered a fraction of an inch from pointing directly at the renegade's chest. Then she picked up Sam's rifle and tossed it back behind her so it was further away from the outlaw.

"Now, slowly stand up and turn your back to me, putting your hands behind you," she ordered.

"C'mon darlin'! I cant eat iffen my hands are cuffed behind my back, now, can I?"

"You can cut out that phony accent of yours. I know you've been well educated and can speak properly. And I'm not your darlin'. Now, do as I told you to or I might just decide to shoot you and save the government from having to hang you."

Dakota Sam took his time complying and kept his coffee cup in his hand, unnoticed by the young deputy. Meanwhile, she pulled her pistol from its holster and leaned her rifle up against a nearby tree. Moving up behind the fugitive, she reached into her coat pocket for her handcuffs. But the cuffs caught on something and the half second distraction was enough time for Sam to toss the hot contents of his coffee cup at her. Dani screamed as the scalding liquid hit her and Sam twirled around reaching out to grab her gun hand. Two things went wrong for the desperado, the coffee missed Dani's face, his intended target, and the deputy recovered quicker than he expected.

Sam had managed to grab hold of the blonde woman's wrist but the six-shooter was still pointed at him. Dani pulled the trigger, creating a large hole in the Indian's stomach. Dakota Sam laid on the ground, gutshot. It was a wound he, like most men, would not survive.

Unfortunately for Sam, it took almost an hour for him to die. He had begged the lawman to finish him off, but she could not bring herself to do so. She didn't regret having shot Sam. However, deliberately killing him was a different story. She had compassion on the outlaw and covered him with a blanket, trying to make him as comfortable as possible under the circumstances. In the end, though, he would die a painful death.

After Dakota expired, Dani saddled his horse and then used ropes to pull him up over the saddle. She tied him facedown so that she could return him to Topeka for a proper burial. Then she ate some of the rabbit Sam had been cooking and laid down to sleep, intending to head back first thing in the morning.

Bright sunshine shone down through the branches of the oak trees covered with early spring buds. A shaft of sun settled on Dani's eyes, waking her up. When she cleared her sight of sleepiness she discovered she was surrounded by half a dozen Sioux Indians.

21

STURGIS

Great Bend, Kansas, April 5, 1875

TWO RIDERS ENTERED Great Bend, Kansas from the east, reined in in front of the town's lone saloon, and dismounted. As they entered the tent that served as the local bar, two more riders rode in from the north.

To the right of the tent's entrance a wooden plank was balanced across two large barrels. The first two riders approached the make-shift bar and ordered whiskey. Making a point of avoiding any hint of recognition, they ignored Ike Sturgis sitting at a table toward the back of the large pavilion. With the arrival of two of his gang members, Ike stood up and quietly left the saloon.

Across the dirt street from the saloon was a combination mercantile and bank. The two riders that had come in from the north were standing next to their horses in front of the store, waiting for their boss man. Without speaking a word, they fell in behind the outlaw as he walked through the wooden structure's front door. As they stepped across the threshold, they pulled bandanas over their mouths and noses, trying to hide their identity. Spreading out, they quickly herded the three customers, two women and a boy, to the back of the store where the owner stood behind a counter.

"This is a holdup," Sturgis intoned. "Stay calm and do what you're told and nobody gets hurt."

The four people stood frozen in place.

"Give me all the money in your cash drawer and in the safe," Ike ordered the owner.

Just then everyone heard a gunshot outside the building. Temporarily distracted, Ike didn't notice the merchant pull a gun out from under the counter. But he did hear the distinctive click the six-shooter made when the man eared back the hammer. Sturgis simply pulled the trigger on his own gun which was still pointed at the store owner.

The bullet tore a hole in the shopkeepers left arm and spun him, causing the bullet he fired to miss Ike and hit one of the women standing nearby. Ike, mad because the owner had done something stupid, fired again, hitting the merchant in the chest and killing him. The owner got off a second shot, but it dug harmlessly into the wooden plank flooring.

Ike's two accomplices, afraid that they might be fired upon, shot the two women and the boy before they could move.

"Let's get out of here," Ike yelled.

The three men rushed from the store just as the other two came running out of the saloon. All five men quickly mounted their horses and raced southward out of town. They rode fast and hard for almost five miles before Sturgis called a halt.

"What happened back there?" the gang leader asked the two men he'd assigned to watch their backs from the bar.

"When the barkeep saw the three of you enter the store he guessed something was up. He picked up a shotgun that'd been leaning against the tent and started heading for the doorway," one of the men answered. "We told him to drop it, but he turned it on us instead. Skel here had to put a slug in him."

Ike cursed.

Hutchinson, Kansas, two days later

Still smarting from the botched robbery attempt in Great Bend, Ike decided to make quick work of the bank in Hutchinson. The result of the robbery was four civilians and two outlaws dead and a haul of less than a thousand dollars.

Exasperated by the blunders committed by the two men still with him, Ike dispatched them to the great beyond and rode off to meet up with the five men remaining from their earlier holdup of the army convoy.

22

MATTIE

San Francisco, April 10, 1875

THE TWILIGHT SKY was a palette of pinks, purples, and oranges as the big locomotive pulled the train into the station near downtown San Francisco. Deputy Marshal Matilda Cochran was awed by the enormity of the city by the bay. Born and raised a country girl, the biggest city she'd ever seen had been Topeka, Kansas, a mere village in comparison to the California city. Her three companions smiled in bemusement at the younger woman's wide-eyed amazement. Despite the fact that they had each spent time in big cities before, they could easily empathize with Mattie's wonderment.

"Excuse me!" a stern voice interrupted the quartet's reverie. "Which one of you gentlemen is Marshal Cochran?" a strict looking uniformed policeman asked.

"That would be me," Mattie answered.

"You're a woman," the officer said dourly before continuing arrogantly, "and women *cannot* be US marshals."

Brody was considering setting the man straight, but a quick glance at the blonde woman's countenance convinced him she could handle this herself.

Mattie pulled back the edge of the duster she was wearing, revealing her Colt .45 and the badge pinned to her shirt.

"Would you care to debate that statement, Sergeant?" the young deputy asked, the tone of her voice clearly indicating the ill-advisedness of such an argument.

Sergeant Petty was in his late thirties, a fifteen year veteran of the San Francisco Police Department. In all that time he had never faced a man whose fiery fierceness could match that of the blue-eyed, five foot seven blonde standing in front of him. Instinctively he knew that he had erred.

"Pardon me, ma'am. I've never heard of there being women in the marshal's service and I realize now that I misspoke. My apologies."

Her fiery look quickly faded and was instantly replaced by a dazzling smile that included her eyes. "Oh, that's okay, Sergeant. My sisters and I forgive you."

"Your sisters?" he asked, searching for more female tigers to be wary of.

"There's three of them," Brody informed the officer, "and they're triplets."

"Oh, lordy! And which one of you is Ridley Adams, or is he a woman also?"

Mattie and her companions all laughed at the policeman's discomfort.

"I'm Ridley Adams," the former soldier answered when the laughter died down.

"Mr. Adams, I'm Sergeant Petty. I'm here to inform you that you are under arrest for the attempted murder of Quincy Ogilvy. Please put your hands behind your back."

After handcuffing Ridley, the officer suggested a hotel where the others could stay while they were in town. Just before he led Adams away, Mattie told the former army man that they'd be there at the trial.

April 12, 1875

On the morning of April 12th, a messenger from the courthouse informed Mattie that the trial would begin in one week.

Mattie met Brody and Lonnie for breakfast and told them about the message she'd received from the court. None of them were particularly happy about the delay, but there wasn't anything they could do about it. All three of them said they wanted to send telegrams, letting others know that they wouldn't be headed back right away. After breakfast, they headed over to the Western Union office.

It took about half an hour for them to prepare all the messages they needed to send out. They were in a jovial mood as they exited the telegraph office and were stunned when they heard a gunshot ring out. A bullet narrowly missed hitting Mattie before it embedded itself into a wooden post holding up the building's awning. Brody and Lonnie had both experienced being shot at and they reacted quickly, rushing back into the building and pulling the young deputy with them. A second shot shattered the front window.

Shrill whistles sounded and a uniformed police officer cautiously appeared in the doorway.

"Is everyone okay?" he asked.

Brody stood up and walked over to the policeman. "We're all okay in here," he informed the officer. "I think the shots came from that rooftop," he said, pointing to a two-story building across the street from the telegraph office.

The officer turned and spoke to two other officers that had arrived on the scene and they quickly rushed off to investigate.

"Any idea why'd somebody would be shooting at you folks?" the policeman asked Brody.

"Not really, officer. We don't really know anyone around here."

"You folks not from around here?" The policeman had removed a small notebook from his pocket and was taking down notes.

"Mr. Harrelson and I are from Colorado. Deputy Cochran here," he said indicating Mattie, "is from Kansas."

"Deputy? As in a lawman?" the officer asked, his tone disbelieving.

Mattie showed him the badge she'd removed from her reticule as she spoke, "I'm Deputy US Marshal Cochran. I'm here on official business."

"Well, I'll be danged. A *female* US marshal. What's this world coming to?" he asked rhetorically.

Before anyone could respond, the other two officers returned from their search of the building across the street. In addition, Sergeant Petty, whom they'd met two days ago when they arrived in the city, was now on the scene. The four policemen held a brief discussion and then the three junior officers left. Sergeant Petty approached the group.

"It looks like you were right Mr. Hancock. My officers found evidence that someone shot at you from the rooftop across the street. So my question for you is who would want to shoot you folks?"

"I'm not sure we can help you there, Sergeant. There's no reason I can think of that anyone would want one of us dead."

"Hmmm. Do you think it might be related to Mister Adams trial somehow?"

"That's always a possibility. But as it stands right now, none of us are scheduled to testify."

"You know," Mattie interjected quietly, "I think whoever it was shooting was aiming at me."

"Maybe someone you put in jail?" the officer suggested.

"The only person I've put in jail is in Topeka, Kansas. Not likely it could be him." She answered.

"What other reason would someone have for trying to kill you?"

"I wish I knew!"

"Do you have any enemies here in San Francisco?"

"This is my first time in your city, so no, I don't think anybody here knows me well enough to want to kill me."

"Who all knows that you're a lawman? Or is it lawwoman?"

"Lawman is fine, and the answer is, only you and these men, as far as I know."

"Well then, I guess my theory is the correct assessment. Someone is trying to kill these two men to keep them from testifying on their friend's behalf. Perhaps you should leave the detecting to those of us with experience."

Mattie turned bright red with indignation.

"I remind you, Sergeant, that I *am* a deputy US marshal and that I outrank you."

"Of course, ma'am. That's why my job just got much harder." With a smug look on his face, the sergeant walked away before the blonde woman could retaliate.

No longer able to suppress her anger, the young deputy just stood there, sputtering as she tried to find words to express her frustration with the fellow lawman. While Brody and Lonnie understood her ire, they also understood that it was a problem she would have to deal with on her own if she were to gain the respect she deserved. The sergeant was clearly out of line, but they were on his turf and she would have to find a way to bring him down.

The young blonde woman told the two men that she wanted to return to her hotel room so she could change into jeans and a shirt. They left her at the door to her room but came rushing back when she yelled out their names. Looking past her into the small hotel room they saw what looked like a tornado had passed through it. The room was thoroughly trashed and a note had been left on top of the room's bureau.

Lonnie pushed past the other two and picked up the note, reading it quickly before passing it to Hancock.

"What's it say?" Mattie asked, a hint of fear in her voice.

"It says," Brody answered as he handed her the note, "that Ridley is a dead man and that you will be too if you don't leave town tonight."

23

Grand Junction, Colorado, April 7, 1875

HE STOOD IN the shadows on the station's platform, staring at her as if he was seeing a ghost. His emotions vacillated between amazement, elation, and abject anger. A debate raged in his mind as to whether or not he should board the train and confront her, but he knew that there was no advantage to be gained in doing so. So he stood there staring.

"Who are those three men she's with?" he wondered in his mind.

It was over three years since David Yarden had last seen his wife. *Is she even still my wife?* When he first spotted her sitting by the train window he was stunned. It seemed impossible to him that she could be here in Grand Junction at the same time as him.

Of all the mistakes Yarden had made in his life, losing his wife was the one that seemed the hardest to take. In all the time he'd wandered over the last five years, he just couldn't get her out of his head. He found himself taking a couple of steps toward the train, thinking that maybe he could speak to her, patch things up. Then he stopped, remembering the encounter he'd had with those two men that caused him to leave Iowa.

The memory of that day was etched in his brain; the feel of the noose around his neck and the words of one of the men just before they let him go never left him.

"If you ever come back to Dewitt, or try to contact Miss Cochran in any way, we will hunt you down and hang you 'til you're dead," the man in black intoned.

And David instinctively knew it was true.

Who are *those two men?* The question still nagged him. When it first happened he thought that it might be Mattie's sisters. But he quickly put that thought out of his mind. There was no way those two girls would have the cheek to pull off a stunt like that.

His next thought was his wife's two brothers, Junior and Cristian. But he'd seen them working in the field with their Pa as he rode out of town.

Would Mattie forgive me? So many questions on his mind, but few answers.

Of course she would forgive me! She believed in all that Bible stuff about forgiveness and mercy and—what was it she called it? Oh yeah! Redemption. But what am I being redeemed from? He couldn't remember.

He had pretended he believed that religious nonsense while he was courting her, but told her he thought it was foolishness once they'd gotten married. Yet he had to admire the way she truly believed in that Jesus fella and what He had preached. There was no doubt that she was convinced that He was God's Son. Mattie was nothing like any other woman he'd ever met.

"Why was that? What did she have that he didn't? What gave her the right to act so holy, so....so....perfect?"

Yarden felt the anger boiling up inside him. His chest started to heave as he gulped big amounts of air, trying to bring the anger under control. He could taste bile in his throat and swallowed several times.

Slipping from the shadows, David started walking away from the train station. Lost in his thoughts, he never heard the sound of the train's whistle or the grinding of the locomotive's giant steel wheels as the conveyance slowly picked up steam. Nor did he notice the sudden look of recognition on Matilda's face or how she twisted around in her seat, craning her neck to watch him walk away.

April 10, 1875

For three days David Yarden prepared to leave Grand Junction. He took some of the money he'd "found" and bought himself a new horse and tack. Then he led the Indian's horse out of town and turned it loose.

With new clothes on his back, a chestnut gelding beneath him, and an older mare as a packhorse, the young man rode slowly out of town, following the westward train tracks having decided to trail his former wife. He had learned that the train she was on was headed to San Francisco, with several stops in between. Why she would be going to California was a mystery to him, but he was determined to try to find her and talk to her.

His plan was to head across southern Utah, heading straight for the big city. He figured that he would arrive a couple of weeks after the blonde woman, but it couldn't be helped. He had considered taking a train, but wanted to be able to change his plans if he encountered any problems along the way. A train was too confining for him.

David wasn't sure how late into the night he rode. Heavy, dark storm clouds had rolled in about midafternoon, blocking out the sun completely and making it difficult to tell the time. He only knew that by the time he made camp he was very tired. After picketing the horses close enough to the water that they could drink when they wanted to, as well as fill their stomachs on the new grass that was growing there, he then ate a quick meal of beans and hard tack before rolling up in his blankets.

Tired as he was, along with the soothing sound of the nearby flowing stream, Yarden slept soundly, until the nickering of the big chestnut invaded his dreams. Something told him to spin to his left, just in time to avoid the sharp-edged knife aimed at his chest. Because of his quick action, the Ute's blade was imbedded into the ground beneath where he'd been laying.

David pulled his six-shooter and fired at a second Indian who was ready to bring a tomahawk right down onto his head. David fired twice, catching him in the chest first and then in the forehead as he toppled forward.

Turning his attention back to the first Ute, Yarden noted that he had freed his knife from the earthly sheath and was getting ready to lunge at him. As the young white man brought his gun up in front of him, the Indian jumped on top, his knife raised above his head. David pulled the trigger instinctively, shooting the native in the gut. The Indian was dead weight on top of him, despite the fact he was still technically alive, so David pushed him off to one side and then scrambled to his feet.

Still feeling the effects of an adrenaline rush, Yarden shot the Ute again. He stood over the two Indians for several minutes before slowly sinking to the ground. How long he laid there, letting the emotions and tensions of the moment slowly seep out of his body, he didn't know. But the thought suddenly occurred to him that there could be other braves in the area and that they may have heard the shots and would come to investigate.

Rising to his feet once more, he quickly gathered up his things, saddled his horse and repacked the mare. Finally, he took a moment to consider the best means of escape. He had been heading directly west and it wouldn't take much of a tracker to discern that. If he rode westward in the stream it would help hide his tracks, but again, it wouldn't take much guessing to figure that out.

David entered the stream, pulling his packhorse behind him, and headed east. His plan was to follow the running water for a few miles and then head south for a day before resuming his westward travels.

Amazingly, even with the traumatic experience of the last hour, Yarden's thoughts returned to Mattie Cochran and why was she headed toward San Francisco with three strange men?

24

CAMI

Chanute, Kansas, April 12, 1875

NURSE CAMI SANDERS was tending to yet another young man who'd been slightly injured in another "unfortunate accident." Dr. Charles Holliday had taken to charging the men double in an effort to stem the tide of these so-called accidents, but was, so far, unsuccessful. The men were more than willing to pay the higher fee for the opportunity to spend time with the pretty blonde "nurse."

"I bet it woodent hert as much if'n yu'd give it a little kiss," suggested Merk Wilkins, the latest accident being a thumb smashed by a carelessly used hammer.

"Yes, and if I did that you would probably come back with a split lip, expecting me to kiss that also," Cami replied.

"Ah now, Miz Cami! Ain't nuthin' wrong wit a man wishin' to kiss a purty gurl now, is thar?"

"No, Mister Wilkins! But this girl isn't looking to be kissed by you, or anyone else, right now."

Wilkins started looking around quickly.

"Is something wrong?" Cami asked, concerned by his abrupt behavior.

"Are we alone?"

Cami took a step back. "Watch yourself, Mister Wilkins," she said firmly.

"No, no, it ain't like that. Thar's sumpthin' I need to tell you, but it's a secret."

Not sure where this was going, Cami put her hand in her right pocket and grabbed hold of the derringer she kept there before speaking. "Doc Holliday left on an errand and you're our only patient right now," she informed the farmer.

"I knows who's killin' the blackies," Wilkins said quietly.

"You should go to Sheriff Blanchard and tell him."

"I can't! They'da kill me!"

"What do you want me to do?"

"Tell the sharif. Everyone knows he's sweet on ya and he'd belief ya."

"But I don't have any proof. I can't just go around accusing folks, especially when I don't even know who it is you're talking about."

"Quinlan Morgan!"

"The banker?"

"Yep!"

"Why?"

"To git dem out sos he can git theirs property."

"Again, Why?"

"The railroad, Miz Cami. The railroads cummin' thru Chanute."

Before Cami could ask any more questions, Doctor Holliday came walking back into the office.

During her late-night visit with Sheriff Blanchard, Cami informed him of Wilkins's claim that Quinlan Morgan was behind the recent harassment of blacks.

"So you think Wilkins was on the level?" Blanchard asked.

"I don't know, Bat. He seemed confident in his accusation and when I suggested he talk to you he got very scared. On the other hand, maybe he thought he could wangle a kiss from me if he gave me a juicy tidbit of gossip."

"What's this about a kiss?" the sheriff asked suspiciously.

Cami shifted uncomfortably in her chair across the desk from the senior lawman. Blanchard's tone told her that she may have had said too much about Wilkins's advances, but it was too late to take back her words.

"Mister Wilkins hurt his thumb and wanted me to kiss it to make it better."

"Is that normally part of your treatment plan?"

Cami blushed, emphatically saying, "No!"

Blanchard stood up and walked past the young deputy. At the rack where he kept his rifles locked up, he removed one of the Winchesters and checked to see that it was loaded.

"I guess I need to pay a visit to Quinlan Morgan—that is, after I visit Mr. Wilkins."

"Bat, it's almost midnight. Surely, they'll be asleep by now." Cami watched Blanchard walk back to his desk, where he stopped next to her and placed a hand on her shoulder.

"Sometimes that's the best time to interview a suspect," he explained. "They're too groggy to know to make up lies.

"As to this kissing business"—he leaned down until his face was in front of hers—"I don't think you should be kissing anyone but me."

With that, he pressed his lips against hers for several seconds.

Camille Cochran jumped out of her chair and backed away from the sheriff. "Bailey Blanchard"—her face turned red from a mixture of embarrassment and frustration— "that was…th—that was…" she stuttered.

The anger quickly left her bright-blue eyes as she looked into the depths of Blanchard's brown doe orbs and saw something she hadn't expected. Her voice thin and soft, she said, "That was very nice. Maybe we should try that again."

Wrapping her arms around his neck and standing on her tiptoes, Cami lifted her face toward him. His hands on her hips, the Chanute lawman drew her body against his own, and their mouths came together for what seemed a great deal longer than it actually was.

"Wow!" Blanchard blurted out when they finally separated.

"Whew!"

"I guess I better get out of here before things get too..."

"Be careful, Bat," Cami implored softly. "I think I'm gonna want some more of those kisses of yours, so don't go getting yourself all shot up."

"You don't have to worry about that. I'm looking forward to continuing our 'discussion' about kissing myself...Why don't you wait until I've been gone for about fifteen minutes before slipping out the back," the sheriff suggested.

"See you at lunch tomorrow?"

"Wild horses couldn't keep me away."

Camille Cochran sat behind the sheriff's desk for more than thirty minutes, daydreaming about that first kiss. She pictured Bat sitting there, a tall, handsome man with curly brown hair she yearned to run her fingers through, and dark brown eyes that shimmered like glistening pools when he smiled. Her dreams wandered through the flower beds of matrimony before she caught herself.

"Stop it!" she said out loud, chiding herself for going too far with her thoughts.

Realizing the time and her need for sleep, she quietly slipped out the backdoor, locking it with the key Bat had given her shortly after she arrived in Chanute. She'd only gone about five feet up the alleyway when something slammed into her back, knocking her to the ground. Somewhere in her subconscious mind, she heard the crack of gunfire and wondered if she'd been shot.

When she tried to rise to her feet, she discovered that none of her limbs would obey her commands. She sensed more than felt the growing expanse as blood spread through the back of her dress. She wondered, *Why would someone shoot me? And who could it be?*

"Please God," she prayed silently, "don't let me die." It was her last thought before she slipped into unconsciousness.

25

MATTIE

San Francisco, April 13, 1875

With Ridley Adams trial still several days away, Mattie skipped breakfast Tuesday morning and slept in. When she woke midmorning she decided to do some shopping. She was just coming out of a millinery shop when she felt something buzz past her ear. Hearing a "thunk" sound on a nearby post and then the crack of a rifle, she quickly ducked down behind a watering trough.

Her six-shooter already in her hand, the blue-eyed blonde peeked around the trough and quickly scanned the rooftops of the facing buildings. She saw no one. So she did a once-over in the doorways but, again, saw nobody with a rifle or drawn weapon.

As had occurred on the previous day when she'd been shot at, San Francisco Police officers quickly arrived on the scene, but their investigation was just as fruitless. Add to the equation the insolence of Sergeant Perry and Matilda's peevishness was understandable. After she was left alone, she decided to prove the officer's ineptness by conducting her own investigation.

Gathering Brody and Lonnie from their hotel room, the trio headed for the building where Mattie was convinced the shot came from. It took a few minutes to persuade the general store's owner to allow them to climb up onto the roof, but once there they discovered something the police had either missed or totally ignored, a brass cartridge. Lonnie bent down to pick it up.

"Don't touch that!" Mattie yelled at him.

Startled, the former First Sergeant stepped back. "It's only an empty shell, Mattie. It's not going to hurt me," he said, confused by her outburst.

"Fingerprints," she responded, squatting down to examine the shiny brass shell closer.

The two men glanced at each other before Brody asked, "Fingerprints?"

Mattie removed the bandana from around her neck and, using a piece of stick that had been lying on the rooftop, carefully picked up the spent cartridge and dropped it onto the bandana.

"There might be fingerprints on the shell," she informed her two friends. Seeing the continued confusion on their faces, she went on, "Brody, hold your hand straight out, palm up. Now, Lonnie, you hold your hand next to Brody's, again, palm up. Look closely at your fingertips.

"Brody, do you see those tiny lines and swirls on your fingers?"

"Yes."

"Now, compare them to the lines and swirls on Lonnie's fingers. See how they're different. About twenty five years ago, scientists studying those patterns concluded that each person has a different pattern and that no two patterns are the same. Even the fingers on your own hand all have different patterns.

"Furthermore, they discovered that the oils in our hands cause these patterns to be transferred to any objects we touch, hence the term *fingerprints*. By comparing fingerprints from this shell casing to a suspect's own finger patterns, we can determine who our mystery shooter is beyond a reasonable doubt.

"That's why we have to be careful not to handle the shell directly. We could smudge any existing fingerprints, or put our own prints on it. I want to take it to the police station and have their lab people do what's called 'lifting the print' off the shell."

"All that's fascinating, Mattie," Lonnie said. "How does the stick and bandana figure into it?"

"I picked it up with the stick for the same reason I told you not to touch it and I put it loosely in the kerchief so I didn't accidently wipe any prints off it. It's just too bad that the bullet itself was so badly damaged."

"Ballistics, right?" Brody asked.

"Very good! How did you know that?" the deputy inquired.

"There was an article in a magazine about a year ago on how they were now using this process called ballistics to prove that a man had shot and killed his wife. It turns out that every gun has a unique pattern of grooves that it puts on a bullet as it goes through the barrel.'

"You know, I remember you showing me that story," Lonnie interjected. "I just wonder what they'll discover next."

"They told me during training that scientists believe that each person's blood is also unique and that one day they will be able to use a drop of blood recovered at a crime incident to prove a person's guilt," Mattie told the men.

A skeptical Lonnie snorted, "Sure they will. Right after they put a man on the moon."

Brody and Mattie laughed at Harrelson's comment.

The three friends headed to the closest precinct station, as they called them in San Francisco. The desk sergeant asked them what they needed. Mattie opened up the bandana, revealing the shiny brass shell, and began to explain.

"We found this on the rooftop of the general store where someone shot at me," she started.

Before she could react, the sergeant picked up the empty shell and rolled it between his chubby fingers as he held it up to the light. "Now ain't this purtty. I ain't never seen an empty shell before," he said, his voice laden with sarcasm.

"You idiot!" the young deputy yelled. "You've just destroyed crucial evidence by wiping out the fingerprints of whoever handled that shell. Who trained you in police science, an orangutan?"

Brody and Lonnie quickly grabbed the blonde woman's arms, fearing that she might jump over the intervening counter and scratch out the man's eyes.

"Look here, missy," the sergeant said, practically hissing the last word, "you come into my stationhouse with some empty bullet shell. I got better things to do then look at a shell that looks like every other .44 caliber shell I've ever seen. Now get outta here before I throw you in jail for insulting an officer of the law."

"What's all the ruckus out here?" a new voice asked.

All four people turned to look at the man who had entered the station's lobby from a back hall. He wore captain's bars on his uniform collar.

"This wacky lady come in here with a piece of brass she found somewheres, hands it to me, and then begins shouting at me because I picked it up," the sergeant informed his superior, revising the story to fit his version.

"This 'wacky lady'"—Mattie spit between clenched teeth—"is a deputy United States marshal here on official business. And that 'piece of brass,' as I was trying to explain to the sergeant, was a piece of evidence from a shooting that occurred early today. I intended to ask the San Francisco Police Department to check it for fingerprints. That is, until this idiot grabbed hold of it and rolled it between his fingers, destroying any prints there may have been on it."

The captain held his hand out toward his subordinate, who handed it to him with considerably more care than he had used when he took it from Mattie.

"I'm Captain Orcutt," he introduced himself. Though he had visibly acknowledged Mattie and Lonnie, he had been staring mostly at Brody. "Do I know you?" he finally asked after a minute or two of silence.

"I'm Brody Hancock," the tall man replied, extending his hand to the officer. "And no, I don't think we've ever met."

"Captain Brody Hancock?"

"I was at one time. But now I'm just Brody Hancock."

Orcutt nodded. "Why don't the three of you come to my office," he invited. As the three friends started walking toward the doorway the captain had come from, the senior officer turned to the desk sergeant and said, sarcastically, "See if you can keep from irritating any more deputy marshals, Sergeant Doyle." He then turned and led the way down the hallway.

Once everyone was seated in Orcutt's office, the captain offered an apology. "I'm sorry for the sergeant's actions. Many of the police officers, especially the old timers, are having trouble adjusting to some of the changes in crime investigations. The concept of finger printing and how it can help solve a case is still beyond their understanding.

"I'm afraid that you're right, deputy. He has probably destroyed any chance of getting a usable print off of this shell. However, I will ask our lab personnel to take a look at it. And I'll have them do a complete workup of Sergeant Doyle's fingerprints, for comparison purposes, of course. Maybe that will give him a new perspective on the subject.

"But out of curiosity, how is it you are a deputy marshal? I wasn't aware the service was hiring females?

"My sisters and I are kind of an experiment, you might say," Mattie replied.

"Your sisters?" the captain inquired.

"There's three of them," Brody interjected.

"Yeah!" Lonnie echoed. "And if the other two are anything like Mattie here, the marshal's service will never be the same."

"Thanks for your votes of confidence," the young blonde retorted.

As Brody and Harrelson laughed, Mattie joined in with them. Captain Orcutt could see that the three of them had quickly become friends.

"Well, I definitely want to hear more about this, but first, Captain Hancock. I don't know if you remember me, Sir, but I was a Union Army sergeant when your rebel army captured my platoon, north of Atlanta. Some of your troops, including your executive officer, wanted to execute all of us, but you had a different plan."

"I remember capturing a platoon," Brody told him, "though I don't remember you specifically. It seems to me that I offered each man his freedom in exchange for a promise to remain out of the remainder of the war."

"Indeed you did, sir. And I am alive today because of your graciousness and mercy. To the best of my knowledge, no other Confederate, or Union for that matter, officer offered his prisoners such a deal. I am proud to say that I upheld my part of the deal, though I know some of the others did not."

"I made that offer because God offered me the same type of grace and mercy by forgiving me of my sins in exchange for simply believing in His Son, Jesus Christ. Because of Jesus's sacrifice on the cross, I not only have forgiveness, I also have eternal life."

"Really? I would be interested in knowing more about that, but right now I have some pressing matters I need to attend to." Though the three friends hoped that the captain meant what he said, his tone suggested that he really wasn't all that interested.

"Anyway, I want to apologize again for the desk sergeant's rudeness and his destruction of your evidence. If our lab is able to recover anything I will let you know immediately. In the meantime, if you come across any other evidence you want us to process, please bring it directly to me Deputy Cochran.

"By the way, have you spoken to Marshal Orcutt here in San Francisco?" Seeing the puzzled look on Mattie's face, he said, "I'm Kevin. My brother, Daniel, is the US marshal for Northern California and has an office about three blocks from here."

"Marshal Winters told me it wouldn't be necessary to contact the local US marshal unless I ran into trouble or there was some type of emergency and I needed his help."

"Since someone has fired at you twice now, maybe it's time you considered this as an emergency. I can tell you that Daniel is a good guy and he won't give you any bull over your being a female deputy. I suspect you'll find him very helpful.

"Now, if you three will excuse me, I really do have other matters I need to see about."

Rising to his feet, the captain extended his hand toward Mattie. "It's been a pleasure to meet you Deputy Cochran, and I wish you, and your sisters, success as deputies." Turning toward Brody after shaking the blonde woman's hand, he said, "Captain Hancock, I again want to thank you for what you did for me on the battlefield. I'm afraid it is a debt I can never repay, but hope, some day, to do so."

"Jesus once told His followers," Brody replied, "that when they did something for someone in need they were doing it for Him.[1] So I would consider the debt paid if you will do something for someone who has a great need like you did."

The captain looked nonplussed as he realized how his 'savior' had just shown him the kind of grace that is beyond

---

[1]   Matthew 25:40 (author's paraphrase)

normal understanding. The thought occurred to him that he really did need to talk to this former military man about who this Jesus was.

Finally, he shook Lonnie's hand and told him that he was pleased to make the man's acquaintance and hoped to see the three of them again before they left San Francisco. Then he led them back out to the front lobby.

As the three friends left the police station, Lonnie asked, "What's next?"

"Maybe we should go back to the scene of the first shooting and see if we can find another empty shell casing there," Brody suggested.

"It wouldn't do us any good if we did," Mattie responded. "Even if we found a shell, we wouldn't be able to prove that the rifle it was shot from was the same one that was shot at me. There's no way to establish when that shell was fired."

"But we know the when," Lonnie countered.

"Yes, we know it, but we can't prove it, not to the standards set in a court of law. Frankly, the only way I can see our getting another shell casing is if the shooter decides to take another shot. That's not something I'm really looking forward to, if you get my meaning."

"So what is your next move?" Brody asked her.

"I guess I'll go see Marshal Orcutt and see if he has any ideas how to catch our erstwhile killer."

The two men parted company with their pretty blonde friend as she insisted on going to see the marshal on her own.

26

DANI

Topeka, Kansas, April 10, 1875

DANIELLE COCHRAN WAS glad to be back in Topeka. The ride back from Southern Nebraska was even worse than the ride up there. Slowed by a sudden snowstorm that didn't stop her, but made travel rough going while also hiding from a war party. She may have escaped from being raped and killed by Two Feathers, but that didn't mean another group of Indians wouldn't be just as deadly.

She thought about that morning, just four days ago.

The bright morning sun was right in her eyes, causing her to squint as she looked around her campsite. Five Sioux braves were off to her left, sitting or standing in a ragged semi-circle. A sixth brave was sitting cross-legged on the ground by her right side, a very large, ugly-looking knife in his right hand.

Slowly she brought her right hand up, making the sign she'd learned for "friend" and saying, "Mi'ye ma kola! Mi'ye ma kola Lakota. Mi'ye ohajsica ni'ye hiya yusica."

The warrior with the big knife paused, surprised at hearing a white woman speak his language. "To'ka ni'ye kte Sam?" he demanded, asking why she killed Sam."

"I'ye un si'ca wicasa. (He was a bad man.) I'ye wi'kte o'ta oyate. (He killed many people). I'ye wi'kte win, nakuj. (He killed women, children)."

The Indian stood up and spoke to the other braves in Sioux, but he spoke so rapidly she could not follow what he was saying. Then he turned to her, making the sign for "friend" and said, "Kola! (Friend)," and extended his hand toward her. Grasping her hand firmly, he pulled her up from the ground with ease.

"I am Two Feathers," he said in stilted English. "Who you?"

"I am Danielle Cochran. I am a deputy US marshal. I've been tracking Sam for the last four days."

"What he do?"

"Sam was under arrest and was supposed to stand trial for his crimes, but he escaped from jail. I didn't want to kill him. But he struggled with me, and I had no choice. The gun went off during the struggle."

"Not right for woman to track man. Not right for woman to shoot man. Woman should keep home. Make lots of papooses. You go! Leave Lakota alone!" Two Feathers commanded.

"What about Sam?"

"Lakota, take Sam. Bury Sam Lakota way. You go now. You not come back."

Two Feathers signaled his fellow braves and the six of them disappeared in the trees, taking Sam and his horse with them. Dani suddenly felt very lonely.

All the way back to Topeka, Dani had this queer feeling that she was being watched. She thought that Two Feathers may not have fully trusted her and sent a couple of his men to spy on her. But now that she was back, the creepy feeling went away.

However, she wasn't prepared for the greeting she received from Marshal Winters.

"Where the—have you been?" he yelled, using the only profanity she'd ever heard him say.

"I went after Dakota Sam," she replied, confused by his angry tone.

"And who authorized you to go off on your own like that? Just who do you think you are?" Winters continued his tirade.

Getting a little mad herself, the usually unflappable Dani shot back, "And who was I supposed to ask? You were on your way to St Louis, and Kyle was on his way back to Wichita. If I had waited to get permission from one of you,

Sam would probably have been in Canada before I could ever get out of Kansas."

"The point is, you endangered yourself needlessly since you didn't even catch him."

"That's because he's dead!" the blonde deputy fired back.

"Dead?" The marshal's tone had softened some because of her attitude. "What happened?"

Letting out her breath slowly, Dani relaxed some and answered, "I caught up with Sam a little ways into Nebraska. He fought with me and I had to shoot him. He died a few hours later."

"So he's at the mortuary, I guess."

"No, the Lakota have him."

"The Lakota? As in Sioux?" Winters asked, a touch of concern in his voice.

"Uh-huh. A small war party woke me up Tuesday morning, wanting to know why Sam was dead. I explained to them what happened and why. After that, they took his body and ordered me to leave the area."

"Now let me get this straight." Winters's tone was one of incredulity. "A Lakota Sioux war party finds a beautiful, young white woman in the middle of nowhere, and they just up and let her go. I'm not buying this, Dani."

"Well, it's the truth, Toby. I guess they were impressed by the fact that I spoke to them in their language and said I was a friend. I also don't think they particularly liked Sam either."

Toby Winters was dumbfounded. "If that just don't beat all! Okay! I guess you done good. But in the future, I don't want you to go traipsing all over the countryside without having talked to Kyle or me." He started to walk away.

"Toby," Dani called out to him. When he turned back toward her, she continued, "Would we be having this conversation if I were a man?"

Winters chose not to answer her and walked away instead. However, he knew he would have to give her question some thought.

27

MATTIE

San Francisco, April 13, 1875

WHEN MATTIE, BRODY, and Lonnie left the police station she told the men that she was going to run some errands on the way to the US marshal's office. Her first stop was a leather goods store where she placed a special custom order. After that, she went to a millinery where she purchased a large hat.

Adjacent to the millinery was a dress shop, and three blocks away she stopped at a drugstore. The dress shop yielded a plain brown dress with pockets and the drugstore sold her several items. Her next to last stop of the morning was the marshal's office.

Mattie spent almost an hour talking to Marshal Daniel Orcutt, explaining who she was and why she was in San Francisco. Orcutt wasn't happy that he hadn't been apprised ahead of time that a deputy from a different district would be operating in his territory, but there wasn't much he could do about it. When he heard her plan for catching her would be assassin, he was impressed by her acumen and offered to assist her in any way he could.

The blonde deputy made one last stop on her way back to the hotel where she was staying, the leather shop to pick up her special order.

April 14, 1875

A blue-eyed, dark-haired woman wearing a large, wide-brimmed hat and a plain brown dress emerged from the front of the Excelsior Hotel in downtown San Francisco at approximately eight o'clock on the morning of April 14th. She moved quickly, but was highly alert to her surroundings. She made her way over to the jailhouse where she met with Ridley Adams for the twenty minutes they would allow her.

As she walked down the steps from the jailhouse she caught a glimpse of sunlight reflecting off of something on the rooftop of the office building immediately across the street. It was the moment she'd been waiting for.

Being careful not to appear to be anxious or in a hurry, Mattie crossed the street and entered the building. The listing of building occupants indicated that the offices were dedicated mainly to lawyers and bail bondsmen.

Up on the roof, the wannabe assassin was becoming increasingly frustrated. Having overheard the blonde woman tell her two friends that she would be visiting Adams this morning, the shooter had found a way up onto the roof and had laid patiently for the girl's arrival. But hours later, the only woman seen entering the jailhouse was a brunette wearing a plain brown dress. If that blonde woman didn't show up soon, the shooter would have to leave or risk discovery.

Back inside the office building, Mattie climbed the interior stairs until she reached the top floor. At the end of a hallway that ran the depth of the building, she found a single window. Carefully opening the window so as not to make any noise, she stuck her head out and looked around. Attached to the back of the building was a set of wooden stairs with a landing right below the casement. Right next to the stairway was a ladder that led up to the roof.

Stepping out onto the landing, Mattie reached into the right pocket of her brown dress. A cutout in the bottom of the pocket allowed her to reach through and draw her Colt .45 from the custom made thigh holster she'd designed. The new holster allowed her to wear her pistol without anyone knowing she had it on.

Moving slowly, eliminating as much noise as she could, Mattie ascended the weathered ladder and peered over the edge of a parapet. There she saw the shooter lying on the ground, watching the street below. Stealthily she climbed over the low wall and moved up behind the shooter. The young deputy took a moment to remove her large hat and place it quietly on the rooftop.

Taking aim at her intended killer, the deputy firmly ordered, "Leave your rifle on the ground and slowly move back from it."

A woman in her mid-thirties looked back over her shoulder, her dark brown hair falling partially across her face. "You!" was all she said, surprised at Mattie's sudden appearance.

"I'm Deputy US Marshal Cochran, and you're under arrest."

"Deputy Marshal?" the woman asked. "I didn't know…I didn't know you were a lawman."

"Get up," Mattie ordered. She was unsure what game the woman was playing. Pausing while the woman stood, she then continued, "Why are you trying to kill me?"

The blonde turned brunette sized up the other woman as she struggled to her feet and stood before her. The woman appeared to be in her mid to late thirties and slightly shorter than the deputy. *Somewhat plain looking, yet with a type of beauty that was much deeper than the skin*, Mattie thought.

"I-I wasn—I wasn't trying to kill you, Deputy," the woman said, stuttering slightly.

"Funny, those shots sure seemed to be aimed at me," Mattie retorted.

"Shots? At you? No, no, I was shooting at a blonde wom…oh, I see…you dyed your hair. Very clever. But I swear, I didn't know you were the law."

"But why were you trying to kill me in the first place."

"Actually, I wasn't trying to kill you. I'm an excellent shot. If I was trying to kill you, you would be dead."

Mattie gave her a look that said, "Give it a rest. You're not helping yourself."

"Okay, this is going to sound silly, but I thought…I thought you were trying to steal Ridley from me," she finished with a rush.

"Ridley? You mean Adams? Whatever made you think that?"

"He…he gave you a hug before he left with that police officer. It was obvious you came on the train with him, along with those two men. When I tried to visit him at the jail, they told me I couldn't because he'd already had a visitor that day," the woman had teared up as she explained. "Another officer told me that some blonde girl had visited him. So I figured that was you."

The deputy eased her Colt back into her holster.

"What's your name?" she asked.

"Jeanette Fishman! I'm Ridley's—or I *was*—Ridley's girlfriend before he left San Francisco. He told me he would write, but I've only received two letters from him," struggling to hold back her tears, Jeanette lost the battle. The waterworks spilled down her cheeks as she said, "I thought…I thought you were his new girlfriend. I just wanted to scare you off."

"If you promise not to try and shoot me anymore, I'll take you down to the jailhouse and get you in to see Ridley. But you can't shoot him either."

"Really?" Jeanette asked, sniffing up her tears. "You would do that for me? You can get me in to see him?"

"Yeah, I figure any woman who would try to kill me to win her boyfriend back deserves some kind of consideration. However, I have an idea I think you're going to like."

"Oh, you're back!" Ridley Adams exclaimed as Mattie approached his cell. "Something wrong?" he asked, seeing the look of concern on her face.

"Yes, there is. Do you know a woman, what was her name, Jeanette something?" Mattie said, pretending nonchalance.

"Jeanette Fishman? Yeah, I know her. Why?"

"Turns out she was the one trying to kill me," the young deputy said, as if it was just another incident in life.

"Jeanette…trying to kill…Wait a minute. You said *was* trying to kill you. What's happened?"

"Well, what do you think happened, Rid? Someone shoots at me, I shoot back! I don't check to see if they are male or female, friend or foe. Shoot at me, and I'm going to do my best to stop you from shooting again, even if I have to kill you."

Mattie could see the tears welling up in Ridley's eyes as he asked, "Is she dead?" Emotion choked his voice.

Pausing briefly, she asked, "What do you care? What was she to you, anyway?"

"She's my girlfriend!" Adams responded, a touch of anger in his voice at the blonde's apparent callousness. "I'm going to—*was* going to marry her."

"Really? Funny that you never mentioned her. All the way from Colorado, we rode together, and I never once heard you say anything about a girlfriend."

"I was waiting 'til Brody and Lonnie made me a partner in the ranch. Then I was going to ask her to be my wife."

"If you truly love somebody, Rid, you shouldn't wait to tell them that, no matter what your reasons are."

"I guess it's too late for that now, thanks to you."

Mattie didn't like the touch of bitterness in his voice. Turning her head to the left, she yelled, "Jeanette!" The older woman stepped into the cell area of the jailhouse. "Ridley has something I think he wants to say to you," she informed her new friend.

"Jeanette!" the former soldier practically screamed, "You're alive!"

Mattie passed the woman as she left the cells, leaving the two to work out their relationship. But she had a huge smile on her face.

28

CAMI

Chanute, Kansas, April 15, 1875

CAMI COCHRAN COULD tell that it was early morning because sunlight was streaming through the window of her room. She knew also that she was in a bed in Doctor Holliday's medical shop. Though she could only move her head slightly to one side or the other, she could see enough of the room to determine that it was a patient's room, the one that faced eastward. Cami calculated that it must be around eight in the morning, but she didn't know what day it was.

The young blonde deputy tried to move her right hand, but it didn't budge. Similar attempts to move other parts of her body failed, with the exception of the aforementioned slight movements of the head.

"Ah, so you're awake," a pleasant female voice spoke, from somewhere off to her right.

"Who…who are you?" Cami asked, her voice cracking from lack of use.

"I'm Hattie Lynch. Doctor Holliday hired me to look after you," she replied, moving into Cami's field of vision.

Cami sized her up. A little shorter and heavier than the deputy, her slightly plump body seemed to fit her comfortably. Her hazel eyes glistened below the bangs of her long black hair. Cami guessed that she was Indian, or at least partly, as her skin seemed too pale in the harsh morning sun. She appeared to be a couple of years younger than Cochran.

"Could I have some water, please?" Cami asked, croaking.

Hattie gave her a glass that was half-full, suggesting she drink it slowly.

"What day is it?" the blonde asked after a couple of sips soothed her parched throat.

"It is Thursday, April 15th. You've been unconscious since Monday night," the other girl offered.

"Why can't I move any part of my body?" Cami asked, her voice now trembling as the full import of the situation crossed her mind.

"I think the doctor better answer your questions," Hattie responded. "I'll let him know that you are conscious now." Hattie left the room before Cami could reply.

"Deputy Cochran?" a male voice, young sounding, spoke from over by the door.

Cami couldn't turn her head far enough to see who it was, but she knew it wasn't either the doctor or Bat Blanchard.

"Who are you?" she asked fearfully.

Realizing she couldn't see him, the young man, who appeared to be around Hattie's age, stepped into the room and spoke. "I'm Deputy Tory Samuels. I work for Sheriff Blanchard. He's had me and another guy guarding you ever since you got shot. If ya like, I could go get him for ya. I know he's been worried 'bout ya."

"Yes...no, wait! Let me talk to the doctor first."

"Yes, ma'am. I'll be right outside the door here if ya need anything. Jes give a hollar and I'll come running."

The deputy sheriff left the room before it occurred to Cami that he had referred to her as a deputy. That meant he knew she was with the marshal's service. She was pondering the implications of that when she heard someone enter the room.

"Hello, Cami," she heard the doctor say as he moved to where she could see him. "Or should I say *Deputy* Cochran?"

"So you know?"

"Bat told me. He thought it was important that I know who exactly I was treating. He also thought that there might be the possibility that you would say something while you were unconscious. He's been very concerned about your safety.

"I gotta tell ya, girl, you gave us quite a scare there. Bat's been here almost constantly, when he hasn't been chasing down the remnants of that gang."

"What's wrong with me doc? I can't move any part of my body except my head."

Holliday walked over and picked up a chair, half dragging it over to near the bed, and sat down. He stared at the young woman for several moments, assessing her condition.

"How do you feel?"

"I don't feel anything!" she replied, angrily.

"Think, Cami! How do you feel? It's very important."

The blonde paused for a minute as she considered his question. "I guess, I guess I feel okay," she finally answered. "Now that I think about it, I'm actually feeling very hungry."

"Good! Excellent! Hattie's fixing you some soup and she'll bring it in when I finish here."

"Now, tell me what you remember about what happened."

"I went to Sheriff Blanchard's office to tell him what I had learned about the gang that's been causing problems for the black people. He left to go talk to someone…did he arrest anyone?"

"He can tell you all about that later. Right now, I need you to tell me exactly what happened."

"Okay. He left the office and I hung around there for a little while, hoping to be there when he returned. After a hour or so, I decided to head back to my room. I went out the backdoor and started walking down the alleyway when, all of a sudden, I felt something slam into my back. I fell face down on the ground.

"I'd never been shot before, but somehow, I knew that I'd been shot in the back."

"Good. Yes, you were shot in the back. The reason you can't move is because the bullet is lodged up against your spine. Actually, it's a miracle it didn't sever the spinal cord or you'd never walk again.

"The problem is, removing the bullet is very risky. One false move and you could be paralyzed for the rest of your life."

Seeing the look of abject terror in her eyes, he continued, "However, there is a doctor in Chicago who has been having considerable success in operating on people in these circumstances, and removing the bullets without further damage. His patients have all recovered completely."

"How does he do it?"

"He's invented some new-fangled machine, which he calls X-ray. It somehow gives him a picture of a person's insides, so he can see precisely where the bullet is.

"But you need to understand, there is no guarantee. But if you're willing to give it a try, he's willing to bring his machine down here and try to remove the bullet."

"What are my chances, Doc?"

"I won't lie to you, Cami. If you decide not to have the surgery, the bullet is likely to stay right where it is, and you would stay in the condition you are currently in. There is a slight chance—a *very* slight chance—that the bullet could shift, relieving the pressure on the spinal cord and making it easier for me to operate. But there is also the possibility that the bullet could shift the other way and end up severing the spinal cord, resulting in permanent paralysis. Frankly, your best option is this doctor, but it is a *big* risk."

Cami lay in silence, thoughts of permanent paralysis bouncing around in her head like marbles in a cup. The doctor had left, Hattie had come and served her some soup, and now she was all alone with her feelings. She reflected on her relationship with Bat and quickly rejected the thought.

There was no relationship with Bat. Not any longer. There was no way she was going to saddle him with an invalid for a wife. Even if he said he wanted her, she would never be sure if it was out of love, or pity. She didn't want his pity, or that of any other man, not under these circumstances.

There was a sound at the door and she twisted her head as far as she could, but still could not see who had entered the room.

"Cami?" a soft female voice spoke. "Are you awake, sis?"

"Dani? Is that you?" the young blonde cried.

Danielle moved further into the room so Cami could see her. She took her sister's hand in hers and said, "Yes, it's me, Cami."

"What are you doing here?" the paralyzed deputy asked. "I thought you had to stay in Topeka until after Dakota Sam's trial?"

"Sam's dead! When we heard about what happened to you Toby, Kyle, and I hurried down here as fast as we could. They're in the other room, but the doctor wants you to have only one visitor at a time. Toby said to tell you that they'd come back later."

"Is Mattie with you?"

"No. She's still in San Francisco as far as we know. I sent her a telegram, but we couldn't wait for a reply. I hope she'll send a message to me here."

"What happened to Sam?"

"He escaped and I had to track him down. He tried to fight with me, forcing me to kill him.

"Sheriff Blanchard filled us in on what he knows, but he doesn't know who shot you. Do you?"

"I'm guessing it was Quincy Morgan, or one of his Klan members."

"Can't be. Blanchard said that after he left you the other night he went straight to Morgan's place with his deputies. They arrested Morgan along with his gang. They were all together, having a meeting to prepare for another attack. Your timing in finding out who was responsible was perfect."

"Maybe there was one member who...Kat!" Cami interrupted herself.

"What cat?" Dani asked, confused by her sister's outburst.

"Not cat...Kat, Kathy Irish. She's supposedly a Pinkerton agent investigating the killing. But I think she's more interested in Bat…Sheriff Blanchard, then she is in catching outlaws."

Dani couldn't help but notice the way her sister referred to the sheriff and wondered if there was something going on between the two of them. She had met the young lawman and was impressed with his mannerisms, not to mention how handsome he was.

"So you're thinking this Kathy Irish person may be the one who shot you?" Dani asked carefully.

"She's the only one that makes sense if it wasn't a Klansman."

After some small talk, Dani told her sister that she was going to go look up the Pinkerton woman and have a talk with her. Cami didn't like the idea of her sister going alone, but there wasn't much she could do about it.

Camille wasn't alone in the room for more than a few seconds before Bailey Blanchard came walking in. He immediately went to her bedside, leaned over her, and gave her a warm, tender kiss before she had a chance to protest. She was surprised to discover that her paralyzed body responded to the affectionate caress. *And what did that mean*, she wondered?

"Thanks to you, we've captured Quincy Morgan and the majority of his gang. They were holding a meeting to discuss further activities. And you'll be happy to know that the good doctor was not part of the group."

"Oh, Bat…you shouldn't have…" Cami stuttered as tears ran down her cheeks.

Perplexed, he asked, "Shouldn't have what? Shouldn't have captured the gang?"

"You shouldn't have…shouldn't have kissed me," she said. "It only makes this harder."

Slightly angry, he told her, "Shouldn't have kissed you? What are you talk…oh, I get it, you think I won't love you now because you're paralyzed. Well, I got news for you, lady. I love you just as much, no, I love you more than I did when I kissed you Monday night."

"But I can't love you back," she blubbered.

Blanchard took some tissues from the box on the nightstand, dried her eyes and then held some up to her nose.

"Blow," he commanded.

He scratched his head as he tried to form his words.

"Suppose the roles were reversed," he said slowly. "What if I was the one lying there with a bullet in my back, paralyzed, and I told you the same thing you're telling me. How do you think you would feel?"

The blonde woman thought for a moment before saying, "I'd tell you not to be ridiculous. I love you no matter what condition your body is in."

Speaking deliberately, Bat said, "Cami…I love you… no matter what condition your body is in. As far as I am concerned, this paralysis is only temporary. This doctor from Chicago is going to come here and remove it and you are going to get all better.

"But even if things don't go the way we hope they do, I will still love you. I want you to be my wife, now and for the rest of our lives, no matter what God has in store for us."

"Kiss me, Bat!"

29

Cedar Creek, Missouri, April 15, 1875

LOCATED IN CEDAR County, Missouri, the small town of Cedar Creek is about ninety miles east of Chanute, Kansas. Neither the railroad nor the stagecoach run through the town, leaving it basically a peaceful and isolated community. The nearest town with law enforcement is Springfield, fifty miles to the southeast.

This made Cedar Creek the perfect place for Ike Sturgis's new plan.

The outlaw rode into the town late in the morning of April 15th. He tied off his horse at the hitching rail in front of the town's only saloon and went inside. Stepping up to the makeshift bar, he ordered a beer and then used the large mirror attached to the side of the tent behind the bar to observe the other occupants.

In addition to Ike and the bartender, there were six other men, seated around two tables that had been pushed together. Five of the men looked like typical small town men such as those Ike had seen in hundreds of other small burgs like Cedar Creek. They were hardworking men who'd become slightly lazy in their quiet, peaceful setting. The sixth man however was huge.

Taller than the rest of his companions, he was heavily muscled with biceps that looked as big around as some men's thighs. Ike surmised that this man was probably the town's blacksmith. He would not be easy to subdue.

Perk Perkins caught Sturgis staring at him and immediately knew that the fellow at the bar was trouble. He slowly stood up, rising to his full 6'5" height. Ike gulped when he saw how big the man really was. Perkins idly made his way over to the bar and sidled up to it just to the left of Sturgis.

"Gimme a beer, Hubie," he said, speaking to the bartender. After taking a couple of slow sips of the brew he turned and spoke to the stranger beside him. "Don' reckon I seen you b'fore, mister?" he stated in a half-question.

"Reckon that's a good thing for you…or you'd be dead already," Ike deadpanned.

Perkins shook his head in disbelief. As big as he was, he wasn't used to being talked to that way. He usually did the intimidating, if there was any to be done.

"Wha's that 'posed to mean?" he asked after a brief pause.

"It means, if you continue to bother me…" the room stilled at the sound of a gun being cocked, "I'll put a bullet in ya."

The blacksmith looked down and saw Ike was holding a big pistol in his right hand, pointing it directly at the big man's oversized belly.

Quickly raising his hands in surrender, Perkins backed off, saying, "Look, mister, we don' wan' no trouble har." He looked back toward the table where his friends sat and noticed that three of them had stood and spread out, their six-shooters drawn and pointed at the stranger. "We gots us a nice, peacefill town har and we don' cotton to no gunslingers han'in' round. Drink up yer beer and git outta har, 'fore you end up bein' the one who's eating lead."

Ike glanced over his shoulder and saw that he was vastly outgunned. Carefully holstering his own gun, he turned and picked up his beer mug, downing the remaining brew. After wiping his mouth with the back of his hand, he slowly stood and walked to the canvas doorway. Not saying a word, he took one last hard look at Perkins and his friends and then exited the saloon. But the four men didn't sit back down until they heard the stranger's horse galloping out of town.

Cedar Creek, April 16, 1875

It was a typical midspring day in Cedar Creek, cool, damp, a morning that started off in the low fifties and would be in the mid-seventies by late afternoon. The populace was winding down from a long, hard workweek, many of them looking forward to the coming weekend. About half of the town's men were gathered at the Dew Drop Inn, the town's only saloon and hotel. The beer joint was a large tent attached to one side of the clapboard rooming building. The men were enjoying a cool mug of brew before heading home. The bar was filled with raucous laughter, which explains why no one heard the large group of horses and riders entering the western end of their burg.

Ike Sturgis and his men rode in fast and hard. After dismounting, Ike signaled for one man to stay with the horses while selecting four men to enter the saloon with him. The remaining four men were ordered to spread out along the town's single street and prevent anyone from interfering.

The five men who walked into the Dew Drop Inn that Friday afternoon already had their guns drawn and began shooting before anyone inside had a chance to respond. Meanwhile, Tolle, the general store's owner, upon hearing the gunfire came running out of his establishment holding a scattergun. He was shot and killed before he could get off a shot of his own.

One of Ike's men had already snuck up behind Perk Perkins, who was still working in his blacksmith shop, and struck him over the head with the butt of his six-shooter. The outlaw then tied up the large man so that Ike could deal with him later. Parson Black stepped outside of the church, where he'd been working on his Sunday sermon, to see what all the commotion was about. He was gunned down immediately.

When the gun smoke cleared only one adult male resident of Cedar Creek was still alive, the blacksmith. Two women were also dead and one of the brigands was severely wounded, having been gut shot by one of the two dead women.

All of the women and children were herded to the church sanctuary at the west end of town, along with Perkins. When everyone was seated and quiet, Sturgis stood in the pulpit.

"My name is Ike Sturgis and I now own this town. You people will serve me and my men. You will do whatever we tell you to do, you will do it quickly, and you will do it without complaint. Or there will be consequences.

"To show you I mean business, I have 'invited' Mr. Perkins here to help me with a little demonstration. You see, yesterday I came to your nice little town here for a visit. While I was enjoying a cool beer in your saloon, Mr. Perkins approached me and let me know that I was not welcome in Cedar Creek."

Turning to one of his men, he said, "Please release Mr. Perkins and stick your gun in his waistband.

"Now Mr. Perkins, let's see if you are still as brave as you were yesterday when you had me outnumbered four to one. Draw whenever you're ready. If you kill me, my men will leave your town and never return. If I kill you, well, I guess it won't matter to you what happens, will it?" Ike laughed at his little joke.

"Yore a gunfighter. I'm jes' a poor smithy. I don' stan' a chance."

"More than the chance you gave me. Some chance is better'n no chance. Draw or I'll kill you anyway!"

Perkins reached for the gun that had been shoved into his waistband, but he was no match for the quick draw of Ike Sturgis, who had his own gun drawn and firing before the big man had barely moved his pistol.

"As for the rest of you," Ike intoned, turning back to face the women and children, "let that be a lesson to you. I own this town now and I…"

"Boss, cav'ry comin'!" one of his men shouted.

Then he rushed into the church's sanctuary, interrupting the gang leader.

"Cavalry? How many?" Ike yelled back.

"Look lik twenty ta thirty," the outlaw replied.

"Let's get outta here, boys!" Ike shouted.

The cavalry troop from Fort Davidson was entering the eastern end of Cedar Creek, a regular stop on their monthly patrols, when they saw a group of men come rushing out of the church at the far end of town. Noticing that there were no residents out and about on a nice Friday afternoon, the lieutenant in charge of the troopers sensed something was wrong. His concern was confirmed when one of the fleeing outlaws took a shot at the soldiers.

"Sergeant Sims, take twenty men and bring those men back here. Something's wrong here, and I aim to find out what's going on."

"Yes, sir!" the sergeant replied. "Squads one, two, and four, you're with me," he commanded. "Forward, ho!"

The blue coats charged forward, chasing Ike Sturgis and his gang at a full gallop.

30

DANI

Chanute, Kansas, April 15, 1875

DANIELLE COULDN'T REMEMBER ever having been as mad as she was right now. She had just left her sister's room and walked out the front door of the doctor's house. Standing on the front porch, she considered what her options were. As she stood there, Toby and Kyle came out and told her they were going to go over to the hotel and secure some rooms. They suggested meeting for lunch, but Dani said she had other plans.

Cami had told her sister that Kathy Irish was staying at the same boarding house where she'd been living since arriving in Chanute. Danielle walked down to the two-story dwelling and around to the back, hiding in some nearby bushes while watching for the redhead to try and sneak out.

Shortly after noon, the rear door of the boarding house opened and Dani saw a woman step out onto the porch and look furtively from left to right. Convinced that the coast was clear, Irish walked down the steps and turned to her right, heading toward the livery stables. Dani waited until she'd taken a few steps before emerging from the bushes that were behind her.

"Stop right there, Irish," the young deputy ordered. "Turn around…real slowly, with your hands in the air."

The phony Pinkerton detective appeared to be unarmed. Nevertheless, Dani kept her hand on the butt of her own six-shooter.

"How…?" Kathy Irish said, confused. "You're…you're supposed to be dead."

The deputy realized suddenly that the other woman thought that she was Cami. She didn't know that the sisters were triplets, so Dani decided to continue the misunderstanding.

"Why'd you shoot me in the back?" she questioned the redhead.

Kathy Irish stared at the deputy marshal for several minutes. Something was wrong, but she couldn't quite figure out what that might be.

"Who are you?" she finally asked, convinced the younger woman couldn't be the one she'd shot.

"Who do you think I am?" Dani responded, angrily.

"But…that can't be. He said that if I shot you in the back it would sever the spinal cord and you would either die or be paralyzed for the rest of your life."

"Who told you that?"

"Holliday!"

"The doctor?"

"No, his younger brother."

"Why would his younger brother tell you to shoot me?"

"Because they were concerned that you were getting close to finding out who was in the Klan. It turns out they were right, but too late. You'd already told Bat before I could get to you."

"Was the doctor in on it too?"

"No. He didn't even know about his brother being part of the group."

Dani drew her pistol and pointed it at the red-haired woman. The deputy's normally bright blue eyes had turned icy cold as she stared at the person who had tried to kill her sister and had paralyzed her instead. She was considering pulling the trigger, but since Kathy Irish wasn't wearing a gun, she knew she couldn't kill her in cold blood. As these thoughts ran through Dani's mind, a tall figure stepped out from the side of the building behind her.

"Don't do it, Dani," she heard a male voice say. "It's not worth it to ruin your life just to get even."

"Toby?"

The momentary distraction was just enough to give Irish time to pull a small pistol from her reticule, point it at Dani, and squeeze the trigger.

"Watch out!" Winters yelled as he watched the redhead and pulled out his own six-shooter at the same moment.

Danielle felt the buzz of a bullet pass her left ear as she ducked to her right. A stinging sensation stabbed the ear as the young deputy fired off a shot that missed the redhead. Irish was still standing and pointing her pistol at Dani. A bright red flame bloomed from the barrel of Dani's gun, the bullet flying through the air and hitting the woman in the chest. Irish squeezed off another shot, but the bullet just plowed into the ground a few feet in front of her as she felt another thump hit her chest. She looked down and saw two red circles expanding quickly on the front of her shirt. She slowly sank down to the ground in a sitting position.

Dani rushed to the fallen woman's side and relieved her of her pistol.

"Who are you?" Irish asked, struggling to speak.

"Danielle Cochran. Cami's sister," she answered.

"You're twins?"

"Triplets actually."

"Hmm! I'm tired now. I think I'll just lay down."

Dani put a hand on the older woman's back and gently ease her down to the ground. Irish was dead. The young deputy closed the red-haired woman's eyes.

The blonde stood up and brushed off her jeans. Realizing that her left ear hurt, she started to reach up and touch it when she heard a low moan behind her. She quickly turned to say something to her boss, but there was no one there. Glancing around, she spied Toby's body lying on the ground about fifteen yards away.

"Toby!" she yelled, running to his side. "Are you all right?"

"I'm okay…I think. Help me sit up," he requested. "Her first shot caught me in the left arm. Looks like it clipped your ear first," he said, pointing to her left ear.

Finally touching the wounded appendage, Dani yelped as her fingers came in contact with the damaged area, which was bleeding profusely.

"Help me up," Winters asked her, "and we'll see if the doctor can patch us up."

Two hours later, Toby Winters and Danielle Cochran emerged from Doctor Holliday's offices and sat in rocking chairs on the front porch. Toby's left arm was in a sling and his shoulder was heavily bandaged. Irish's bullet had passed straight through the soft tissue below the shoulder bone. Dani's wound was considered minor despite the fact that she was now missing a small chunk of the outer rim of her left ear. The bright white bandage she was wearing made her self-conscious.

When the doctor had completed treating the two lawmen, they spent some time visiting with Cami, who found her sister's plight quite amusing. The paralyzed girl seemed to be in very good spirits, despite being frustrated that it would take almost two months for the doctor from Chicago to arrive. He would need to first dismantle his x-ray machine, ship it to Chanute, and then reassemble it before he would be able to operate and remove the bullet. The blonde deputy was calculating that it would be nearly the end of June before she'd be able to start walking again. At that point, she'd probably have to relearn how to.

Nevertheless, Cami's faith was in God and she knew in her heart that she would indeed walk again. God was in control, she believed, and He had given her a real peace about the situation, which is why she could laugh at her sister's ridiculous looking bandage.

Cami remembered her Bible studies where she heard the story about Jesus healing a paralyzed man,[1] and all the Old Testament prophesies that proclaimed the Messiah would heal the lame, the blind, and the deaf,[2] and all of our diseases.[3]

Laying in the bed, alone again, Cami knew she would walk again. She would walk and she would marry Bailey "Bat" Blanchard…she just didn't know when.

---

[1] Matthew 9:1–7 (author's paraphrase)

[2] Isaiah 35:5–6 (author's paraphrase)

[3] Psalm 103:2–3 (author's paraphrase)

31

San Francisco, California, April 14, 1875

WEDNESDAY MORNING FOUND Mattie Cochran nervously pacing the train station platform, awaiting the arrival of the eastbound train that would return her to her sister's side. Brody Hancock and Lonnie Harrelson sat in matching rocking chairs watching the pretty female deputy get increasingly agitated. Since she'd received word the previous day of Cami's injury she'd been a nervous wreck and the two men had been unable to calm her down.

Adding to her worries, Mattie had tried to no avail to contact Danielle, whom she believed was in Topeka. Now the train that would take her eastward was more than an hour late.

As Mattie paced she remember an article she had recently read in an old magazine from New York. The article talked about the possibility of man flying in some type of craft one day, making travel across the country considerably faster. While she was skeptical of the concept, right now she'd give just about anything if she could climb aboard Leonardo da Vinci's amazing flying machine the article mentioned.

Finally, she heard the train whistle and she gathered up her belongings. She hated to leave before Ridley's trial, but Toby Winters had recommended that she return to Kansas as quickly as possible. Unfortunately, his telegram did not specify the extent of Cami's injuries, which contributed to the blonde's anxiety.

Meanwhile, Ridley would have to depend on Brody and Lonnie making sure he received a fair trial. One piece of good news was that his girlfriend, Jeanette Fishman, knew someone who was an eye witness to the events and was willing to testify on Adams's behalf.

Once the train came to a stop, Mattie gave Brody and Lonnie each a hug before boarding. She would miss her two new friends and gave them a last minute promise to visit them in Colorado the first chance she had.

The eastbound train crossed a bridge into Oakland, had stops in Tracy and Modesto, and then headed to the Nevada border. Mattie was deeply occupied with her own thoughts and had paid scant attention to those passengers boarding or disembarking at the various stops. Consequently she didn't notice the thin man dressed in black that stood by her seat until he spoke.

"Good morning, ma'am!" he greeted politely. "Would it be all right if I took this seat opposite you?"

Mattie looked the stranger over. He was of average height, clean shaven except for a pencil thin mustache, and had salt and pepper hair, leaning more toward the pepper. She placed him in his late forties or early fifties. He was wearing a single Colt .45 ensconced in a tied-down holster on his right hip. Thinking that he was probably a gunslinger, the young deputy quickly scanned the rest of the rail car to see if other seats were available, but discovered the car was practically full.

Seeing her discomfort, the man introduced himself. "The name's Reverend Keith Whiteman," he simply said, removing his flat-brimmed black hat.

Mattie glanced at the walnut handled six-shooter and then drifted her eyes upward until they met his. "Reverend?" she said, her inflection making the word a question.

"Yes, ma'am," he answered. Tapping the butt of the weapon, he continued, "Sometimes it becomes necessary to defend oneself during one's travel. God said we aren't to murder one another, but He never said we shouldn't defend ourselves."

Motioning to the seat across from her, Mattie said, "I remember you now. You're the minister that came to our church in Dewitt when I was still a young girl. My sisters and I accepted Christ as our Savior after hearing you preach one night."

"Dewitt? As in Dewitt, Iowa? Parson Edelman's church?" the reverend asked.

"Yes. My family has attended there since before I was born."

"Let me think now...yes, I remember, weren't you and your sisters triplets?"

"That's right. My sisters are Danielle and Camille."

"So what's a pretty young Iowa girl doing way out here in California, if I may ask?"

"Delivering a prisoner for trial."

Whiteman looked confused. "A prisoner for trial?"

"I'm a deputy US marshal. I had to escort a man from Colorado to San Francisco so he could stand trial. I was supposed to stay until the trial took place in a few days."

"Well now, if that don't beat all. A deputy marshal you say. If you didn't go to Parson Edelman's church, I'da thought you were lying to me. You aren't funning me are you?"

"No, sir!"

"If I had known that deputy marshals were going to be as pretty as you, I might've taken up criminaling instead of preaching."

"Criminaling?" the blonde laughed.

"Making up new words is kind of a hobby of mine. But you said you were supposed to stay for the trial, so how come you're on this train?"

"One of my sisters has been hurt and I'm going back to Kansas to see her.

The train came to a stop and the two of them looked out the window to see where they were. The conductor came through their car and informed everyone that they were a few miles from the Nevada border and that they'd stopped to take on water and pick up the mail. He told them that they would be underway shortly and that the next stop was in Tonopah, Nevada.

For the next couple of hours, Mattie and the Reverend talked about their lives. She told him about growing up in Dewitt and what life was like on the farm (though she didn't tell him about David and her disastrous marriage). He was surprised when she told him that her two sisters were also deputies in the Marshals Service. He told her about life as an itinerant preacher and some of its frustrations.

"I tell you, Mattie, there are few things I've found more frustrating than standing in front of a crowd for an hour or so, pouring your heart out as you tell people of their need for Jesus and how much He loves them and wants to save them from their sins, only to watch them walk away as if you'd never spoken. I want to lead people to Jesus, but sometimes I just feel like telling them to go to—well, anyway, guess you know what I mean," he ended, sheepishly.

Mattie laughed. The older man decided he really liked her laugh.

"So tell me more about this dangerous assignment that took you halfway across the country?"

Still smiling, she answered, "Oh, it wasn't all that dangerous, and I was in the company of three handsome men. Of course, with my luck, two of them are already married and the third one will be as soon as his trial is over, if he knows what's good for him, that is.

"The story is that Rid helped a friend of his rescue his wife and daughter from some evil men. Apparently an innocent bystander caught a stray bullet and now he's suing Ridley."

"Ridley?" Whiteman repeated the name. "You don't mean Ridley Adams do you?"

"Yes, but—"

"Were his two friends Lonnie Harrelson and Brody Hancock?"

"How did you—of course, they told me that you helped them rescue Katherine and Jamina."

"And would the man with the hole in his hand be Hiram Ogilvy?"

"Hole in his hand? Reverend Whiteman, I'm confused. What do you mean by 'hole in his hand'? Hiram Ogilvy is confined to a wheelchair."

"Wheelchair? Now I'm the confused one. Let me tell you what I know.

"I met Brody and Lonnie—let me think. I guess it was eight—no, *nine* years ago. Several months later, I met them again on a train to San Francisco. They told me how Lonnie's wife, daughter, and son had been kidnapped years earlier and that they had heard that they'd been spotted in the city. Lonnie's wife was being enslaved in a jeans factory while his daughter was being held hostage in order to insure the mother's cooperation. They were on their way to meet Lonnie's friend, Ridley, and rescue his wife and child. I asked if I could go along, my being somewhat handy with a pistol and the odds likely against the three of them.

"We set up a plan after we'd cased the place. Lonnie and Brody would go in through the backdoor while Ridley and Amanda, Brody's wife, would—"

"Miranda!"

"Excuse me?"

"Miranda. Brody's wife's name is Miranda."

"Oh, yes, so it is. Anyway, Ridley and Miranda would go in from the front. I was stationed on the roof of a building across the street. I had a rifle and was there to make sure no one went in behind Adams and Brody's wife.

"Just as the shooting began, a man came walking up the boardwalk. When he heard the commotion he hid behind a water trough and drew his gun. I kept an eye on him and as Miranda came out of the factory, he aimed at her. I shot him in the hand and he ran off.

"It wasn't until later, after Brody and the rest were well on their way on the eastbound train, that I learned that the man I shot was Hiram Ogilvy, one of the owners of the jeans factory."

"You're the one who shot Ogilvy? Not Ridley?"

"That's correct! And I only shot him in the hand. There's no reason for him to be in a wheelchair."

"Ogilvy's story is that he was simply walking down the street when he heard this gun battle break out. He claims he was trying to hurry past it when Ridley emerged from the building and shot him in the back. A doctor is supposed to testify that he is permanently paralyzed from the waist down," Mattie informed the minister.

"I've got to get back to San Francisco," Whiteman exclaimed. "I've got to make sure the truth is told."

In the hour it took to reach Tonopah, Nevada, Reverend Whiteman spoke to the conductor and obtained information about the westbound train. He was told that the train wouldn't arrive in Tonopah until the sixteenth, but that he would still arrive in San Francisco almost as quick as he would on horseback, without the potential problems.

The minister parted ways with Mattie in Tonopah as she continued on her way back to Kansas. The young deputy arrived in Wichita early in the morning on April

17th, about six hours before Reverend Whiteman arrived back in California.

Southeastern Kansas, April 17, 1875

Mattie Cochran saddled up her mare, Miss Molly, later that Saturday morning, intent on heading to Chanute as quickly as she could. She met briefly with Deputy Kyle Branch, who had returned to Wichita the previous day. Branch filled her in on her sister's condition before he joined a group of federal marshals that were heading up to the Dakotas because of problems with the Sioux.

There had been a discovery of gold in South Dakota and it was on the Indian Reservation. The Sioux were not happy about the influx of white men who they claimed were desecrating their sacred territory with their prospecting. The president had ordered a contingent of deputy US marshals to go up there and restore order. He told Mattie that Marshal Winters was counting on her and her sister Danielle to help him keep the peace in Kansas.

Having left Wichita shortly after her meeting with Branch, the blonde rode into the early evening hours, covering nearly thirty-five miles before making camp for the night. She built a small fire to boil coffee and cook up some beans and bacon. As she sat eating she caught a glimpse of movement on the far side of the fire.

She removed the leather thong off her pistol's hammer and slowly eased the six-shooter from its holster. As quietly as she could, she pulled back the hammer and prepared to shoot at whoever was sneaking up on her. Straining her eyes to see through the smoke and light of her campfire, she spied a gray wolf staring at her.

The light-gray animal inched its way forward until it was close enough for the blonde deputy to see that it wasn't a wolf but a rather mangy-looking dog. Determining that it didn't appear the animal was going to attack, she set her pistol down by her leg, picked out a piece of bacon from the pan, and tossed the morsel off to the dog's right side.

The dog jumped back and then ran back into the dark woods. A couple of minutes later it slowly crawled out of the trees on its belly and approached the slice of bacon while keeping a wary eye on Mattie. Mattie watched in fascination as the canine took several minutes to get to the rasher, sniff it suspiciously, and finally take it in his mouth, practically inhaling it.

Mattie threw a second strip of the fried pork off to the dog's left and watched as it went through the same routine, running into the trees and then slowly crawling back out to get the bacon. Mattie quickly cooked up some more bacon, but it took four slices before the dog no longer ran back into the trees between slices. The deputy now began throwing the pieces of bacon short, bringing the animal closer to the fire and to her. Finally she held a slice out in her left hand, keeping her right hand on the butt of her pistol just in case.

Approaching cautiously, the mangy dog sniffed the bacon in Mattie's hand and then gulped it down like it had the other rashers. The blonde continued to hold her left hand out, allowing the canine to sniff it. After a couple of minutes, she slowly slid her hand onto the dog's head and gently ruffled his fur. She petted him for several minutes and then slipped her hand off his head and onto her left knee. The dog immediately stood up and used its nose to nudge the girl's hand until she began petting him again.

Once he settled back down onto the ground she moved her hand back to her knee until he nudged it again with his nose. They played this game several times until the gray animal got smart and rested his chin on Mattie's knee, giving her a look that said, "What are you going to do now?"

"So that's how you're gonna be, huh?" she asked, teasingly. "Think you're pretty smart, do ya?" Mattie laughed out loud. "Well, tell me smarty, you got a name, or should I just call you Dog?…Not gonna tell me, huh? Guess it's Dog then."

The gray canine closed his eyes and seemed to relax. He'd shown no response to being called Dog, so Mattie checked the leather collar to see if a name was written on it, but came up empty.

"What am I going to do with you?" Mattie asked herself out loud. "It looks like you've belonged to someone, but where are they?"

Just then the wind shifted, momentarily blowing the smoke from the campfire at them. The dog jumped to its feet, faced the fire, and began barking.

"Don't like the smoke, boy?" Mattie asked.

At the word *smoke*, the canine turned back toward the young woman and sat as if at attention. Puzzled, the deputy decided to try something.

"Lay down!" she commanded, and the dog promptly laid on his belly. She picked up a stick from the wood she'd collected for her fire and threw it, yelling "fetch" as it left her hand. The dog immediately bounded away, coming back moments later with the stick held in its jaws.

"Smoke!" the deputy said and the dog dropped the stick and sat at attention. "So your name is Smoke?" she asked. The greyhound answered with a single bark.

The blonde patted her knee and the dirty, mangy looking dog settled back down on the ground next to her, resting his chin on her left thigh.

"Nice to meet you, Smoke. My name's Mattie. I have a feeling we're about to become good friends," she said softly.

The animal glanced up at the blonde as if he understood every word, then settled back down as she gently stroked his head.

32

CAMI

Chanute, Kansas, April 20, 1875

"No, Bat, no!" Cami shouted.

Hattie lurched from the chair where she'd been dozing and rushed to the side of the bed.

"Wake up," she urged her charge. "You're having a bad dream."

"Oh, Hattie, it was…" Cami started to say before she noticed the strange look on the younger girl's face. "What's wrong, Hattie?" she asked.

"Yo—you're—you're sitting up," the nurse stuttered.

Cami looked at herself. Her knees were drawn up against her chest, her feet flat on the bed. She had her arms wrapped around her knees.

"Hattie, what just happened?"

"I…I don't know. Let me get the doctor," she said as she rushed from the room.

Camille swung her legs over the side of the bed and sat there for a moment. Slowly she stood up, placing her right hand on the bed to steady herself.

"What do you think you're doing?" the doctor all but shouted as he roared through the open doorway. "Get back in that bed this instant."

"But, Doctor, I feel fine. There's no pain and I can move again."

"Please, Cami, lie back down," the doctor said, softening his voice. "Let me examine you before you start strolling around the room. We don't want you to do something that might permanently harm you."

"Okay, Doc," the deputy replied as she lay back down.

"Now, tell me exactly what happened," he inquired.

"Well, I was praying, thanking God for letting me live, and for letting me love Bat, and for Bat loving me despite my condition, and for the doctor coming from Chicago, and—well, I guess I fell asleep. Next thing I know, I'm sitting up, yelling at Bat."

"Did you have a dream about the sheriff?"

"I guess so. I don't remember anything other than yelling at him."

"Okay. I want you to slowly rollover onto your stomach so I can examine your back."

When she had complied, Doctor Holliday parted her gown and gently probed the area of her back near where the bullet had entered. After several minutes of poking and prodding her, the doctor got a strange look on his face.

"What's wrong, doctor?" the patient asked.

"I don't understand. Before, I could feel the bullet that was lodged against your spine. But now, there's nothing there. You must have dislodged it when you sat up, but I've never heard of such a thing.

"As a matter of fact," he continued after more probing, "I can't feel the bullet at all. It's like it's completely gone."

The doctor and Hattie joined her in prayer as she thanked God for the miracle He had performed. Then Cami asked the young nurse to go get Sheriff Blanchard but instructed her not to tell him about what happened.

It was almost three hours before Bailey Blanchard could break free from his duties to go see Cami. When he arrived at the doctor's office his future wife was still lying flat on her back. He leaned over her and gave her a kiss.

"You know, Bat, you're a pretty good kisser," she told him tenderly. "I think there may even be some powerful medicine in those kisses."

The sheriff laughed. "You think so, huh?"

"Why, I think…Is it possible?"

"Is what possible?" the young man looked at her suspiciously.

"I think…yes, I think I can feel the warmth of your kiss all the way down to my toes. Kiss me again, Bat," she exclaimed.

Not needing a second invitation to kiss the woman he loved, Bat leaned over the bed and placed his lips against hers. Finding it difficult not to start laughing, Cami slowly slid her legs from under the covers and began to stand up, holding the kiss the whole time.

Bailey Blanchard, realizing that something extraordinary was happening, stepped back and looked at his girlfriend.

"What's going on here?" he asked, stunned to see Cami standing in front of him.

"I've been healed, Bat. God moved the bullet and Doc can't find it at all. He wants me to stay here for a little while to ensure that it's really gone, but he thinks I'm going to be just fine."

Tears of joy began to run down the young woman's cheeks.

"What's all this?" a female voice demanded from the doorway. "I thought you were supposed to be paralyzed from the neck down?" Mattie questioned.

"Oh, Mattie! It's a miracle," Cami cried, running into her sister's arms.

Danielle was right behind her newly arrived sister, a stupefied look on her face.

"God healed me, Mattie!"

The three sisters hugged each other for a long time. When they finally stopped, Cami introduced Mattie to the sheriff and informed her that they were planning on getting married. This elicited another round of hugs and congratulations. Then the four young adults decided to get down on their knees and pray, thanking God for His healing and for all the wonderful things He's done for them.

33

REVEREND WHITEMAN

San Francisco, California, April 19, 1875

THE TRIAL OF Ridley Adams began at nine o'clock on a Monday morning. Reverend Keith Whiteman had met privately over the weekend with his friends Brody Hancock and Lonnie Harrelson. Knowing that Ogilvy's charges against Ridley were a sham, they decided that Whiteman would not acknowledge that he knew the other two when the trial began. They knew that Ogilvy wouldn't know about the minister's involvement in the rescue event and the good reverend had a plan to expose Ogilvy's true condition.

Outside of the courtroom, the morning was like so many others in San Francisco—foggy and chilly. But inside, the overpacked legal facility was hot and stuffy. Whiteman sat in the front pew, about five feet behind the wheelchair Ogilvy sat in. The plaintiff's attorney called his first witness, the doctor who had treated the plaintiff.

"Doctor Karrup, you examined Mr. Ogilvy, did you not?" the attorney asked.

"I did, sir."

"And what did you determine were the extent of his injuries?"

"Mr. Ogilvy was shot in the back. The bullet is lodged between some vertebrae and his spinal cord. He is paralyzed from the waist down and will never walk again."

The judge looked at Ridley's attorney and said, "Your witness counselor."

Standing, the defendant's lawyer addressed the doctor, "What type of doctor are you, sir?"

"The type that treats people who are injured," Karrup replied, drawing a laugh from the audience.

"I mean, sir, are you a specialist in a particular field, such as dentistry or ophthalmology?"

"I am an ophthalmologist."

"An eye doctor then?"

"Yes, but I also treat a number of people who have been patients of mine for many years, like Hiram Ogilvy."

"Did you consult with a back specialist or spinal cord specialist while examining Mr. Ogilvy?"

"I didn't need to. I've seen plenty of gunshot wounds to the back to know what his condition was." Doctor Karrup was getting surly in his responses.

"Do you keep up with the latest advances that are published in magazines such as the *Philadelphia Journal of Medical and Physical Sciences?*"

"I don't have time to read all that stuff. I have a lot of patients to take care of. I'm a very busy man."

"No further questions, Your Honor," the defense lawyer said, retaking his seat at the table.

"Your Honor, the plaintiff calls Sergeant Peter Cranston of the San Francisco Police Department," the attorney for Ogilvy said.

Once the sergeant was sworn in, the attorney asked him about the night that Ogilvy was shot.

"Yeah, we got somebody come in to the station and tell us there was a big gunfight going on at the jeans factory on Border Street. A bunch of us rushed over there to see what was going on and found that a gang of hoodlums had raided the factory and stolen all the workers who lived there away."

"And what about Mr. Ogilvy? Where did you find him?"

"Oh, he come into the station while we were at the factory. Said he'd been shot in the back."

"No further questions, Your Honor."

"Mr. Stanley?"

"Thank you, Your Honor. Sergeant Cranston, you just testified that Mr. Ogilvy walked to the police station with a bullet in his back, is that correct?"

"That's my understanding, but I never actually talked to him until the next day."

"That would be after Doctor Karrup treated him?"

"Yes, sir."

"Have you ever actually seen the wound to Mr. Ogilvy's back?"

"No, sir."

"What about a wound to Mr. Ogilvy's right hand?"

"His right hand was bandaged, but no one ever told me why."

"Okay, sergeant. Now, you also testified that it was a gang of hoodlums trying to steal women that caused the gun battle, is that correct?"

"That's what we were told by the owners of the factory that night."

"And what, if anything, have you since learned about what happened that night?"

"It's been reported to the police that the defendant and his two friends, the ones sitting behind him, were rescuing one of them's wives and daughter."

"And has that been investigated?"

"Yes."

"And do you know the outcome of that investigation?"

"The detectives concluded that the owners of the factory were engaged in using women as slaves to manufacture their jeans." The sergeant was obviously getting uncomfortable.

"And do you know who those owners were?"

"Yes, sir."

"And was one of those owners Hiram Ogilvy?"

The police officer paused for a long moment, looking around like one looking for help from somebody.

"Answer the question," the judge commanded.

"Yes, sir."

"No further questions, Your Honor."

"Next witness," the judge intoned. The look on his face told everyone that he wasn't pleased with the direction this case was taking.

"The plaintiff calls Hiram Ogilvy." Ogilvy's attorney was hoping that the man would be able to get things back on track.

Ogilvy began to wheel his chair toward the witness box when Reverend Whiteman suddenly stood up and grabbed the handles.

"Here, let me help you, Hiram," he said. Then he tipped the wheelchair forward, causing the supposedly paralyzed man to stand up or fall on his face. Whiteman raised his hands toward the ceiling and proclaimed, "It's a miracle! The man is healed."

"Order in the court!" the judge shouted, banging his gavel several times and repeating his demand until the hubbub settle down.

"What's the meaning of this?" the judge directed his question at Whiteman.

"Your Honor, I beg your forgiveness, but I knew Mr. Ogilvy wasn't shot in the back. I knew that because I'm the one who shot him, and I shot him in his right hand because he was about to ambush Mrs. Brody Hancock."

"Who are you, sir?"

"My name is Reverend Keith Whiteman. I am an itinerant minister. I was assisting these three gentlemen," he waved his hand indicating Ridley, Brody, and Lonnie, "in rescuing Lonnie Harrelson's wife and daughter. They had been kidnapped by Mr. Ogilvy's business associates and were being held captive as Mrs. Harrelson was forced to work in the factory."

"Mr. Ogilvy, is this true?" the judge asked the plaintiff.

"I don't know what this man is talking about. I've never seen him before in my life, and I don't know anything about any kidnappings or forcing women to work."

"So you are calling a man of the cloth a liar?" the judge asked.

"No, no, of course not. I just don't know what he's talking about."

Ogilvy could see from the judge's expression that he was losing ground. "Wait a minute," he yelled. "How do you even know he's really a minister?"

"Aside of the fact he's dressed like every preacher man I've ever met, I don't. But I do see that you are standing just fine even though you and your doctor claimed you were confined to a wheelchair. So you tell me, whom would you believe?"

Before Ogilvy could respond, the judge turned to his bailiff and ordered, "Bailiff, take Mr. Ogilvy into custody. Mr. Ridley Adams, you are released and I offer you the apology of this court for any inconvenience it has caused you.

"As for you, Doctor Karrup and Sergeant Cranston, I am ordering the district attorney to investigate your involvements in this case. This court is adjourned." He banged his gavel one time as he rose and left the courtroom.

Pandemonium broke out as the judge exited through a doorway at the back of the courtroom. Brody and Lonnie embraced Ridley and congratulated him. Jeanette came up and gave him a big hug and then stepped aside so that Adams could thank Reverend Whiteman for his part in what had just happened. The five of them decided to have lunch to celebrate the case's outcome.

While they were all in a celebratory mood, Ridley turned to Jeanette Fishman and asked, "How do you feel about marrying me and moving to Colorado?"

"Just try to leave town without me again, Ridley Adams, and I'll hunt you down like the polecat you are," she replied, jokingly.

"I take that as a yes?"

"Yes, Ridley, I will marry you and move to Colorado."

After more congratulations and hooplas, the five left the restaurant and headed back to the courthouse. There, the same judge who had presided over Ridley's trial performed the marriage ceremony. The next day, all five boarded the eastbound train. Brody, Lonnie, Ridley, and Jeanette were headed to the Double H Ranch while Reverend Whiteman resumed his trip, headed for a conference in Philadelphia.

34

DAVID

San Francisco, April 21, 1875

DAVID YARDEN WAS angry. He had been following the men he had seen on the train with Matilda back in Grand Junction, but she wasn't with them any longer. And now they were getting ready to board the eastbound train themselves. So where was his wife?

Of course David knew that Mattie wasn't really his wife any longer, but he wasn't going to let that little detail prevent him from finding her and trying to win her back. He'd spotted two of the men she had been on the train with shortly after he arrived in the city on Friday. However, there had been no sign of the pretty blonde haired won. .n over the weekend. Now the men, along with three other people, were waiting at the station, leaving the city.

All sorts of thoughts were running through his head. *Should he approach the group and ask them where Mattie was? How would they react?* The men looked tough, even the one dressed like a preacher man. Maybe Mattie had left San Francisco. *Should he get on the train and try to befriend the men? Could he trick them into telling him where she'd gone?*

Before David could arrive at answers to his myriad of questions, the train arrived at the station. The group boarded one of the passenger cars and Yarden was soon left all alone on the station platform.

I need a drink, he thought.

April 24, 1875

It was nearly midnight on Saturday. David Yarden had either drank or gambled away all of the money he had, and it wasn't his money to begin with. In his mind he had justified spending the funds because he decided it was probably stolen from somebody before he stole it. It didn't occur to him that stealing stolen money was as wrong as stealing it in the first place. David's values and beliefs, such as they were, were tainted by his "need" for alcohol and gambling.

Now he was out of money and just shy of falling down drunk. So when the two men accosted him in the alley beside the saloon he'd just left, he was ready to fight someone, anyone.

"Hey, you!" one of the men demanded, "You the one owns that chestnut gelding?"

"What's it to you?" David spat back.

"Heard you bought it with some of my money," the stranger said.

"Nope, bought it with my own money," Yarden replied, slightly slurring his words.

"Way I hear it, you used the money you got out of my saddlebags that you stole when you stole my gray horse. Now I want my money back, all six thousand seven hundred and fifty three dollars of it."

"Ain't got it!"

"Then you better get it. I'm giving you 'til Monday night to come up with the money or I'll take it out of your hide. And don't even think of trying to leave town, or go to the sheriff. My friend here and I will be watching you day and night."

"Where am I su'posed to get that kind of money?"

"That's your problem. You stole it from me, steal it from somebody else for all I care. Just make sure you come up with it by Monday."

The two men faded back into the shadows of the alleyway. But David knew they were still watching him. He went back to his hotel room to sober up and figure a way out of his predicament.

April 25, 1875

Just after midnight, Yarden entered a different saloon. He carefully watched the various groups of gamblers taking note of who was winning and who was losing. Around one thirty in the morning, he saw one of the gamblers he'd been watching get up and leave the saloon.

David followed at a distance until he was sure he could attack the man without interference. He was reasonably sure the man was too drunk to put up much of a resistance. Tapping the man on his head with the butt of his pistol, Yarden then checked to make sure the man was only unconscious and not dead. Then he rifled the drunk's pockets until he came up with the small amount of his winnings. It barely amounted to two hundred dollars.

Having gotten himself a small stake, David proceeded to a third saloon where he sat and watched the new tables of action. He had to pick his table carefully as he couldn't afford to lose any money. About an hour later an opening came up at one of the tables he felt he stood a pretty good chance at being able to succeed.

It took almost two hours, but he eventually cleaned out everybody that had been at the table when he'd joined them. However, when he counted up his loot he discovered he now had only about five hundred dollars. The problem David had was, any poker player he was able to beat consistently wasn't likely to be betting very much money. If he was going to raise the nearly seven grand by playing poker, he was going to have to find a higher stakes game. Unfortunately, that also meant playing against better skilled players.

By Sunday night, David had played poker in six different saloons; and though he won regularly, he had only amassed a total of $2,400. *There's only one option left*, he reasoned. *I'm going to have to find a gambler who wins big, and I'm going have to rob him.*

April 26, 1875

All day Monday and into the early evening hours, David Yarden wandered from saloon to saloon in San Francisco, looking for that one gambler that appeared to be winning enough money to make it worth his while to try and rob him. He finally settled on a man he could tell was a professional gambler. He watched the man rake in pot after pot until he had what appeared to be several thousand dollars in front of him.

Sitting at a table toward the back of the saloon, David slowly sipped whiskey, knowing that he had to remain sober yet loving the effect the alcoholic beverage had on him. He saw the stranger that had demanded his money Saturday night enter the saloon, but there was nowhere for him to hide, and no way for him to slip out the back as the man's friend was now standing just inside the rear door. The man came directly to David's table and sat down without seeking permission.

"You got my money?" he asked.

"Not yet. I'll have it by midnight," Yarden replied.

"How?"

David nodded toward the table where the gambler was now raking in another winning hand. The stranger looked back over his left shoulder and then back at Yarden.

"You talkin' 'bout the gambler over there?"

"Yeah. He's been winning big. I think he's probably won enough for both of us to come out ahead."

The stranger just grunted. "You are one stupid…never mind. Just make sure you bring me my money by midnight. And don't make me come looking for you."

He got up from the table and walked over to where his friend was standing. David watched as he said something to the other man. They both looked over at the table David had been watching, and laughed. As they walked out the front of the bar, the second man pointed his index finger at David, and acted like it was a gun he was firing. David Yarden felt a shiver run down his spine.

April 27, 1875

Police Sergeant Petty of the San Francisco Police Department stood over the body of the unknown man lying dead in an alleyway next to one of the city's most notorious saloons.

"Any identification on this gent?" he asked the officer who had been the first one on the scene.

"No, sir. I've asked around too, and nobody seems to know who he is. Just another drifter, I guess."

"'Kay, get him over to the morgue and let the coroner know. Looks like cause of death is probably gonna be gunshot, but we'll let him make that decision."

Two men lifted David Yarden's body onto a stretcher and carried him off.

35

IKE

Outside of Chanute, Kansas, April 21, 1875

IKE STURGIS WAS angry. He was holed up in an abandoned farmhouse about four miles northwest of a small town. He'd been evading a platoon of army troopers for almost a week now and though he believed that he had finally shaken them, he couldn't help but feel that he was still only barely one step ahead of them.

The sudden appearance of the cavalry in Cedar Creek, Missouri had spoiled his plans to take over the town. Added to that frustration was the knowledge that in their escape attempt two of his men had been shot and, presumably, killed. Two others had been captured and were probably in the stockade at Fort Davidson, Missouri. This left his gang severely diminished. He would have to try and pick up some new boys before he could resume his robbing of banks.

Ike was also thinking about maybe trying what he'd done at Cedar Creek on some other town. Maybe even this Chanute town that was nearby. Toward this possibility, he had sent one of his men into the farming community to learn what he could about the prospects. But the man was supposed to return nearly two hours ago. This really steamed Ike. He expected complete obedience from his men and didn't suffer it easily when they failed to carry out his instructions.

As Sturgis sat at the farmhouse's kitchen table mulling over these thoughts he heard the sound of approaching horses. Two of his men quickly jumped up and rushed to separate windows.

"Riders comin'!" one of the men yelled.

"I kin hear that," Ike responded sarcastically. "Can you tell who they are?"

"Yeah! It's Rowdy and some other guy," the second man answered.

Ike jumped up and headed toward the window. "Is the other guy the law?" he asked.

"I don't think so. Looks like a gunny."

After peering out the window at the man riding in with Rowdy, Ike went to the front door and stepped out onto the small porch.

"Who you got there, Rowdy?" Ike asked when the men reined in their horses and began dismounting.

"His name's Goren Young."

"Goren Young, the man who killed Kid Roberts?"

"One and the same," Rowdy answered.

Ike walked up to Young and stuck his hand out. "Nice ta meet ya Young."

"Likewise Sturgis. Heard a lot 'bout you. When I saw Rowdy her', figured I'd see if I could latch on to yore outfit."

"You're mighty welcome. We lost a couple of men on our last job, so we can definitely use tha help. Why doncha come inside and have some coffee."

The three men proceeded to enter the cabin and sit down at the table.

"First, I want to hear what Rowdy found out in town," Sturgis said.

"I gotta tell ya, Ike, it looks bad. The town sheriff is supposed to be a real hard-case and there are four marshals in town."

"Four marshals? As in *US* marshals?"

"Yeah," Goren answered him. "Been some trouble in Chanute with the KKK and the marshal for Kansas sent some woman deputy down to check it out. Seems she got shot and now the marshal himself, along with two other deputies are hanging out there."

"Wait a minute. You said it was a woman deputy got shot?"

"That's the rumor goin' 'round town. Apparently, Winters, that's the marshal, has hired him some female deputies."

"Sounds like easy pickin's to me," Ike commented.

"Don't be too sure 'bout that. I been trav'lin' 'round the state and been hearing lots of talk about these here females. Seems like they're plenty tough enough. Story is they escorted Dakota Sam from Colorado to Topeka and wiped out almost his entire gang en route.

"Then, when Sam escaped, one of them chased him all the way to Nebraska, by herself, and kilt him and a war party of Sioux. I wouldn't be too anxious, if'n I was you, to take on these girls."

"You ain't scared of some dress wearer are you?"

"No, but I try not to bite off more'n I can chew. And these girls sound hard for females. Besides, I know of a nice little town in the northern part of the state that would be ideal if'n yore lookin' to try that little gambit you attempted in Missou."

"Okay. Tell me about this town."

"It's called Jewell City. It's only been around for a few years and isn't got a lot of people. But when I rode through there a couple munts ago, there were some good looking women, including some young girls, and the men were mostly farmers. There also wernt any lawmen."

Ike decided that Jewell City sounded like a good prospect and asked Young to fill him in on more details.

April 23, 1875

Ike, Goren Young, and the gang left the farmhouse outside of Chanute and headed toward Wichita. Ike had a plan to rob some banks along the way to Jewell City so that they could stock up on supplies before hitting the town.

36

THE CHASE BEGINS

Wichita, Kansas, May 12, 1875

US MARSHAL TOBIAS Winters called Mattie and Dani Cochran into his office. The three of them had returned to the city from Chanute just before the end of April, having left Cami Cochran in Chanute to continue healing from her gunshot wound.

"There've been a string of bank robberies," he said, addressing the two sisters, "over the last couple of weeks. Banks in Hutchinson, Emporia, and Salina have all been hit and the information I have makes me believe it's the same group of outlaws.

"I received a report from a lieutenant at Fort Davidson, Missouri about a gang that tried to take over a town called

Cedar Creek around the middle of last month. It just so happened that this lieutenant was leading a full platoon of cavalry troopers out on patrol. It was their normal routine to pass through this town and make sure everything was okay as they don't have any sheriff. He and his troopers arrived in time to thwart the bad guys, but not before they had killed every man in the town as well as a couple of women.

"From the lieutenant's description of this gang, and from the information I've been able to garner about these robberies, I believe we are dealing with one gang and that their leader is a man named Ike Sturgis.

"I want you two to go to Cedar Creek and interview anybody that's there still and then go to Davidson and talk to this lieutenant. From there I suggest you go to each of the banks that have been robbed and talk to any witnesses. I want you to locate this gang, but I don't want you to try to apprehend them by yourselves. When you find them, contact me and I will bring as many deputies as I can round up."

"Didn't the lieutenant try to pursue the gang?" Mattie asked.

"Yes. He sent a squad of troopers after them. They ended up killing two of the outlaws and capturing another two. They are currently in the stockade at the fort, awaiting trial. It probably wouldn't be a bad idea to try to question them, though I suspect they won't be very helpful."

"When do you want us to leave?" Dani asked.

"Tomorrow morning. You can stop in Chanute and see your sister, but she is not to go with you, no matter how much she begs."

Winters asked if there were any further questions and when neither of the deputies asked anything he finished by saying, "Do not approach this gang on your own. Are we clear on that?"

"Yes, sir!" the two women replied in unison.

Chanute, May 16, 1875

Two bedraggled women and a dog entered the town of Chanute in the late afternoon on Sunday. They had been caught in a midspring rainstorm that had pelted them from Thursday noon until early that morning. They checked in to the only hotel in the small town and changed into dry clothes. Then they went to see their sister, who was now back at Miss Edna's boarding house.

"Hey, you two! What are you doing here?" Cami asked her sisters in greeting.

"We're on our way to Missouri and thought we'd stop in and see how you're doing," Dani replied.

"Well, it's really good to see you. Oh, and you too Smoke! Has Mattie been taking good care of you?" she cooed. "If she doesn't treat you right, you just come and live with me."

Smoke was no longer the mangy looking mutt Mattie had found staring at her over a campfire a month ago. His gray fur was smooth and shiny now and he no longer had that gaunt body he'd had. Mattie was taking good care of her dog, as her sister well knew, and he was faithful to her.

"So why are you two going to Missouri, and can I come along?" Cami now asked.

"We're investigating a gang of outlaws that shot up a town there and killed all the men," Mattie answered. "Toby told us that you have to stay here. He doesn't want you riding until he's confident you're completely healed."

"Come on Mattie, I've been stuck here for over a month since God moved the bullet and doc couldn't find it. I am completely healed. What more does he want?"

"Cami, this investigation is going to take some time and we're going to be doing a lot of riding," Dani explained. "Since the gang shot up the town, they've gone on a spree of bank robberies. Toby wants us to go to each bank and question witnesses."

"We're going to be on the trail probably for the next couple of months," Mattie said, trying to sound reasonable. "Doc says he's not sure your back is ready for that grueling amount of riding a horse."

"But I want to be part of what's going on," their sister whined. "You two are getting to have all the fun. This was supposed to be the three of us together."

"It is Cami. And when we find this gang, we're going to make sure you are part of the group that takes them down. In the meantime, just do what you've got to do to get fully well," Mattie said.

"Besides, think of all the time you'll get to spend with Bat. Talk about fun. You'll be having a lot more fun than Mattie and I will," Dani said.

Mattie and Dani hung out until Tuesday, the eighteenth, to allow the roads to dry out.

Cedar Creek, Missouri, May 21, 1875

Mattie, Dani, and Smoke entered the small town of Cedar Creek midmorning. Smoke had already scouted ahead of the two women and given them an all clear indication. Yet as they rode slowly in, they noticed that the town appeared empty. Not quite a ghost town, yet abandoned looking. The two young deputies came to a stop in the middle of the town's only street, glanced all around themselves and then stared at each other for a moment.

Mattie was just about to speak when a female voice shouted, "You men turn dem ponies 'round an' ride back out the ways you come!"

"Ma'am, we're deputy US marshals," Mattie shouted back. "We've come to talk to you about the trouble you had last month."

"Hol' yer fire, ladies," the same woman shouted. Then to Mattie and Dani she yelled, "Ya got any pruf youse the law?"

The two girls reached under their dusters and unpinned their badges, holding them up in the air so they could be seen.

"'Kay, slide off'n dem horses and hol' yer hands in the air 'til we check you out," the woman commanded.

After glancing at each other a second, the Cochran sisters slipped out of their saddles and stood on the street. Smoke growled softly as two women came out of a building and approached the deputies.

"Quiet, Smoke!" Mattie ordered the dog. "Everything will be okay."

The gray canine settled back on his haunches, but his owner knew that he was ready to spring at the slightest signal from her. Over the last month, the two of them had become closer than many married couples when it came to knowing what each other was thinking.

Having looked closely at the two sister's badges and determined that they were really deputies, one of the women that had come out turned and yelled at the front of the general store.

"They's wimmen, Maude!"

"Whose wimmen?" Maude yelled back.

"Dem deputies! Who'd ya think I talkin''bout?"

Suddenly, about two dozen women—all of them armed with rifles and holsters strapped around their waists—emerged from the various buildings that made up the town. They all gathered around the Cochran sisters, which made Smoke nervous until Mattie ran a hand over his head and told him to relax.

As the women closed around the girls one of them yelled out that they were twins.

"Actually," Dani responded, "we're triplets. Our other sister is back in Kansas, healing up after being shot."

The woman, who apparently was Maude, spoke up, "So's how com' yer jes now comin' to Cedar Creek to talk to us?"

"We've been tied up with other affairs," Mattie answered. "I was in California and my sister here was in Topeka. Then we had to go see my other sister and make sure she was okay and that the person who shot her was dealt with."

"And how was he dealt with?" one of the other women asked.

"I shot and killed her," Dani answered, matter-of-factly.

"Why don' you ladies com' to da saloon and hav' a drink on me?" Maude asked.

"We don't drink liquor," Mattie stated, "but we sure could use a cup of coffee to wash down the trail dust."

The three women and Smoke headed to the town's only saloon, followed by all the other women. Maude had detailed two women to take the deputies' horses to the stables and bed them down. For the next three hours, the women of Cedar Creek filled Mattie's and Dani's ears with the story of Ike Sturgis's attack on the town.

Finally, Mattie asked, "And there's no doubt that this man, the leader, was Ike Sturgis?"

"No!" one of the women said, "He told us his name when he stood up on the platform in the church."

"Jes 'fore he kilt Perky," another woman chimed in.

"Perky?" Dani asked.

"Perkins was the town blacksmith," the first woman said. "Everybody called him Perk, except for a few women who got away with calling him Perky."

A number of women looked toward the second girl, who blushed brightly.

"Lo'k, you gurls mus' be famished," Maude suggested. "Why don' we go ta my house and grab us a bite?"

The two young deputies stayed in Cedar Creek for two days, listening to the women that survived the attempted takeover tell their stories. But then it came time to move on and they said their good-byes.

"Ya rea'ly think yer goin' ta catch this Sturgis?" Maude asked them as they sat on their horses, ready to head to Fort Davidson.

"Ladies," Mattie addressed all the women gathered around, "my boss has tasked my sister and I to find Ike Sturgis so that he, and his men, can be brought to justice. We aim to do just that, and you have my word that we will accomplish our mission."

Nodding to the women, the two sisters put their spurs to their mounts and trotted out of town with Smoke running on ahead to scout.

Fort Davidson, Missouri, May 28, 1875

It took the two sisters close to a week to get to the fort outside of Pilot Knob, Missouri. Unfortunately, upon their arrival they learned that the lieutenant they wanted to speak to was out on patrol. However, as he was expected to return by the beginning of the week, they elected to remain in town. After telegraphing Marshal Winters as to their status, they then checked into the Pilot Knob Hotel.

The hotel itself wasn't much of a building. Two stories tall, it only had ten rooms on each floor and each room had only one bed. Fortunately, the bed was just big enough to accommodate both women. The downside was the hotel was mostly there to cater to the soldiers from the fort, who were in town to have fun. That made the place very noisy late at night (during the day and evening they were in the saloons, drinking, gambling, and trying to score with the pretty girls). Monday couldn't come soon enough for Mattie and Danielle.

———•••◦◧◦•••———

Lieutenant Jacoby "Jake" Staley didn't arrive back at Fort Davidson until midday on Tuesday. He spent the remainder of that day meeting with his Commanding Officer and other superiors, giving them a debriefing on his patrol. Consequently, it was Wednesday morning before the deputies had an opportunity to talk to him about Cedar Creek.

"So, Lieutenant Staley, please tell us about what happened when you arrived at Cedar Creek back on April 16," Mattie began after the three of them were seated at a table in the Mess Hall, cups of coffee steaming in front of them.

"Please call me Jake. I don't know what all I can tell you that the women there couldn't. You really should talk to them."

"We already did, Jake," Dani replied. "We just want to get your perspective."

"Well, Deputies, when my men and I entered the town, I suspected something was wrong. We've been to Cedar Creek a few times before and it's always been fairly active. But when we arrived on the sixteenth there wasn't a soul in sight. Then suddenly, some men came pouring out of the church at the far end of town, so that added to my suspicions.

"When the men all jumped on their horses and started to ride out, I ordered one of my sergeants to take his squad and chase the men. He was told to catch them and bring them back to town. However, the men began shooting at my troopers, who were forced to return fire.

"I know we killed two of the outlaws and were able to capture two others. Whether or not any others were killed or wounded, I couldn't say."

"What about your men?" Mattie asked compassionately.

"Fortunately, my men escaped fairly unscathed. Two of them received minor wounds, creases on the arms where bullets barely hit them."

"We're glad to hear that," Dani said. "We'd like to speak to the prisoners also, Jake."

Mattie glanced at her sister. It was obvious from the look on Dani's face that the triplet was taken with the handsome young lieutenant. She wondered how that affected her sister's earlier interest in Toby Winters.

"I'm not sure how much good talking to them will do you, but you're welcome to try."

The officer led the two women over to the stockade and arranged for the prisoners to be brought to them in a conference room, one at a time.

Two hours of grilling the prisoners elicited no information from either one and the two deputies grew tired. They headed back to their hotel, slightly discouraged. The trip to Fort Davidson had been unproductive and lasted too long. Next stop: Emporia, Kansas.

37

CAMI

Chanute, Kansas, May 18, 1875

HER SISTERS HAD left earlier in the day and Cami was feeling very lonely once more. True, Bat Blanchard was nearby, but he was tied up with his work and she was under strict orders not to do any activity that might cause a relapse in the paralysis.

The bullet had moved over a month ago. However, Doctor Holliday was being overly cautious as there wasn't a great deal of medical information available about the subject. Researchers were always studying the effects of back injuries and bullet wounds, but there were few experts in the field. Consequently, the good doctor was telling her to take it easy, no, he was telling her to not do anything at all, she thought.

Cami was miserable, sitting in her boarding house room, with nothing to do.

There was a knock on the door, waking Cami from the sleep she hadn't intended to take. Opening the door, she found Miss Edna standing there.

"Hi, can I help you?" Cami asked.

"You have some visitors," Miss Edna replied.

"Visitors? Who?"

"Come see for yourself."

Cami closed her door behind her and followed the older woman down the hallway. When she entered the sitting room she found her parents standing there, waiting for her.

"Mom! Dad!" the young woman yelled, rushing into her mother's arms. "What are you doing here?"

"We thought you might need some company," her father answered, "what with your sisters gallivanting all over the countryside."

"But how did you know?"

"Someone named Bailey Blanchard telegraphed us a week ago and said he thought it might be a good time for us to visit you," her mother said.

"That's right," her dad agreed. "Now, just who is this Blanchard fella?"

"He's the sheriff of Chanute, and a very good friend."

Her mother looked at her suspiciously before stating, "It sounds like he's more than just a good friend, Camille."

The daughter took a couple of minutes to respond to her mother's assertion, motioning for them to sit in the interim.

"Yes, mother, Bat—Bailey is more than just a friend. I don't know a lot about how to know when you're in love, but I think I'm learning very quickly."

"Sounds like I better meet this man real soon," her father said.

"Oh, dad, I think you are going to like him, as much as I do. He's a real man, not like that guy Mattie married. Bat knows how to handle himself without mistreating others."

"What are you talking about?" Cami's mother asked.

"I'm talking about how David Yarden treated Mattie."

"Matilda never told us anything about Yarden mistreating her," her father said, looking at his wife for confirmation.

Realizing that she'd opened the door, Cami knew she'd have to tell the whole story. Mattie was going to be mad at her for sure, but it was too late. Why hadn't her sister told her parents?

"David Yarden used to hit Mattie whenever he was angry or felt like she hadn't done something the way he wanted it done."

There was a long silence as her parents processed the information. When her father spoke next it was with trepidation in his voice.

"Did Mattie kill David?"

"No! Dani and I dressed up as men and took him into the woods. We pretended we were going to hang him and when he begged for his life we offered to let him go if he promised to leave Dewitt and never return.

"We had found out that Yarden was suspected of killing a wife he'd had in New York, so he was anxious to get out of there as fast as he could."

"And Mattie went along with this plan of yours?" her mother asked.

"No. She didn't know anything about what we did until a few months ago when we accidently said something and ended up having to tell her."

"I can't believe you and Danielle would do such a thing," Mr. Cochran said, the disapproval evident in his words. "Whose idea was it, yours?"

"Not exactly, sir," Cami tried to affect a contrite tone. "Dani and I talked about what we could do to stop him from hurting our sister, and together we came up with that plan."

"Why didn't you come to your mother and I instead?"

"Because, Mattie is our sister!" Cami was near tears when she realized her father was angry with her. "She's one third of who Danielle and I are. You hurt one of us and you hurt all three."

"I think I understand, sweetheart," her mother said softly. "Cami's right, dear," she turned to her husband. "You can't hurt just one of them. They aren't like our other children, they're triplets."

"I guess I don't understand, but I'll take your word for it, darling," Cami's dad said after thinking over his wife's remarks. "I think it would be best if we keep this discussion just between the three of us. No sense in adding to Mattie's burdens.

"Do you have any idea where David Yarden is?"

"There's a chance he's in Colorado."

"What makes you say that?"

"Mattie told Dani and I that when she was on the train heading for San Francisco it made a stop in Grand Junction, in the western part of the state. As it was leaving the station, she thought she saw David at the train station in town, but she's not really sure if it was him or not."

"Maybe we should have your friend—the sheriff—alert the authorities in Grand Junction and, if he's there, have him arrested. If the police in New York want him, don't you have an obligation as a law enforcement officer to assist them in locating him?"

"I guess so. I never really thought about it that way, but I see your point. I'll ask Bat at lunch about sending a telegraph to the New York police and to the sheriff in Colorado."

"Well, then, let's go join this young friend of yours and have some lunch," her mother suggested.

"Let me grab my things and lock my room," Cami said.

"Bat, these are my parents, Charles and Lydia Cochran. Mom, dad, this is Bailey Blanchard," Cami formally introduced her parents. "I've invited them to join us for lunch, Bat."

Now that Cami was no longer pretending to be Doctor Holliday's nurse, it was also no longer necessary for her and Blanchard to pretend there wasn't an interest in each other.

"It's nice to finally meet you folks," Bailey said as he shook Mr. Cochran's hand.

"It's nice to meet you also," Charles replied. "Apparently our daughter didn't see fit to tell us about you, though."

"Dad!" the young deputy yelped, concerned that Bat would take it the wrong way. "I couldn't tell you about him because I was under orders to act like we were just acquaintances."

"Still, you could have written your mother and me."

"I assure you, Mr. Cochran, your daughter cares about the two of you very much. She talked about you every time we were together."

"My husband knows that, Sheriff Blanchard. He's just giving our daughter a little of her own medicine," Lydia interjected.

"Please, call me Charles," Cami's father said, addressing the young sheriff.

"Thank you. My friends call me Bat," he replied.

"And why is that?" Lydia asked.

"When I was a child, I got lost in a cave that was full of bats. I was very scared of them, so when I got rescued, my older brother starting calling me the bat boy. Later it got shortened to just Bat, and it's stuck with me since."

"Shall we take a table and have lunch?" Cami asked.

38

WAYNESVILLE

Waynesville, Missouri, May 18, 1875

ACCORDING TO THE map of Missouri that Lieutenant Staley had given the two sisters, they were getting close to Waynesville, a town they hoped to stop at and get fresh supplies *and* maybe a good night's sleep before trudging on to Emporia. Just as Mattie was about to make a comment on how peaceful their trip was, gunshots went off.

Reining in their horses, the two young deputies listened, trying to ascertain where the shots came from.

"It sounds like they came from over there," Dani suggested, pointing toward the woods to the south.

"I agree. Let's take a look, but I suggest we split up and flank the area."

"I'll go this way," Dani said, pointing.

"Okay, I'll swing around the other way," her sister indicated.

Moving cautiously and quietly through the woods, the deputies heard some more gunfire coming from the direction they were headed. Soon they could see a group of men that had another man pinned down behind some rocks and were shooting at him.

"Hold your fire!" Mattie yelled from behind a tree. "We're US marshals. Hold your fire!"

"This don't concern you, Marshal," a man yelled back.

"Looks to me like you have someone outnumbered and outgunned and are trying to kill him. That makes it our business. Now, hold your fire and holster your weapons or you'll deal with me."

"All right, boys, hold your fire like the marshal says," the man instructed his men.

"And lady, I never heard of a female marshal before, so if you ain't for real you're gonna have to answer to me."

While Mattie was getting the group of men to surrender, Dani had worked her way behind the man hiding in the rocks, who was now trying to slip away.

"Hold it right there, mister," she said softly. "I've got my Winchester pointed right at your belly. Holster that mule hog of yours and put your hands in the air. We're going to join that group over there and find out what's going on here."

The lone man slipped his pistol back in its sheath and raised his hands. At a nod from Dani, he began walking over toward the group. When everybody was together, Mattie spoke.

"My sister and I are deputy US marshals. Here are our badges to prove it. Now someone explain what is going on here and why you are shooting at this man."

The man who'd spoken before explained, "We caught this man trying to steal a horse from my ranch. When I tried to stop him, he shot at me. We chased him here and he took cover and began shooting again."

"Is that right?" Mattie asked, addressing the man Dani had caught.

"Not exactly ma'am. The horse he says I was stealing belongs to me. It was stolen from me four days ago down near Springfield."

"Did you go to Mister...?" she looked toward the accuser.

"Drysdale, ma'am."

"Drysdale, and tell him you thought it was your horse?"

"I did, but they had already branded over my brand, so he said I couldn't prove it was mine."

"Actually, deputy," Drysdale said, "the horse was sold to me a couple days ago. The man who stole it, if it was stolen, musta rebranded it."

"Show me the brand," Dani said to the man who claimed it was his horse.

He led Dani over to the horse and she took a long look at the brand.

"Mattie, it does look like someone recently rebranded this animal," Dani informed her sister.

"Okay, here's what we are going to do. My sister and I will escort Mr. Drysdale and this other man into Waynesville and they can tell the sheriff there their stories. He can decide how to proceed with the situation. Meanwhile, the rest of you men go back to your homes. There won't be any more shooting today."

Dani escorted the horse's owner back to the horse where Mattie and Mr. Drysdale joined them. They then headed toward town while the rest of the men rode off.

Town Marshal Abner Wortham was in his late fifties with a seemingly permanent three-day growth on his face and bloodshot eyes. It was immediately apparent to Mattie and Dani that he preferred whiskey to coffee. If they had to sum up his appearance in one word, they would say he was grizzled.

Wortham made it plain right from the beginning that he didn't like marshal deputies, especially female ones, sticking their noses, no matter how pretty they might be, in what he considered to be his business. And Drysdale's and Windom's dispute was part of his business.

After about fifteen minutes of listening to Wortham's complaints Mattie grabbed him by the arm and propelled him toward the back room where the jail cells were located, telling Dani to stay with the other two as she exited the main room.

"Marshal Wortham," she said sternly once they were behind closed doors, "I don't care what your opinion of female marshals is. I don't care if you don't like our bringing this dispute to your attention. I don't even care whether or not you like me. But I *do* care whether or not you do your job and do it correctly.

"Now, it just so happens that my sister and I *are* deputy US marshals. That means you are under our authority. You will take care of this matter or I will remove you from the office of the town marshal."

"You can't do that. The mayor of Waynesville appointed *me* marshal!"

"Yes, I *can* remove you. When I tell the mayor that you are in dereliction of duty, he will have no choice but to appoint someone else as marshal."

"Derek what?"

"Derelic—never mind," she could see the blank look on his face. "It means that you have failed to do your job. And if the mayor refuses to do his job, I will contact the governor of Missouri.

"Now, are there any more questions?" Mattie asked rhetorically.

Deputy Cochran led Marshal Wortham back into the main room and addressed the two men waiting. "I think I have convinced the marshal here of the wisdom of settling this dispute in a peaceful manner. However, if you gentlemen have any further problems, please don't hesitate to inform either my sister Dani here or myself and we will see to it that the marshal takes appropriate action."

Without further word, the two deputy sisters left the marshal's office.

Waynesville, May 20, 1875

Dani and Mattie were having breakfast in Annie's Café before heading out of town when they saw Mr. Drysdale enter the restaurant and look around. After he spotted them, he walked over to their table.

"Ladies, I just wanted to stop by and thank you for stopping me from making an awful mistake the other day. It turned out that Matt Windom was correct, the horse was his. After your little talk with the marshal he decided to be more helpful. When I told him that I had seen the man who sold me the horse in town on Monday he began to ask around. It turned out the thief was still in town yesterday.

"Marshal Wortham brought the man to his office and had Matt and I waiting there to confront him. He admitted, after some time, that he had indeed stolen the horse from a ranch in Springfield. Fortunately, he still had the money I'd paid him, so I was able to recover my money and Matt was able to recover his horse. Then the marshal locked the man up.

"There will be a trial next week when the circuit judge is in town and I imagine the man will probably hang. We don't cotton to horse thieves in Missouri, but it will all be legal this time."

"You're welcome Mr. Drysdale," Mattie responded for both of them, "and we're glad everything worked out. But please let this be a lesson, it's better to take your time and get it right then to jump to conclusions and get it wrong."

"Don't worry, deputy. I have learned my lesson. However, I will say that you two surprised me. I wasn't aware there were female deputies working for the Marshals Service or that they would be twins."

"Triplets!" Dani informed him.

"Triplets? You mean there's another one somewhere?" he asked, looking around as if he expected a third young woman to suddenly appear.

"Yes. Our sister Camille is in Chanute, Kansas. She's recovering from being shot in the back," Dani answered.

"Shot in the back, you say! Well, you three are definitely made of sterner stuff then what is apparent on first look. It is indeed my pleasure that I was able to make your acquaintance, and I wish you well in whatever you are up to next. Oh, and I must say, the bad guys had better look out."

Jared Drysdale walked away as Mattie turned toward her sister and said, "He's got that right!"

39

EMPORIA

Emporia, Kansas, May 29, 1875

IT WAS LATE in the afternoon when the Cochran sisters finally arrived in Emporia, Kansas. A sudden thunderstorm had delayed them and forced them to hole up in Butler, Missouri for more than a day. However, their arrival on a Saturday meant that they could attend church services on Sunday. So they checked into a hotel and went in search of a bath.

For two days, the pretty deputies interviewed witnesses to the robbery at First Emporia Bank. The descriptions they heard of the robbers fit those of the citizens of Cedar Creek, so there was no doubt that it was Ike Sturgis and his gang. On Tuesday morning they were preparing to leave and head for Hutchinson, Kansas, just north of Wichita, when the telegraph operator came running up to them bearing a message from Marshal Winters.

Winters's message informed his deputies that another bank robbery had occurred, this one in Jefferson City, Missouri, and that it sounded like the work of the gang they were chasing. He suggested that they go to that town next, while the event was still fresh in people's minds. So instead of heading west, Mattie and Dani turned their horses eastward.

Jefferson City, Missouri, June 7, 1875

A week after leaving Emporia the Cochran sisters arrived in Jefferson City. They spent the afternoon checking into a hotel, getting a bath, and eating a good meal before they went to see the town sheriff.

"I'm afraid you ladies are a little late to the party," Sheriff Tom Holbrook informed them. "My posse and I ran down the murdering thieves that robbed the bank and killed three of our good citizens. I have two of them locked up right now, waiting for their trial. But the rest of them were killed in a gun battle with me and my men."

"Was Ike Sturgis one of the ones you killed or is he locked up?" Mattie asked.

"Who is Ike Sturgis?" Holbrook inquired.

"The leader of the gang," Dani answered.

"Guess you two have been misinformed. I don't know anybody named Sturgis, but the man who led this gang is locked up in my jail. His name is Rufus Whittler."

"May we see Mr. Whittler?" Mattie asked.

"Sure! Right this way."

Mattie and Dani followed the sheriff into a back room that was lined with jail cells on the left side of a narrow aisle. The sheriff stopped in front of one of the cells and pointed, "That's Rufus right there," he said.

The girls took a long look at the outlaw and realized that he didn't come close to matching the description they had of Ike.

"Hey, sheriff, mighty nice of you to bring me a couple of saloon girls to play with," Rufus commented, eyeing the two very attractive women.

"They're not saloon girls, Whittler, they're deputy US marshals, and I don't think they're interested in playing with you, so mind your manners."

"Well, I'll be. Are you really genuine marshals?" he asked.

"Yes," Dani said bluntly as the two turned and walked away. Catcalls and whistles erupted from the two men locked behind bars until the sheriff threatened to withhold their dinner if they didn't settle down.

Back in the front office, Holbrook echoed Whittler's surprise, "I gotta say, I agree with Rufus. If I hadn't seen your badges and the papers authorizing you to be deputies, I would've had a hard time believing it myself.

"So the Marshals Service is now hiring females? Are there more than just the two of you?"

"Actually, there are three of us," Dani responded.

"And is the third one as pretty as you two?"

"I guess you could say so," Mattie said, "since we're all triplets."

"Okay! I don't think I want to know any more. The three of you will be confusing outlaws for the next twenty years. I wish you the best, and I'm sorry you came all this way for nothing."

"Not your fault, Sheriff. It's been a pleasure meeting you, and we're glad you were able to capture or kill all the men who robbed your bank," Mattie said in parting.

Hutchinson, Kansas, June 18, 1875

It took the two young deputies over a week and a half to travel from Jefferson City to Hutchinson. When they arrived late Friday afternoon, they were exhausted and dirty. A hot bath took care of the dirt, and some of the exhaustion, a nap took care of the rest.

Unfortunately, Hutchinson yielded little more information than the sisters had found in Emporia. Convinced that the local bank was robbed by Sturgis and his gang did little to bring them closer to capturing him. However, they did receive one surprise.

On their third day in the Kansas town there was a knock on their hotel door. Dani opened the door slowly, not sure what to expect, and was greeted by her sister Cami.

"Cami!" the blonde deputy screamed, excitedly. "What are you doing here?"

"Toby sent me a telegram a week and a half ago, telling me to come to Wichita," she answered when her sisters finally stopped hugging her and allowed her to breathe. "Then, a few days ago he told me to ride up here and join you two. I guess he finally realized that you weren't going to get anything done without me."

"Yeah, yeah, yeah. More likely he got a complaint from Doc Holliday that you were driving him crazy and decided to save the poor man," Mattie rejoined.

"Hi there, Smoke. How's my puppy doing? Are these two yahoos taking good care of you?" Cami said, petting the gray dog.

"You're probably right, Mat! Holliday seems to be really happy having Hattie helping him. Since I don't need to work uncover there anymore, it was getting pretty boring."

"Being around a good looking man like Bat Blanchard is boring?" Dani asked.

"No, of course not. But Bat has his duties as sheriff, so I only got to spend a couple of hours a day with him. And in case you didn't notice when you were there, there isn't a whole lot to do in Chanute."

"So did Toby say you could travel with us to Salina?" Mattie inquired.

"Yep! He has returned me to full time duty."

"Great! We'll be leaving first thing in the morning."

The three girls spent the rest of the evening getting caught up on all their various news, finally getting to bed after midnight.

40

JEWELL CITY

Jewell City, Kansas, August 21, 1875

FOUR MONTHS AGO, Ike Sturgis left Chanute, Kansas and began a bank robbing spree across the state of Kansas. In addition to robberies in Hutchinson, Emporia, and Salina his gang hit the banks in Great Bend, Dodge City, and Concordia, as well as in five other towns. Now the day had finally come for the group to take over Jewell City in the northern reaches of Kansas.

Ike's band of desperados now numbered twenty hard-eyed men, including himself. He divided the group up into two, putting one bunch under the command of Goren Young, who had proven himself a very capable lieutenant during their recent binge. Young was directed to take his group around the town and enter from the east while Ike would bring his company in from the west.

Jewell City was a quiet peaceful town, much like Cedar Creek had been that Saturday morning, as the two clusters of riders slowly rode into the city. No one suspected anything was wrong until the first shot rang out, killing the town sheriff who had just stepped out of his office. Planning to go to the hotel's restaurant for his breakfast, the sheriff stood watching as Goren Young rode up to him, drew his pistol, and shot him point-blank in the chest.

Caught completely unawares, the town's inhabitants were quickly rounded up and ushered into the Baptist church located in the settlement's center. Men were separated out from the women and children and then hustled off to the jailhouse. Ike then addressed those remaining at the church, telling them that the men would be safe, as long as they rest of the community cooperated with him and his men. But cooperation had an entirely different meaning in Ike Sturgis's mind.

September 13, 1875

For three plus weeks, the Sturgis gang terrorized the women and older girls of Jewell City, raping and beating them according to their whims. While Mattie, Dani, and Cami continued to traverse the state, trying to locate these vicious killers, they remained holed up in the tiny town located less than twenty miles below the Nebraska state line.

Around noon on a gorgeous September day, Nathan Grinnell slowly rode into town, having left his home in southern Nebraska early that morning en route to Junction City, Kansas. He reined in his big chestnut gelding in front of the lone saloon, dismounted, and went inside to get a beer.

Young and several other men were in the saloon at the time and he closely watched the stranger cross the floor to the bar. One of the gang members was tending bar and eyed Grinnell suspiciously.

"Wha'll ya haf?" he asked.

"The coldest beer you got," Nathan answered.

Placing a mug of warm beer in front of the stranger, the bartender asked, "Yew passin' thru?"

"Yeah! Just wanted to wash down some of the trail dust."

"Whar yew frum?"

"Up in 'braska, headed to Junction City. This beer's awfully warm. Don't you have any cold beer?" Nathan asked, almost spewing out the first sip.

"I's da col'est we got. Don' like it yew cin mosey on."

"That's not very friendly, pal." Nathan said, offended by the man's attitude.

"The bartender said you can mosey on if you don't like it here," Goren Young spoke up from the table where he sat. "I suggest you do just that."

Grinnell turned and looked at the speaker and considered saying something in response, but he noticed that every eye in the place was staring at him. Several of the men, including the man who had just spoken to him, had their hands either on their pistols or close enough they could draw fast. Nathan quickly decided he was not in a position to stand up for his rights.

Tossing a fifty-cent piece on the counter, Grinnell said to the bartender, "Thanks for the beer. Keep the change." He then slowly walked out of the saloon, cognizant of the eyes following his every move.

Without looking toward the bar any more than necessary, Nathan climbed up on the chestnut and turned it eastward. Just as he started to move, Young and some of the outlaws came rushing out of the tavern.

"Hold up there, fella," Young started to say.

Nathan kicked his horse hard in the flanks, spurring the horse forward into a gallop. Shots rang out behind him and Grinnell ducked down hoping to avoid being hit. Urging his horse on, he rode out of town as quickly as he could, putting space between him and the outlaws he was sure were now chasing him.

Fifteen miles from Jewell City, Nathan pulled up when he got to a large outcropping of rocks. He had been headed south-southeast for much of the way and it had been about half an hour since he last saw any evidence that he was being followed. He rode up into the rocks and found a spot where he could watch the road below while remaining hidden from view. He ground-reined his horse behind some other rocks and hoped the gelding wouldn't make any noise if it heard other horses approaching.

For over an hour, Grinnell watched the road and the surrounding countryside, but saw no sign of the desperados. He was just about to relax and take a nap when he heard the sound of a horse whinnying. There below him on the road were five men on horseback. He recognized a couple of the men from the town he'd been in.

So, Grinnell thought, *I didn't shake them after all.*

Nathan was never one to be a bushwhacker, but he also knew that he couldn't continue to try to outrun these men. So he leveled his Sharps .50 rifle at the lead man and yelled, "You men go back to where you came from. I've got a fifty cal rifle aimed at you and I will shoot if you don't leave me alone."

Unfortunately, the men weren't so easily swayed, choosing instead to quickly dismount and take cover, firing their pistols at Nathan. Grinnell's first shot eliminated the lead man, leaving only four to go. He had chosen his vantage point wisely and soon eliminated two more outlaws. The remaining two men decided that flight was better than death, grabbed their horses and rushed out of there.

Nathan went and got his own horse and expeditiously rode out of there himself.

Fort Riley, Kansas, September 16, 1875

Early Thursday morning, Nathan Grinnell arrived in Junction City, just outside of Fort Riley, Kansas. He went to see his friend, whom he had ridden all the way from Nebraska to see. After exchanging several personal news stories, Nathan told his friend about his encounter in the northern town in Kansas. His friend urged him to go to the nearby fort and report the incident to the provost marshal there since Junction City only had a local police department.

Friday morning, Nathan spoke to Major Conrad Noble and told him the whole story, including the fact that he'd killed three men.

"Seems to me that they would have killed you," the major opined. "So I'd say you acted in self-defense."

"Thank you, major. I too believe that way, but it's nice to hear you say that."

"Look, it's really not within my purview to investigate the situation. What I suggest is that I contact the US marshal's office in Wichita and tell him your story. He'll probably want to talk to you in person, so you may have to go down there."

"I don't have a problem with your contacting the marshal, but I don't think I have the time to travel to Wichita. I have a farm back in Nebraska I have to get back to."

"Well, let me cable Toby Winters and see what he wants to do, okay?"

"Yeah, sure!"

Saturday afternoon a soldier from the fort came to Nathan's friend's house and told Grinnell that Major Noble wanted to see him. Nathan rode back to the fort with the soldier.

"I heard back from Marshal Winters," Major Noble informed Nathan after he'd been seated. "It turns out that he has a couple of deputies in Concordia, Kansas right now. He says he can tell them to stay there and wait for you if you're going to be headed back that way soon."

"I was planning on leaving here a week from Monday."

"I'll let the marshal know and advise you as to what he wants to do."

"Thank you, major. You've been very helpful. I would really like to see those men captured and brought to justice."

41

RECONNAISSANCE

Concordia, Kansas, September 14, 1875

THE COCHRAN SISTERS received a telegram from Marshal Winters informing them that Nathan Grinnell would be meeting them in Concordia in nine to ten days and that they were to remain there until he arrived. The girls weren't happy about sitting around for almost two weeks when there was a better than good chance that Ike Sturgis and his gang were holed up in a town less than thirty miles from them.

After much discussion, and not too little argument, it was decided that Cami would wait in the town in case Grinnell showed up early. Meanwhile, Mattie and Dani would pull reconnoiter duty on Jewell City. Cami wasn't officially engaged to Bailey Blanchard (he hadn't formally proposed nor given her a ring), but her sisters felt that she should stay behind for her own safety. This really rankled the normally demure young woman. Nevertheless, she finally acceded to her sister's insistence that she remain behind.

Mattie and Danielle left Wednesday morning, arriving at a glen in the middle of the woods southwest of Jewell City at mid-afternoon. They set up a campsite and sat there discussing their strategy for spying on the town. Smoke had sauntered off shortly after their arrival, presumably to perform his own reconnaissance of the area.

Outside of Jewell City, September 16, 1875

Mattie left camp early in the morning, skirting the town to the west and finding a spot to the north where she could easily observe the small community with binoculars while remaining hidden from their view. Dani had taken up a similar position just to the south of town.

For three days, the two girls watched the goings-on in Jewell City, meeting back up in the late afternoon to discuss their notes. Mattie watched from the north on the first and third day, exchanging places with her sister on the second day. Interestingly, neither had seen any sign of Ike Sturgis, though they were convinced they had spied some of his men based on descriptions they had obtained from numerous witnesses over the course of the last several months.

Concordia, September 20, 1875

Danielle and Matilda arrived back in Concordia late Monday afternoon. They spent the evening with Camille, filling her in on what they had seen up north. Then they waited.

September 29, 1875

Nathan Grinnell showed up in Concordia just after the sisters had finished their lunches. After guzzling down a mug of cold beer at the local watering hole, he went looking for the deputy marshals he was asked to meet with. When he found them, his jaw dropped with surprise.

"Why, you're girls!" he exclaimed.

The three sisters took stock of the stranger. He was tall and rangy, in his late thirties or early forties they judged, with a shock of black hair tinged with gray around the temples. He hadn't shaved in a couple of days, but the rugged look looked good on him. His dark brown eyes were like pools of deep mud, there was no smile or laughter in them.

"I'm sorry," he apologized, "that didn't come out the way I meant it."

"That's okay," Mattie responded, "we're used to people being surprised when they meet us.

"I'm Mattie Cochran, and these are my sisters, Camille and Danielle. As I imagine Marshal Winters has already informed you, we are deputies under his authority."

"Yes, the marshal did tell me that in a telegram. But all he said was that I would be meeting with a couple of deputies of his. He didn't tell me that there were three of you, or that you were women, or that you were, what do they call you?" he ended, searching for a word.

"Triplets!" Cami answered.

"Triplets, huh? Well, he also didn't tell me that I'd be meeting triplets."

"Well, here we are, Mr. Grinnell," Dani spoke up. "And we are very anxious to hear your story about your visit to Jewell City."

"I rode into the town on the thirteenth. All I was looking for was a mug of cold beer to wash down some of the trail dust and a bite to eat before I pushed on to Junction City. I didn't think much of it at the time, but there were no saloon girls hanging around like there are in most places.

"The bartender was not very friendly, but I ordered a beer anyway. However, I almost spewed the first swig back out, it was so warm. When I mentioned that it wasn't cold, I was told that I could leave if I didn't like it.

"Then some cowpoke sitting at one of the tables told me to get out."

"Describe him," Mattie asked.

"Let's see. He was young, maybe early twenties. Had mean blue eyes. Couldn't see his hair too well because of his hat, but I think it was blonde."

"Any scars?" Dani inquired.

"Yeah, now that you ask, he had a nasty-looking one. Went from his right eyebrow down his cheek and to the middle of his chin."

"Goren Young!" Mattie said.

"*The* Goren Young?" Nathan asked, astonished.

"One and the same," Cami said.

"I…I didn't know. My lord, I almost drew on him." Grinnell was stupefied.

"It's probably a good thing you didn't," Mattie commented. "So what happened next?"

"I saw all the men staring at me and I realized I was in a bad place. I paid for my beer and made my exit as quickly as I reasonably could without seeming like I was scared, which, by the way, I was.

"I got on my horse and was turning to leave when several men came rushing out of the saloon. One of them, Young it was, yelled at me to stop, but I dug my spurs into the horse and made a mad dash out of there.

"Fifteen or so miles out of town, I found a place where I could have a good vantage point to see the road and find out if I was being followed. Five men rode into view and I ordered them to return to town and leave me alone. They rushed to cover and began firing at me, so I fired back. I killed three of them and the other two turned tail, skedaddling out of there."

"Mr. Grinnell…"

"Please, call me Nathan," he interrupted.

"Nathan," Mattie continued, "thank you for meeting with us. You have been a tremendous help. However, I recommend that you make a wide detour around Jewell City on your way back north."

"Believe me, I will do just that. It's been a pleasure meeting the three of you. And now I have an even better story to tell my male friends. None of them are going to believe me when I tell them that there are three gorgeous female deputy marshals here, but that's okay, it'll be fun watching their faces as they try to figure out if I'm telling the truth."

The Cochran sisters laughed, knowing that there were probably several men in Kansas that had Nathan Grinnell's "problem."

42

GAUNTLET

Wichita, Kansas, October 4, 1875

ONCE NATHAN GRINNELL had left his meeting with the Cochrans, they discussed the situation among themselves. Both Mattie and Dani had seen Goren Young when they were spying on the town, so they knew that it was likely that Ike was also in Jewell City. Mattie sent a telegram to Marshal Winters apprising him of what they had learned. His reply ordered them to return to Wichita "fastest possible." They rode in on Monday, the 4th of October.

Tuesday morning, Toby Winters called a meeting with his Chief Deputy, Kyle Branch, all available deputies in town, and the three sisters.

"Mattie, brief everybody on what you learned from Mr. Grinnell," he requested.

"Mr. Grinnell stopped in Jewell City on his way to Junction City. He only wanted to get a cold beer and something to eat. When he was served a warm beer he started to complain and was told to get out of town. However, when he tried to leave a group of men tried to stop him. From his description of one of the men, we believe it was Goren Young, whom we had earlier learned has become second in command to Ike Sturgis.

"While we were waiting for Mr. Grinnell to arrive in town, Dani and I rode up north and camped out just outside of Jewell City. For three days we watched the town through binoculars. Both of us saw Mr. Young along with several other men eyewitnesses had described to us as members of Ike's gang. While we didn't see Ike himself, we believe that he is hiding out there."

"I don't remember giving you and your sister permission to conduct surveillance," Winters said, a touch of anger in his voice.

"No sir, you didn't. But Dani and I were extremely careful. I felt that the intelligence we would bring back was worth the risk."

"You aren't paid to make those decisions Deputy Cochran. You and your sisters and I will discuss this later. In the meantime, the three of you are dismissed."

Mattie considered arguing with Winters, but Kyle Branch gave her a little shake of his head to warn her, so she and the other two girls quietly left the room.

An hour later, Branch came to the room where the Cochran women were staying.

"Toby wants to see you three in his office," he told them. "Mattie, you made a mistake not advising him of your plans before you went off on your own. He's furious because he thinks the three of you are acting on your own too much, so all of you need to be contrite and apologetic when you meet with him. Keep in mind that he's under a lot of pressure from the Governor and DC over this Sturgis guy. So he doesn't really mean to take it out on you, but you're the easiest choice."

"Thanks, Kyle, for the heads up," Dani said. "We'll try to keep ourselves calm and act repentant."

"Good. By the way, just between the two of us—er, *four* of us—I thought you did a great job. Toby just doesn't like rookies to have too much initiative."

The sisters made their way over to the marshal's office and reported in. Katie Winters looked at them with sympathy. She knew from the way her brother had been slamming around his office for the last hour that he was mad at them though she didn't know why.

"Toby said to go right in," she told them when they entered the building, "but you probably better knock first."

"Thanks, Katie," Mattie said in reply.

The sisters were happy that the receptionist had warmed up to them over the past months and now seemed to accept them as she would any other deputy.

"Come in!" Winters growled when they knocked on the door to his office. "Have a seat!"

He let them sit there for several minutes before he continued, "I'm going to be taking a contingent of deputies to Jewell City to capture Ike Sturgis and his gang. While we're gone, the three of you will be in charge of keeping the peace here in Wichita as well as dealing with any problems in the surrounding area."

The whole time he was speaking, he was staring straight at Mattie, and when he saw that she was intending to protest, he said, "This is an order and is not open for debate. If you don't like following my orders, you can turn in your badges right now."

In the silence that followed, Winters made eye contact with each of his female deputies before saying, "Good. If there are no further items for discussion, you are dismissed."

The Cochran sisters quietly stood and left the room. They waited until they were back in their hotel room before saying anything.

"This is so unfair," Cami complained first. "We did all the hard work of tracking these outlaws down, and now he's going to take all the credit for capturing them."

"I'm sorry, girls. This is all my fault. Kyle is right. I should have sent Toby a telegram telling him of our plans before we went off like that," Mattie said apologetically.

"Don't take it all on yourself, Mat," Dani said. "Cami and I were just as responsible for helping you make that decision. Frankly, I think we did the right thing. Toby's just too stubborn headed to admit that sometimes others have good ideas too."

"What are we going to do, Mat?"

"We're going to stay here and keep the peace, just like Toby told us too.

Jewell City, Kansas, October 20, 1875

Marshal Toby Winters gathered nineteen deputies around him and split them up into two groups. Just like Ike had done, Toby would take one group and enter the town from the west while Kyle would take the other group, circle around to the south, and enter from the east. He didn't know that he was copying Sturgis's plan or he might have chosen a different path.

Ike Sturgis hadn't survived as long as he had by being careless. He had posted sentries at either end of town and had drilled his men to respond to the alarm if they came ur attack. Consequently, as the marshals rode into Jewell City, the outlaws opened fire. Toby Winters was the first to fall.

"Pull back! Pull back!" Chief Deputy Branch began yelling as soon as he realized they were caught in a gauntlet. When the deputies reconvened outside of rifle range there were only twelve of them left.

Branch led them away from the town until they came to the same outcropping of rocks Grinnell had found. There he had them take up defensive positions while he considered his options. He knew that he had to drive Sturgis from Jewell City and free the people there, but he also knew that it wasn't going to be easy with only twelve men.

October 22, 1875

Acting US Marshal Kyle Branch had sent a man to Concordia to obtain as much black clothing as he could. Now he and his eleven remaining deputies were dressed in black. His plan was for a small group to enter Jewell City under the cover of darkness and as silently as possible, take out the sentries at either end of town. Then the rest of the deputies would come in and capture, or kill, as many of the outlaws as they could.

He also wanted to collect the bodies of Marshal Winters and the seven deputies that had been killed in the failed attack. Branch implemented his plan at ten o'clock at night on October 22nd. By midnight, every outlaw in the town was either dead, captured, or had fled to parts unknown.

Branch's one regret was that Ike Sturgis was not among the dead or captured. However, Goren Young would never commit another crime in this world.

43

Wichita, Kansas, October 21, 1875

KYLE BRANCH ARRIVED back in Wichita around dinner time on a Thursday evening. With him were five of the twelve surviving deputies. Three deputies had remained in Jewell City to help the town recover, while the last four returned to their homes in various parts of the state. Friday morning he sent word to the Cochran sisters that he needed to see them.

"As you probably have already heard, our initial raid on Ike Sturgis's gang was a disaster," he informed them when they'd been seated. "Toby was the first one shot and killed. Altogether we lost eight good men.

"I've sent Katie home to tell her folks rather than sending them a telegraph. She leaves this morning by train, and she'll take Toby's body with her so he can be buried there in St. Louis.

"In the interim, I need one of you to fill in for her at the front desk, until she gets back or I hire a replacement. Katie was kind enough to leave some instructions on what needs to be done."

"Who did you have in mind?" Mattie asked.

"I'll do it," Cami responded before Branch could answer.

"Do you have any experience with a typewriter?" the acting marshal inquired.

"No, but I've watched Katie use it, and I think I can manage. Besides, as my sisters will undoubtedly tell you, I am the most organized of the three of us."

"She's got that right!" Dani ventured.

"Okay. You can get started after you go and change your clothes."

"Change my clothes?" Cami enquired.

"Sorry, but I can't have you wearing jeans if you're going to be the receptionist. You are the first impression anyone coming through that door has of this place. You'll need to wear dresses while you are working up there."

"Oh, okay. I'll go change and get back as quick as I can then."

"Thanks!" After she left, Kyle turned to the other two women. "I want the two of you to go visit the wives of the other men who were killed. A telegram seems too impersonal for this type of news. You can either split up and each take three families, or you can travel together to all six of them."

"Six? Don't you mean seven?" Dani asked.

"One of the surviving deputies lives near to where Deputy Simmons's family is, so he volunteered to inform them of their loss.

"Look, I know this is a difficult assignment, but think of how you would feel if you received a telegram saying that your loved one has died while trying to capture a desperado gang?

"Also, Ike and a few others got away. So this will give you a chance to gather some information, hopefully, that will help us find him again. When we do, this time I promise you, he will not escape."

"One condition, Kyle," Mattie said pensively. "If we find Ike Sturgis and his gang, my sisters and I will take him down this time." Her tone of voice suggested it was not debatable.

Branch sat thoughtfully for a couple of minutes before answering. "Okay, you have a deal. You find him, you can take him down…And, ladies, I don't care if you take him down hard. We don't need for there to be a trial, if you know what I mean."

Mattie and Dani left Wichita Monday morning, October 25.

October 26, 1875

Cami was sitting at the front desk, her head down as she concentrated on writing up a report so that she could type it and send it off to Washington. She heard the door open and close, but since she was expecting one of the other deputies to bring her lunch, she didn't look up right away.

"How's the prettiest girl in all of Kansas doing?" she heard a male voice say.

That brought her eyes up, followed by her jumping out of her chair and racing into the arms of the speaker. "Bat, what are you doing here?" she cried out into his shoulder.

"Heard you were on desk duty and just had to come and see for myself," he replied.

"Oh, Bat! I've missed you so much. I'm glad you came," the young woman blubbered.

"I've missed you too. Think Branch will let you go to lunch with me?"

"Wait right here. I'll go ask, though I'm sure it won't be a problem."

Cami returned less than a minute later and grabbed Blanchard by the arm, practically dragging him out the door. Over their lunch, Cami told him all about the attempt to capture Sturgis and the deputies who were killed in the skirmish that ensued. He told her how he had unearthed some more Ku Klux Klansmen in the surrounding area and was fairly certain there were no more now.

———•∘○❦∘•———

Sunday morning, Bat and Cami attended church together and then went on a picnic at a nearby lake. Over a luncheon of fried chicken, potato salad, corn on the cob, and tea, they talked a lot about the future.

"So tell me…do you think you want to have kids someday?" Bat asked after a brief discussion about Cami's family.

"Sure. I think I'd like to have at least a boy and a girl. Maybe even two of each," the blonde mused.

"Don't you think being a deputy marshal might interfere with that plan?"

"Oh, I don't think I'll be a deputy for very long. This was really more of Mattie's dream than mine. Dani and I went along because we felt we should stick together after her marriage…you know."

"You don't think Dani will stay a deputy either?"

"At first, I didn't think so, but she's changed over the last year. I think she really likes being a deputy marshal. She and Mattie aren't even working together right now. They each took three families and are visiting them separately.

"Mattie has Smoke to keep her company, and I think Dani wants to team up with somebody else, at least for a while. She was hit pretty hard with Toby's death. She had fantasized about the two of them marrying though I don't think he had the same interest. For now, Dani just wants to be alone, I think."

"And what about you?"

"What about me?"

"Do you want to be alone?"

"What are you asking me, Bat?"

Blanchard paused for what seemed like an eternity to Cami before saying, "Camille Cochran, would you be my wife?"

The pretty blonde woman threw her arms around the sheriff's neck and buried her face in his shoulder.

"Bailey Blanchard, I thought you'd never ask," she cried.

"Is—is that a yes?" he stuttered.

Pressing her lips against his, she held them there for several seconds before saying, "Yes, Bat, yes I'll marry you."

Wichita, Kansas, November 23, 1875

Danielle Cochran arrived back in town just before lunch time. When she went into the marshal's office to report in, she was greeted by Katie Winters, who had returned to her job the previous week.

"Hi, Katie. How are you doing?" she asked, pleasantly.

"I'm doing okay. How are you?"

"I'm fine. Is Kyle in?"

"He is. He said that if you or your sister showed up, to send you on back. He's still using his old office, by the way.

He says he doesn't feel right about using Toby's office, at least not until his promotion is confirmed by Washington."

"Thanks! Oh, yeah. Do you know where Cami is? They told me she isn't staying at the hotel."

"She's down in Chanute. She said she would be back up here on Wednesday. She also said to tell you and Mattie that your parents will be here for Thanksgiving."

"Really! That's great! I can't wait to see them! Thanks again, Katie. And it's great to see you back."

Mattie showed up late that afternoon. After reporting in to Kyle, she and Dani got together to compare notes on what they'd learned about Ike Sturgis.

"From what I've gathered, the gang has all split up," Mattie started. "Apparently they get together occasionally, pull off a robbery, and then disappear again."

"That's pretty much the impression I've been getting. I spoke to a sheriff that led a posse after them when they had just robbed a train. He said they were all together for about two miles, and then they slowly started peeling away, one or two at a time."

"Okay, after Thanksgiving, I want to go back out on the trail and see if I can pick up some more information. Do you want to go with me?"

"Yeah, that sounds like a good plan."

"So what's Cami doing in Chanute?" Mattie asked.

"I'm not sure. I asked Katie and Kyle and they both just smiled and said she was visiting down there."

"You think she's seeing the sheriff?"

"Well, wouldn't you be if you were her?"

"Yeah, I guess so."

"Anyway, she'll be back here tomorrow, Katie said, so we can ask her then."

"Good! When are mom and dad supposed to arrive?"

"I think their train comes in tomorrow around noon."

"All right. I'm hungry. Let's go get something to eat."

44

ENDGAME

Wichita, Kansas, November 25, 1875

THE COCHRAN FAMILY gathered around a dining table in the Fairmark Hotel in Wichita. Charles and Lydia Cochran had traveled to the city to join their three daughters, Camille, Danielle, and Matilda, for the Thanksgiving holiday. Also present were Bailey Blanchard, the newly elected Sheriff of Neosho County, and all three of the girl's siblings, Charles Junior, Cristian, and Suzanna. Everyone, except Mattie and Dani, were in a jovial mood.

"Would someone please tell Mattie and I what is going on?" a frustrated Danielle complained. "Why is everybody in the family here?"

"I think perhaps the answer to that lies with your sister," her father answered quietly.

Everyone quieted down and looked at Mattie for a comment.

"What? I don't know what's going on."

"I think Father is referring to me," Cami said finally. "I have an important announcement to make. Bailey, Bat, has asked me to marry him, and I have agreed."

The group erupted into chaos as everyone tried to congratulate the couple and hug one another. This time, the only one sitting back was Cami's father. When things finally quieted back down, Cami noticed a smug look on her father's face.

"Aren't you happy for me, Father?" Cami asked.

"Absolutely! I wouldn't have given Bailey permission to ask you if I wasn't happy to have him as a son-in-law."

"Permission? What's this?"

Charles looked to his future son-in-law, signaling him to explain.

"Before I came to Wichita and asked you to marry me, I went to Dewitt and talked to your father. I asked him for his consent as I believe that is the proper thing to do."

"Charles?" Lydia looked at her husband questioningly. "You knew about this and didn't tell me?"

"Sometimes, dear, the best-kept secrets are the best surprises. Bailey asked me not to tell anyone until the two of them could announce it together. I simply honored his wish."

"We'll talk about this later, Charles."

"I'm sure we will, but what's done is done."

"In the meantime," his wife continued, "have you set a date?"

"We've decided on June 17th. And we plan on getting married in Dewitt."

"But, dear, it's customary to wait about a year first."

"I know, Mother. But Bat and I have talked about it, and we think that seven months is long enough."

When their mother started to protest, Mattie stepped in. "Mom, Cami and Bat are adults. They have a right to make their own decisions as to what is appropriate. Frankly, I agree with them."

"I do too, Mother," Dani chimed in.

November 29, 1875

The train carrying Mr. and Mrs. Cochran and their three children left the station early Monday morning. As it pulled out, the snow began to fall. It wasn't heavy at first, but by noon, it was coming down harder and beginning to collect in deep drifts. For the next two and a half months, there wasn't a day in Kansas when it didn't snow. By Groundhog Day, the snow was over a foot deep just about everywhere and was considerably deeper in the drifts. The three blonde deputies were pretty much snowbound for the entire time. Bat had managed to get to Chanute before it got too bad.

However, there was very little traveling one can do during the cold, bitter winter.

In mid-February, the weather started to turn pleasant, and the snow started melting away. Mattie, Dani, and Cami ventured out on the first of March, seeking information as to the whereabouts of Ike Sturgis and his gang.

Hays, Kansas, March 18, 1876

Two plus weeks of searching had given the female deputies no clues as to the location of the outlaws. They were sitting in a restaurant in Hays, Kansas, eating their dinner and discussing their failure so far.

"Hey, isn't that one of Sturgis's gang members?" asked Cami suddenly.

"Where?" Mattie replied.

"He just came in. He's sitting down at a table by the window. He's looking out like he's expecting someone," Cami informed her sisters.

The other two women surreptitiously checked out the man their sister was talking about.

"I think you may be right," Dani said after stealing a couple of glances.

"He definitely meets the eyewitnesses' description of one of them," Mattie noted after consulting a notebook with descriptions of many of Ike's compatriots.

"Should we arrest him, do you think?" Dani asked.

"No. Let's wait and see what he does. I think Cami's right about his waiting for someone. Maybe we'll catch more than one of them."

For two days, they shadowed the outlaw, rotating watch and using disguises as much as they could. On March 20th, he made contact with another man. When Mattie looked through her notes, she couldn't find any description that matched him more than just generally. They concluded that he was probably a new recruit.

The two men spent a great deal of time in one of the town's saloons, a place where none of the three women wanted to go into, nor would they have been welcome in. Instead, they took turns watching the saloon from across the street. As the evening wore on, raucous laughter erupted from the tavern confines; shortly thereafter, the two outlaws (Mattie was convinced that the new man was also a desperado) emerged from the bar, stumbling around in a drunken stupor. The three deputies decided this was a good time to make an arrest, while the men would find it difficult to put up much resistance.

Marshal Clete Adams of Hays, Kansas, didn't like having deputy US marshals coming to his town and making arrests, especially when there were three of them—and females to boot. But he was hardly in a position to do more than verbal protest once he learned who these men were. He allowed Mattie to lock the men up in his jail and to contact Acting Marshal Branch. Then the three women took turns questioning the man they were certain was a member of Ike's band of ruffians.

The man's cagey, Mattie had to admit. No matter how they asked the questions, they couldn't trip him up. They knew he had the information they wanted, but they also knew that he wasn't going to give it up easily.

"Look, Arizona," Mattie said, frustrated (he had told them his name was Arizona Kid but refused to acknowledge anything else), "we know you ride with Ike Sturgis. We've had several witnesses identify you as one of his bunch. You're going to get hanged unless you cooperate with us and tell us where we can find him."

After hours and hours of asking Arizona the same questions over and over and getting no helpful response, Mattie was shocked when he finally said, "Okay, I'll tell you where he's going to be next month! But you have to get the prosecutor to agree not to hang me."

Mattie sat up fast in her chair. "What did you say?"

"I said I'd tell you where he's going to be in April, but I want a written guarantee from the prosecutor that I won't be hanged. I'm scared of hanging. I've seen some men get hanged, and I don't want to die that way!"

Salina, Kansas, April 14, 1876

Mattie watched from the shadows of two buildings until she saw the flicker of matches lit by her sisters. She then lit her own match and quickly blew the flame out, signaling to her siblings that she was ready. She knelt down beside the large gray dog that had been her constant companion for a year now.

"Hey, boy," she said soothingly as she ran her hand over his head, ruffling the fur. "I want you to stay here, Smoke. If anything happens to me, go with Dani or Cami, okay?"

The formerly mangy-looking animal was now a slick, well-muscled canine; its part wolf, part husky background was now evident in its features. Mattie buried her head in the dog's shoulder briefly before rising to her feet.

"Stay!" she ordered then walked purposefully across the street.

The batwing doors of the Dog Ear Saloon squeaked back and forth as Mattie pushed through them.

"US Marshals, you're all under arrest," she said aloud.

The space quickly filled with flying bullets as the outlaws attempted to fight her off, resisting arrest. Out of the corner of her eye, Mattie saw a silver blur flying through the air, its jaw wide open and teeth bared. Despite the gunfire, one could hear the cracking of wristbones as Smoke's mandible clamped down on the arm of an outlaw who had had his gun pointed directly at the deputy's head. The shot went wide, the bullet embedding itself into a wooden post as the six-shooter went flying and the desperado screamed.

Fifteen seconds later, the shooting stopped. The air was filled with the pungent smell of cordite. Eleven men lay either dead or wounded. The remaining criminals raised their hands in surrender. Once the three deputies had secured the weapons the fugitives had, Mattie looked around for her dog. Smoke was lying on the ground, blood pooling on the floor.

"Smoke!" Mattie cried out.

Rushing to his side, she gathered him in her arms and began crying.

"Oh, Smoke, what did you do? Please, God, don't let Smoke die!" she pleaded, looking to the heavens.

Salina's sheriff came barreling into the saloon, followed by a dozen townsmen.

"What's going on here?" he demanded.

"We're deputy US marshals," Dani answered as she and Cami continued cuffing the brigands. "This is Ike Sturgis and his gang. Or what is left of them, anyway."

"Ike Sturgis, you say? Heard of him but didn't know he was in my town. Um, you ladies got proof that you're really deputies? Never heard of female deputies 'fore."

Dani and Cami both showed the middle-aged lawman their badges.

"You got a doctor in town?" Cami asked.

"Yeah! Woody, go fetch Doc Stanley. Tell him that there's several wounded men in the saloon."

"Tell him too that his first priority is our dog, Smoke," Cami said in a tone that brooked no debate.

Despite having told Cami that she could escort the five prisoners to his jail herself, the sheriff finally instructed three men to take the prisoners to the jailhouse and lock them up. When the doctor arrived, he began treating the wounded crooks first, but Cami put a quick halt to that.

"Smoke comes first, Doctor," she informed him, pointing toward the wounded dog.

"Sorry, I'm not a veterinarian. You'll have to send for Doc Kristel, over in Abilene."

"That dog saved my sister's life. You will take care of him first or deal with me," Dani joined in. "And I guarantee you the former will be much more pleasant than the latter."

Seeing the determination in the sisters' eyes, he went over to where Smoke lay. After getting Mattie out of the way, he examined the hurt animal.

"Looks like the bullet skidded along his side. There's no bullet to remove. I'll only have to stitch him up, and with a few days' rest, he should be as good as new. You two men"—he pointed to a couple of bystanders—"carry this dog over to my office. And be gentle. I don't think you want to infuriate these ladies."

As the two "volunteers" carried Smoke out, with Mattie following close behind, the doctor noticed the blood on

Cami's arm. "Let me take a look at that arm now, young lady," he said. After tearing off her left shirt sleeve, he gently examined the wound.

"Looks like a through-and-through."

"What's that, Doc?"

"Means the bullet went all the way through. It didn't do much damage. I'll sew it up. You won't be able to use that arm for a while, but you'll survive just fine…Now, if it's okay with you ladies, I'm going to treat these men so they can stand trial."

Not waiting for a response, Doctor Stanley spent the better part of an hour checking the wounds of four men, determining that two of them weren't going to last through the night. The remaining two, along with their five friends already in jail, would live long enough to stand trial and then be hanged.

Epilogue

Dewitt, Iowa, June 17, 1876

THREE WEEKS BEFORE her wedding, Cami noticed a dark lump on her left side, a couple of inches above her waist. Since she was living in Chanute until the wedding day, she went to see Doctor Holliday. The doctor incised the area where the lump was and the bullet (which had been missing since it moved in April of the previous year) fell out. Holliday stitched Cami back up and told her to take it easy for a few days.

The wedding of Camille Cochran and Bailey "Bat" Blanchard was an incredibly festive occasion. Mattie and Dani Cochran were fellow maids of honor while Bailey's brother, Ezekial, was his best man. Many of Bat's friends from Chanute made the long trip, as well as Marshal Kyle Branch and several of the sisters' fellow deputies.

A promise by Mattie and Dani, and Smoke too, to keep an eye on Neosho County allowed the newlyweds to take a trip to San Francisco. Mattie's stories of her trip to the west coast city had only spurred on Cami's desire to see the country.

Seven outlaws were hanged in late May for their part in terrorizing the families in Jewell City the previous fall. The outlaw who had given Dani and Mattie the information on Ike's whereabouts was found hung in his cell at Fort Leavenworth, where he was serving a life sentence. The investigation concluded that he had committed suicide.

When Camille returned to Wichita in July, she turned in her deputy's badge and resigned. She now lives in Erie, Kansas, where her husband is the elected county sheriff of Neosho County.

Matilda and Danielle Cochran are still members of the Marshals Service under US Marshal Kyle Branch. Mattie's dog, Smoke, fully recovered from his gunshot wound and is now an honorary deputy.

CPSIA information can be obtained
at www.ICGtesting.com
Printed in the USA
FFOW02n1501091016
28227FF

9 781682 376843